NINE LIVES TO DIE

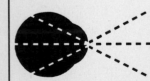

This Large Print Book carries the Seal of Approval of N.A.V.H.

A MRS. MURPHY MYSTERY

NINE LIVES TO DIE

RITA MAE BROWN
& SNEAKY PIE BROWN
Illustrated by Michael Gellatly

THORNDIKE PRESS
A part of Gale, Cengage Learning

GALE
CENGAGE Learning®

Farmington Hills, Mich • San Francisco • New York • Waterville, Maine
Meriden, Conn • Mason, Ohio • Chicago

GALE
CENGAGE Learning®

Thorndike Press, a part of Gale, Cengage Learning.
Copyright © 2014 by American Artists, Inc.
Illustrations copyright © 2014 by Michael Gellatly.

Thorndike Press® Large Print Basic.
The text of this Large Print edition is unabridged.
Other aspects of the book may vary from the original edition.
Set in 16 pt. Plantin.

LIBRARY OF CONGRESS CATALOGING-IN-PUBLICATION DATA

Brown, Rita Mae.
  Nine lives to die : a Mrs. Murphy Mystery / by Rita Mae Brown & Sneaky Pie Brown.
    pages cm — (Thorndike press large print basic)
    ISBN 978-1-4104-6919-9 (hardcover) — ISBN 1-4104-6919-0 (hardcover)
    1. Murphy, Mrs. (Fictitious character)—Fiction. 2. Haristeen, Harry (Fictitious character)—Fiction. 3. Women cat owners—Fiction. 4. Women detectives—Virginia—Fiction. 5. Mystery fiction. 6. Large type books.
  I. Brown, Sneaky Pie, 1982- II. Title.
  PS3552.R698N57 2014b
  813'.54—dc23   2014017854

Published in 2014 by arrangement with Bantam Books, a division of Random House LLC, a Penguin Random House Company

Printed in the United States of America
1 2 3 4 5 6 7 18 17 16 15 14

Dedicated with admiration
to
Gracie, a Yorkshire Terrier
living in Cape Town, South Africa.
She has her human beautifully trained.

CAST OF CHARACTERS

Mary Minor Haristeen — "Harry," just forty-one, a Smith graduate who wound up being Crozet, Virginia's postmistress for sixteen years, is now trying to make some money by farming. She survived breast cancer and prefers not to think about it. She more or less lives on the surface of life until her curiosity pulls her deeper.

Pharamond Haristeen, D.V.M. — "Fair" specializes in equine reproduction. After graduating from Auburn he married his childhood sweetheart, Harry. He reads people's emotions much better than his wife does. He is a year older than Harry.

Susan Tucker — Outgoing, adept at any and all social exchange, she's Harry's best friend since cradle days. She loves Harry but worries about how Harry just blunders into things.

The Very Reverend Herbert Jones — A Vietnam Veteran, Army, he is pastor at St.

Luke's Lutheran Church, which is well over two hundred years old. He is a man of deep conviction and feeling. He's known Harry since her childhood.

Deputy Cynthia Cooper — Tall, lean, and Harry's next-door neighbor as she rents the adjoining farm, she loves law enforcement. Harry meddles in Cooper's business from time to time but the Smith graduate has an uncanny knack of finding important information.

Aunt Tally Urquhart — This 101-year-old aunt of Marilyn Sanburne, Sr., does what she wants when she wants. She's not in too much evidence in this volume, which gives everyone a rest.

Marilyn Sanburne, Sr. — "Big Mim," known as The Queen of Crozet. She runs everything and everyone except her aunt. Big Mim is a political animal.

Miranda Hogendobber — A second mother to Harry, a devout member of the evangelical Church of the Holy Light, she, too, isn't much in evidence in this volume. Like Big Mim, she's in her seventies and has no idea how she got there so fast.

Sheriff Rick Shaw — The sheriff of Albemarle County, he is overburdened, underfunded, and overworked. Despite that, he likes law enforcement and has learned to trust Cooper. Originally, he wasn't thrilled about having a woman in the department.

BoomBoom Craycroft — Another childhood friend of Harry's, she had an affair with Harry's husband years back. It was a mess, of course. Everyone has recovered and in many ways is the better for it. BoomBoom runs her late husband's concrete business. She is conventionally beautiful.

Alicia Palmer — Now here's a showstopper. Alicia was a movie star in the fifties, whipped through a few husbands, affairs, etc., made pots of money, inherited more from an old flame. She returned to Crozet, fell in love with BoomBoom, and is blissfully happy.

Jessica Hexham — Well-educated, outgoing, ready to help a good cause, she's becoming part of the girls' group with Harry and her old school friends.

Brian Hexham — Jessica's husband leads a nonprofit, Silver Linings, organized to help disadvantaged boys. No one involved in this organization, housed at St. Cyril's Church, takes any salary.

Arden Higham — A bit high-strung, married to a successful businessman, she tries to keep peace between her husband and her son. She does the books, again for no

11

pay, for Silver Linings.

Louis Higham — Started and runs an ad agency that is quite profitable. He's a former high school football star as are many of the men involved with Silver Linings. He has a domineering streak.

Tyler Higham — At fourteen he's a tech head, gets along well enough with his classmates but is woefully unathletic to the embarrassment of his father.

Coach Al Toth — Retired and in his early seventies, he was head coach at Crozet High School during their glory football days throughout the 1970s and 1980s. He helps at Silver Linings and is admired by all.

Esther Mercier Toth — She, too, does her bit for Silver Linings and is utterly devoted to Al. Once one of the math teachers at Crozet High, she is burdened by caring for her older sister.

Peter Vavilov — Another football star guided by Coach Toth, he became a Ford dealer, makes pots of money, and loves the car business.

Charlene Vavilov — She, too, runs the dealership and like her husband has learned to love a tough business. She hopes her two sons, once out of college, wind up somewhere in the auto industry.

Father O'Connor — As a young parish priest at St. Cyril's, he was sent to help the aging Father O'Brien. Regarding church politics, he keeps his head down and concentrates on his parishioners.

Cletus Thompson — Once one of the math teachers at Crozet High, a school well regarded for their math department. He is retired and lives with his ancient dog, The Terminator. Battles with the bottle have ravaged his once handsome face. He is a decent man struggling with a demon.

Flo Rice — Peculiar doesn't really cover it, but she's bright, well-read, suspicious of most people. She fights with Esther Toth, her younger sister. Buster, her dog, is a happy spot in her life.

Odin — A young coyote who lives behind Harry's farm on the eastern slope of the Blue Ridge Mountains, leads Mrs. Murphy, Pewter, and Tucker to a frightening discovery.

THE REALLY IMPORTANT
CHARACTERS

Mrs. Murphy — She's a tiger cat who is usually cool, calm, and collected. She loves her humans, Tucker the dog, and even Pewter, the other cat, who can be a pill.

Pewter — She's self-centered, rotund, intelligent when she wants to be. Selfish as this cat is, she often comes through at the last minute to help and then wants all the credit.

Tee Tucker — This corgi could take your college boards. She is devoted to Harry, Fair, and Mrs. Murphy. She is less devoted to Pewter.

Simon — He's a possum who lives in the hayloft of the Haristeens' barn.

Matilda — She's a large blacksnake with a large sense of humor. She also lives in the hayloft.

Flatface — This great horned owl lives in the barn cupola. She irritates Pewter, but the cat realizes the bird could easily pick her up and carry her off.

Shortro — A young Saddlebred in Harry's barn who is being trained as a foxhunter. He's very smart, young, and good-natured.

Tomahawk — Harry's older Thoroughbred. He and Harry have been friends a long time.

THE LUTHERAN CATS

Elocution — She's the oldest of the St. Luke's cats and cares a lot about the "Rev," as his friends sometimes call the Very Reverend Herbert Jones.

Cazenovia — This cat watches everybody and everything.

Lucy Fur — While she's not interested in church dogma, she is interested in the Very Reverend Herbert Jones whom she thinks of as "Poppy."

1

"Gin!"

"I don't believe it." Susan Tucker stared at the cards that her childhood friend, Mary Minor Haristeen, "Harry," had smacked down.

The six other women in the room, all slack-jawed, came over to view the winning card.

"Well, Susan, she did," BoomBoom Craycroft, another childhood friend, said and smiled.

"Harry can't play cards worth squat," Susan complained.

"Well, I did tonight." Harry beamed. "Susan, mark your calendar, Tuesday, December third, my best friend Harry knocked the stuffing out of me at gin."

Jessica Hexham was petite and middle-aged, well dressed even though the evening was relaxed. She murmured, "Maybe something less exuberant for the calendar — just

17

a red-letter day?"

"Do you remember when Miss Donleavey lectured us about red-letter days on the ancient Roman calendar?" Susan rolled her eyes.

BoomBoom, Susan, and Harry had been in the same class at old Crozet High School. While the buildings still stood, students now attended Western Albemarle High School, a large complex consolidating former small community schools. Jessica Hexham, Alicia Palmer, Charlene Vavilov, and Arden Higham had not. Jessica had attended Miss Porter's; Alicia, Orange High School; Arden, Buckingham High; and Charlene, older than the others, had attended St. Catherine's in Richmond.

With the exception of Jessica, all were central Virginia natives. Jessica, born and raised in Concord, Massachusetts, often found them amusing while contradictory at times, and they were reliably solid friends.

"Alea jacta est," Susan pronounced with emphasis.

Harry translated. "The die is cast. Said when Julius Caesar crossed the Rubicon in 49 B.C. at the head of the Thirteenth Legion. He knew civil war would follow."

"Talk about a red-letter day," said Boom-Boom.

"Isn't it something, though, how a device thousands of years old still works, I mean, a red-letter day? God bless Miss Donleavey. She taught us well."

Jessica also recalled her Latin teacher at the expensive private school, perhaps less fondly. "I would never bless Miss Greely."

The others laughed.

"Charlene, bet you took Latin at St. Catherine's," Alicia wondered.

"You couldn't go to college without two years of it," said Charlene. "I took four. It's helped me more than I could know when I hated memorizing those conjugations." She laughed.

"Funny, isn't it?" the uncommonly beautiful Alicia said. "What we use? What we remember?"

"What I remember, apart from *amo, amas, amat,* was Miss Donleavey's mysterious disappearance. Never found her." Harry picked up the cards to shuffle.

Susan reached across the card table, placing her hand on Harry's forearm. "Don't you dare."

"Huh?" Harry blinked.

"I'll shuffle."

"Are you calling me a cheat?" Harry's voice rose.

"No, but you won the last hand, so it's

19

my turn to shuffle. Plus, what if you have a hot hand?" Susan used the gambling term.

"I'd better tell that to my husband."

This evoked more laughter.

The lights flickered, once, twice, then no light.

"Dammit," Susan cursed the dark. "Stay put, ladies. I'll get the candles."

"You need my little flashlight." Harry reached into her pocket, pulling out a two-and-a-half-inch LED flashlight made in China.

Susan pressed the button. "Wow."

"What else do you have in your pocket?" Jessica asked.

"One pocketknife," BoomBoom answered for Harry. "She always has a pocketknife and a little money."

"The emphasis is on *little*," said Harry, emptying her pockets onto the card table as Susan returned with candles.

"Let me help you." Thanks to the tiny LED flashlight, Alicia could see. She reached for some candles.

"There's a hurricane glass lamp. Well, here, let's do it together. Girls, we'll be right back."

True to her word, Susan and Alicia returned to the living room with small brass candleholders, which they placed about and lit. The large hurricane candleholder glowed on the card table. All held six- to eight-inch candles.

Susan noticed the small pile of debris.

"Harry, what's your stuff doing on the card table?"

"Jessica wanted to know what was in my pocket."

"In the dark?" Susan questioned.

"We knew there'd be light," Harry shot back.

Jessica dutifully investigated the contents: one Case pocketknife, a folded cotton handkerchief, twenty-two dollars in small bills, one dog cookie.

Harry pointed out the cookie. "Never know when I might get hungry."

The ladies laughed again as Alicia walked to the large triple-sash windows. "Girls, we're in for it."

"No kidding?" Harry hurried over, as did the others.

"The storm's early." BoomBoom, like all country people, paid intense attention to the weather.

"We have a little time before we need to worry about the roads," Harry confidently predicted. "Everyone has four-wheel drive, right?"

"If not, I'm happy to sell you one." Charlene smiled. She and her husband, Pete, owned the Ford dealership.

"We're good," the others replied.

"Well, let's not play cards by candlelight. Ladies, I whipped up vegetable hors d'oeuvres, and they're really tasty, if I do say so myself. I can't eat them all. You have to help me. Harry, use your flashlight again and let's bring the food out from the kitchen. BoomBoom, you know where the bar is. Give the girls what they want."

BoomBoom picked up a candle as she glided to the well-stocked bar. Susan's husband, Ned, was a delegate to the state legislature in Richmond, and the couple entertained frequently. In this part of the world, good liquor was considered an essential by any host and hostess. Southerners did drink wine, but many still preferred a high-octane bourbon or scotch, and then there were the legions of vodka drinkers who believed it didn't linger on their breath.

Once settled in the living room, comfortable in decidedly not-modern décor, Jessica, curious, asked, "So what did happen to your Latin teacher?"

"Nobody knows." BoomBoom shrugged. "She disappeared after a Friday-night football game. Her car was in the parking lot. Monday, she didn't come to school."

"We played the Louisa Dragons that night," Harry recalled. "Good game. Miss Donleavey never missed a football game."

"She dated the coach, Mr. Toth," Susan filled in. "Handsome, handsome, handsome."

"Coach Toth? That Toth?" Jessica asked. "Silver Linings?" She mentioned a youth organization the coach supported, as did all the husbands of the women in the room. Apart from helping young men, business leaders and former athletes ran Silver Linings. To belong was beneficial to one's career.

"Jessica, this must be irritating, being in the middle of a bunch of old friends." Harry handed her a napkin.

"No, it's fascinating. A vanished Latin teacher."

"You know the stereotype of the old-maid Latin teacher? Well, not Miss Donleavey. She was voluptuous, raven-haired, so pretty," BoomBoom noted, herself voluptuous.

"Suspects?" Jessica's eyebrows raised.

Miranda answered. "At first, people thought it might have been a rival of the coach's. Men were crazy for her."

Susan added, "Lots of men were questioned. Everyone had an alibi."

"Anyone else?" Jessica persisted.

"Esther Mercier. Hated Miss Donleavey, just hated her." Harry bit into a carrot incised with a tiny trench filled with rich cream cheese.

"In love with Coach Toth." BoomBoom filled in facts. "An attractive enough woman, but not in Miss Donleavey's league."

"What was her first name?" Jessica asked. "Miss Donleavey?"

"Uh, Margaret. It's funny, but I still have a hard time calling my teachers by their first names. I mean, Coach Toth is always Coach Toth." Susan smiled. "And eventually he did marry Miss Mercier, one of the math teachers."

"You'd think someone would have known something. Crozet is still a small place," Charlene wondered.

"If they did, no one noticed. Crozet, like any place anywhere in the world, is full of secrets that people take to their graves," Harry remarked. "Miss Donleavey's kin, all older, are gone. It's one of those persistent small-town mysteries."

"Well, people don't just disappear off the face of the earth." Alicia twirled a fresh bit of broccoli.

"The Black Dahlia," BoomBoom countered.

"You're right, to a degree," said Alicia. " 'Course, I wasn't in Hollywood then. And she didn't disappear, Sweetie. They never found the killer."

"You're right." BoomBoom got up and walked over to the window, nose almost on the windowpane. "It's really coming down now. We'd all better head home."

"Let me help you clean up," Harry offered.

"A tray of vegetables and a couple of glasses? Anyway, no power, no water. Go on. If your cellphones don't work you can still text if you have a Droid."

Arden said, "I hope the Silver Linings fund-raiser isn't canceled."

"We'll cross our fingers." Charlene crossed hers.

After a long, careful drive, Harry slowly finally drove down her long farm driveway, windshield wipers flipping as fast as they could. She pulled in front of the old white frame farmhouse, cut the motor, the lights with it.

Golden candlelight cascaded over the snow. The frosted windows glowed pale gold, the wavy imperfections of the hand-blown glass all the more obvious with the candles behind her.

"Mom's home." Inside the house, Tucker the corgi barked joyfully.

Pewter flopped on the kitchen table, lifted her head. *"About time."*

Mrs. Murphy, the tiger cat, walked alongside Fair, Harry's husband, as he opened the kitchen door to the porch. He carried a huge flashlight, which he focused on the path to the back porch, screened-in in summer, glassed-in in winter.

"Honey, I'm glad you're home." He stepped into the snow.

"Fair, get back inside. I can see."

He didn't, of course, kissing her as she hurried onto the porch, Tucker and Mrs. Murphy at her feet.

Pewter considered a welcoming meow when Harry walked into the kitchen, then thought better of it. It's never wise to indulge humans.

Harry stamped her feet again. "Boy, it's really snowing."

"I'll get the generator going. Just got home myself about ten minutes ago. Buried in paperwork today."

Hanging up her coat on one of the Shaker pegs inside by the kitchen door, she shook her head free of snow. "Honey, do you have your Droid?"

"Yeah, sure."

"May I borrow it?"

Fair retrieved the device, which he'd placed on a kitchen counter when he walked into the kitchen, handing it to his wife.

Harry texted Susan: "I won."

She then recounted her small triumph with her husband, who celebrated with her.

Tucker also laughed, for she knew how frequently Harry lost at cards.

"I shredded a pack of cards once," Pewter crowed. *"Good cards, they had Susan's initials on them."*

"We know," both Mrs. Murphy and Tucker replied. *"Thanks to you, the girls won't play cards here,"* Tucker added.

"Who cares?" Pewter saucily called down from the table.

"I do," the intelligent corgi said. *"The girls always drop food."*

"Well —" Pewter had no comeback for that.

While the fire blazed, Harry and Fair cuddled on the sofa.

"First big snow of the season. Even though it creates all manner of problems, I do love it." Fair smiled.

"Any horses at the clinic?" Harry asked. Fair was an equine vet.

"No, which is why I can enjoy the snow. I don't have to drive back there until the roads are plowed." He glanced out the

27

window. "They'll have their work cut out for them."

"At least the refrigerator is running with the generator, and the stove is on propane gas."

Fair pulled Harry closer. "I like the candlelight."

"Me, too, and I like the silence, especially when the fridge cuts off. Say, we got to talking about Miss Donleavey."

"Haven't thought of her in years. That was a good game the night she disappeared. We creamed Louisa. And someone got away with murder."

"Maybe." Harry's voice, light, lifted a bit higher.

"Oh, honey, she's gone forever."

But she wasn't.

2

Snow bits stung Harry as she drove the 80hp tractor outfitted with a snowplow down the long drive. The old, big tractor emanated power. She wished that it had a covered cab, but such a convenience was too expensive when she bought the tractor years ago. It was even more expensive now.

An emergency call had pulled Fair out of bed at four in the morning. Although a foot of snow had fallen by then, his one-ton four-wheel-drive truck managed to crawl through. Now, at seven-thirty in the morning, gray and dark, Harry plowed as snow piled up.

As she approached the secondary state road she could see the snowplows had passed over it at least once. They'd need to come back. Making a big circle, she headed back down her drive. With the wind-driven snow at her back, she felt a bit better.

Harry could take most any weather. Growing up on a farm, farming for most of her life, she was tough. The four years at Smith College were the softest she'd known. Even when she'd worked at the post office in Crozet, she'd come home and do chores, also doing them at dawn before heading east to the small town.

A new post office had been built by the railroad tracks. She left the job because she couldn't take her cats and dogs. The little country post office, so warm, felt like home. The big new post office, while impressive, felt like one more government building.

Whenever people mocked the postal service for its monetary losses, she still defended it. It was a department of government held to different standards, hemmed in by various monetary restrictions, some concerning its pensions. She didn't believe the P.O. could ever make money. A one-cent rise in gas prices would cost the postal service more than a billion dollars. Just one cent.

She missed seeing everyone in town five days a week and she missed working with Miranda Hogendobber, an older friend. And one more thing: Harry missed a regular paycheck.

Despite that, she loved farming full time and, like every farmer, she accepted that

Mother Nature was a demanding, difficult business partner. No one day was like any other.

A honk startled her. She turned around, snow hitting her in the face again, to see her neighbor, Deputy Cynthia Cooper, in a four-wheel-drive sheriff's vehicle.

Harry cut the motor on the tractor, climbed down.

"Hey," she greeted Cooper.

Window down, Cooper responded, "You'll freeze your butt off."

"Not much to freeze," Harry joked.

The lanky law enforcement officer smiled back. "Well, that's the truth, and how many women can say the same? Do you need anything?"

"Oh, no, Coop, thanks. Fair's on an emergency call. He'll bring back supplies."

"Where is he?"

"At the de Jarnettes'."

"He'll have slow going coming home. This is supposed to stop by mid-morning, clear. Then more snow tomorrow night. Well, it will keep me busy."

A gust made Harry duck her head for a moment. "It's the wind that gets you."

Cooper nodded. "Does."

"Speaking of picking up things," said Harry, "Jessica Hexham and I are going to

31

Nordstrom's tomorrow. I desperately need a dress for the Silver Linings fund-raiser. Need anything?"

"An entire wardrobe." Cooper smiled. "If I don't see you before the 'do,' have a good time. Raise money." She wiped some blown snow off her face. "I'll be on duty that night. Should be a great party."

3

"One hundred and fifty dollars?" Harry whispered into Jessica's ear.

Nodding back, the always well-dressed woman cooed, "Worth every penny."

"Well —" Harry stalled.

Both women stood on the second floor of Nordstrom, located at the town of Short Pump, outside of Richmond. Charlottesville contained the usual complement of shops catering to middle-class women in a suburban environment; neither Harry nor Jessica felt at ease in such outfits.

However, Nordstrom was always expensive, and Harry, ever tight with the buck, balked at one hundred and fifty dollars for a silk scarf.

"Now, look, you have as many Christmas parties to go to as I do. Do you really want to look like the frosted-hair set?" Jessica was ruthless. "I have to look good — my husband is president of Silver Linings. I can't wear the same outfit twice. It's the fund-raising season. You have to look good, too."

"Uh, now, Jessica, some of my best friends have frosted hair and look good."

"It's over. I mean over. Too seventies. Just don't do it."

"My hair's not turning gray." Harry paused. "Yet."

"When it does, just make sure it's a good gray. Now, buy the scarf and throw it around your neck when you wear that fabulous emerald-green cocktail dress. That wasn't cheap, so why drag your heels at the scarf? And I do mean heels."

"You're right." Harry dug into her leather purse for her credit card. Resistance was futile.

As Jessica stood with her at the counter, both women scanned the large second floor. "Finding good clothes in Virginia is like finding the Holy Grail," said Jessica.

"That's a fact." Harry thanked the clerk after the clerk thanked her.

The two women headed for the escalator, stepping aside as two teenage girls attached to their mother ducked in front of them.

"Adriana, you turn around and apologize right this minute," ordered the mother, West End Richmond all the way.

Red-faced, Adriana, rail thin, ears pierced,

did turn around, looked up at Harry and apologized.

"Accepted," Harry replied with some warmth.

The mother turned around. "If you don't have children, don't start."

This made both Harry and Jessica laugh. Christmas always brought out the best and worst in people. If this mother insisted on proper deportment, maybe things weren't so bad. Jessica carried her bags with aplomb. Good manners eases one's path in life. So does a good mother. "Are you sure you only want the one dress? I don't mind going to another department or even driving over to Saks."

"I can't take anymore. Shopping gives me a headache."

Jessica laughed. "Let's go home. I have Motrin in the car and a bottle of water. Just knock those orange pills back, girl."

They walked through the plowed parking lot, skies lowering.

"Thank you for coming with me." Harry peered up at the clouds.

"You've worn everyone else out." Jessica hit the remote to open the car.

Once inside, Harry ruefully agreed. "Susan only goes with me if Alicia and BoomBoom come along as her enforcers.

She says I am the worst person ever to shop with or for. I don't think I'm that bad."

"What are best friends for if not overstatement?"

"Funny. Just yesterday Susan reminded me she's my best friend and therefore can give it to me both barrels."

"She's right. Let's cruise down 250 for a bit. Getting back onto 64 will be a mess and" — she craned her neck to look up through the windshield — "it really is going to snow again. The weather report was right."

"Winter truly has arrived." Harry also looked up at the sky.

"Snow or not, the fund-raiser is going to be held tomorrow night. Anyway, you need to show off that wonderful dress."

Harry, with a devilish smile, clicked shut her seatbelt. "Wouldn't it be fun to show up with as much showing as possible?"

Jessica cruised onto the highway. "That depends. Whenever I have a moment where I question the Almighty, I remind myself He gave us fashion and I am comforted."

"Well, girl, you will be comforted tomorrow night, as there will be a lot of fashion."

"Harry, clothes cover a multitude of sins."

The two women giggled.

But some sins are harder to cover than others.

4

Unbeknownst to Harry and Jessica, Lou Higham and Tyler were also at the large shopping center in Short Pump. Lou wanted to buy surprising and expensive gifts for Arden without driving up to Washington, D.C., or flying to New York or Atlanta. Although a man who expected to be in charge, Lou proved generous. He liked adorning his wife with jewelry, alluring clothing. Sometimes he'd surprise her with a fancy piece of luggage all packed and ready for a trip, even if only overnight to a bed-and-breakfast he liked in Orange County, Virginia. A forty-minute drive from Charlottesville beat a clogged flight to Manhattan.

Tyler, with some reluctance, tagged along with his father, who was determined to start the young man early on the ways to please women. He bribed Tyler by promising he would take him to the Apple store to buy a new iPhone.

"Dad, you're not going to buy Mom anything from in here?" Tyler felt miserable as his father marched him through the aisles of Victoria's Secret.

"No. I'm looking. The day will come when, if you're smart, you'll buy a special woman special lingerie. It makes her feel, uh, beautiful, and she appreciates that you think of her that way. Just park that in the back of your mind."

Outside the store, Lou determinedly strode to a high-end men's store. Tyler couldn't imagine being with a woman that way. He liked the girls in school who, like him, were computer nerds or liked chem lab. One girl in particular, Yasmine Dulaney, sat next to him at the lab. She was a year older, smarter than smart, and they could talk endlessly about the properties of sulfuric acid or why and at what rate iron rusts. For Tyler, connections started in the mind. For Lou, with women, they started below the belt. While connections have to start somewhere, Lou's approach, direct and simple, might lead to more. Tyler, slow, halting, uncertain, in time might have a better way to approach girls. But girls, at this point in Tyler's life, were a separate species.

The oaken walls and display shelves,

enhanced by a woodsy scent artfully released from tiny nozzles hidden throughout the store, inspired Lou to buy a three-ply cashmere sweater in a heavy heather.

"Tyler, I'll spring for a turtleneck if you find one you like."

Smiling shyly, the thin young man said, "Dad, I'm going to hit you up in the Apple store."

Lou smiled back. "I just bet you will, Son. I just bet you will."

The two had traipsed through the many stores for two hours. Lou did find a bracelet for Arden. Large lapis lazuli rectangles set in gold. It wasn't cheap, but it was a wonderful Christmas gift. Even Tyler admired it and said, "Mom will love it."

Checking his watch, Lou commented, "I'm done. Checked off my list. Okay, your turn."

With a brisk step, Tyler headed toward the Apple store. None such existed in Charlottesville, although one could buy an Apple computer at the University of Virginia bookstore, but only if a student, or a member of the faculty or administration. So everyone else had to hit the road, and Richmond was closer than the Washington area, plus the drive was considerably more pleasant. Once in the orbit of Washington, traffic clogged, people flipped the bird at one another, and too many horns blared. Lou always said those were not true Virginians, but who knew? Even Virginians were not immune to an erosion of manners under driving and shopping duress. Those who worked for the government endured even more duress, or so it seemed.

Thinking he had lucked out on the drive, at least, Lou walked into the store with his son, who zoomed directly to the iPhones.

Picking up a gold one, he said, "This is it, Dad."

Immediately Lou checked out the price. "Not too bad."

"Yeah, but I want," and Tyler rattled off such a long list of apps that Lou's eyes glazed over. "And, Dad, I need to get a cover for the glass. Gotta protect your investment." Tyler tried to talk his father's language.

"Uh." Lou's head ran up calculations while the overworked salesperson nodded that he would reach them as soon as he finished with the prior customer.

Lou eyed the many covers, some more expensive than others, but all overpriced to his mind. "The phones are cheap. They hit you up on all the other stuff. What a damned cash cow." Lou knew chargers for the car, and different ones for the house, would also be added to the bill.

"Once it's loaded, that's it. And they're fast now, Dad."

"Right." Lou could use about anything techie.

It was the cost that choked him.

Tyler carefully scanned the various covers, picking out a hot turquoise.

"Don't get that."

"Why?"

"It's girly. Get something dark. Black leather."

"If I buy a bright color, I'll always find my phone." Tyler picked out a hot pink.

Lou practically slapped it out of his hand. "Never! Buy the goddamned black leather one or I'm not paying for a thing."

Tyler did as he was told.

Outside, Lou looked at the few snowflakes twirling down. "Let's hit the road. Maybe we can get home before it really comes down."

Saying nothing, Tyler opened the door after his father unlocked the Acura. They drove in silence for ten minutes; cars and trucks had their lights on. Most people adjusted for the weather. A few idiots still fired down I-64 at seventy-miles-plus.

Finally Lou said, "The phones are so thin

now. Back in the eighties, they looked like small bazookas." As his son remained silent, Lou became falsely cheerful. "Wait until you pull your phone out. The guys at school will want one, too. You'll be the first."

"I'm not the first, but I'm close enough."

"Cool stuff."

"Right."

"Tyler, there's a logic to what you said about being able to find your phone, but believe me, you'll thank me for making you get the black leather. You don't want guys looking at you sideways."

"They don't look at me at all. I don't even exist."

"Of course you do. You're not real outgoing, but you're really bright, Tyler. And success is the best revenge. Just wait, you'll beat all those dudes to the bank." Lou laughed.

Tyler wanted to say, "Does everything have to be a competition? I don't care what other guys think. I don't care what you think. You don't know me." But he didn't, of course.

5

As snow fell outside, people young and old danced in the ballroom at the Keswick Club. As partygoers entered through the front door, a brand-new Ford F-150 sat right out front, bright red, though becoming covered with snow. Given the weather, Pete Vavilov put the raffle drawing sign inside the front door on an easel. Those supporters of Silver Linings who had paid a thousand dollars for a ticket were each given a key. Near the end of the evening, each one would get inside the truck. Whichever person had the key that started the truck would win it.

Inside, downstairs, a fat blue spruce festooned with colored balls, garland, and twinkling lights announced it was Christmas, as if all the other decorations did not. Arden Higham, in charge of the color scheme, had outdone herself. She and her team found and copied Victorian pictures of sleighs in the snow, beautiful ladies with their hands in muffs, reindeer, Scottish terriers. The entire spectrum of what was popular during those times formed the table centerpieces. Small baubles hung from sconces and a sleigh filled a corner, overflowing with gifts for the boys. Silver Linings worked with young men, twelve through eighteen, most of them from poor homes headed by single mothers.

St. Cyril's, the Catholic church in Crozet, allowed the organization to use its rec room. Tonight Father O'Connor — young if not a bit portly — beamed at the turnout. Although Silver Linings operated independently of St. Cyril's, the association was close.

Brian Hexham; Pete Vavilov; Lou Higham; Coach Toth; Nelson Yarbrough, former UVA quarterback; and many others mentored the young men, coached them in various sports leagues, and brought their own sons to the activities. The original idea was to pair a privileged boy with an underprivileged boy, a buddy system, but the boys found their own compatriots. Over time the natural buddy system faltered and a more accurate buddy system took its place.

The sponsors had given the young men money for tuxedos. For most of them this

was the first time they were in black tie. Most of them loved it. Then again, most people are not averse to being the center of attention.

Young ladies from the church attended, as well as the daughters of participants and sponsors.

"I had no idea Arden was so artistic," Darlene de Jarnette said to Harry as they both waited on the sidelines of the downstairs ballroom. Like most ballrooms, it was rectangular, neutral in palette and with a raised dais for the band. Arden's décor added color and excitement to the bland setting. Their husbands lined up at the bar to get them drinks. "I think of her as the detail type, bookkeeping. I guess I don't associate those skills with décor." Darlene laughed. "I'll revise my opinion."

"Girls, how about if a thorn stands between two roses?" Reverend Herbert Jones, a Lutheran minister, put his arms around the ladies as a photographer snapped a photo.

"Your red cummerbund is appropriately seasonal." Darlene smiled.

"At these events, you ladies get all the colors, beautiful gowns and jewels. We're stuck looking like penguins." He smiled as he waved at Father O'Connor. "Harry, looks like Susan whipped the food operation in order."

"She has. St. Luke's can be proud. Jessica Hexham has everything organized for St. Cyril's."

Harry, Susan, and the others were parishioners at St. Luke's. Reverend Jones had been the pastor for decades.

"Good. Good." He released them, walked through the crowd, shaking hands, giving ladies kisses.

Each Christmas, churches distributed food and clothing. Some of the boys in the room would be receiving those items with their mothers, grandmothers, siblings. But tonight the excitement was high, thanks to the truck raffle, the band, the food, the music.

Susan Tucker joined Harry and Darlene just as Fair and Max de Jarnette delivered the drinks.

"Susan, let me get you whatever you need," said Fair. "Your husband is over there talking about a bill on the floor that I think has something to do with cameras at stoplights. I tuned out, but if you wait for him, you'll be parched."

Glancing over at Ned, Susan said, "Fair, I would kill for a scotch and soda."

Seeing the crowd at the bar, Harry

quipped, "You may have to." She handed her best friend her own drink.

"Thank you." Susan gulped down the entire restorative cocktail, to the amazement of Harry, Fair, and Darlene.

Jessica Hexham joined them as Harry said to Susan, "I've never seen you do that."

Jessica laughed. "And it looks as though it will be a long night. She may do it again."

As the small group complimented Jessica on the festive event, Fair trudged back to the bar to replace his wife's drink and buy a scotch and soda for Susan. Given his six feet five inches, he could usually command the bartender's attention with ease. He wedged in next to Pete.

"The truck's a beauty."

Pete beamed. "The city gas mileage is eighteen mpg, out on the highway about twenty-six mpg. Now, I give or take a mile or two. I like to get about twenty-thousand miles on an engine. I know, I know, I'm supposed to spout the company line, but I always give a little wiggle room on the estimated mileage."

"All three truck brands have made such improvements."

"They have, Fair, but you drive a Ford and you praise the Lord." Pete slapped him on the back. "Your wife drives a 1978 Ford

F-150. You know how good they are."

"Tyler," Pete called over Lou and Arden's son, a weedy, pale fourteen-year-old. "Did your dad get in on the raffle?"

"Yeah."

"You tell him to let you see if you can start the truck, hear?"

"Yes, sir." Tyler scooted off.

"One of those brainy ones," Pete remarked. "I sure hope the kid puts on a few pounds these next few years. No way he can play football skinny as he is."

Al Toth rolled up to the bar. "If you boys had done this in high school I would have benched you." The coach and two of his former outstanding players liked to joke about old times.

Harry, still waiting for her drink, waved to BoomBoom and Alicia. They would eventually reach her, but first she felt a hand on her shoulder.

"That is so becoming on you. Harry, your body is the same as when you took Algebra Two." Esther Mercier Toth circled round to face Harry.

"That's the truth," said Susan. "I fight to lose every extra pound. She never puts them on." Susan kissed her former teacher on the cheek, as did Harry.

"You look just the same," Harry said to

50

Mrs. Toth, and it was mostly true.

Esther smiled. "It's thrilling what modern medicine can do. A nip here, a tuck there. Sooner or later, though, girls, the edifice comes tumbling down."

They all laughed.

Pete took the floor as the band put down their instruments for a much-needed break. "Ladies and gentlemen, thank you for your support of Silver Linings. Young men, come here." The boys, varying heights, from barely five feet at twelve years to over six feet at seventeen, joined him. "Here is where your money goes. Our high school graduates will have funds for college thanks to you. Fellows, raise your hands."

Five young men did just that, and one kid — not the best-looking fellow, but with a killer smile — called out, "Thank you." He was then joined by the others.

Pete listed the event's donors — an insurance company paid for the food, et cetera — thanked Father O'Connor, the Hexhams, Arden and her decorating crews. "I won't bore you with a long-winded speech. I know you want to know who wins the truck, so come on, let's find out."

Up the stairs they trooped, ladies grabbing coats, for the snow fell harder now. Those with keys, one by one, tried the truck. No ignition. Tyler, key in hand, father by his side, tried. No.

Alicia Palmer, sliding into the bucket seat, swooping in her long gown, rolled down the window, put the key in the ignition. *Rumble.*

"I can't believe it," said the woman, who should have won an Oscar. "I never win anything."

Arden whispered to Jessica, "She has more money than God. Ain't it always the way?"

The group inside the front door cheered as Alicia came back in, key firmly in her grip. BoomBoom kissed her.

Alicia held up her hands. "Thank you, Pete. This is a wonderful occasion and I'm glad to be the lucky winner. I have been fortunate in so many ways and I have noticed that Father O'Connor's old Mercury is fading away. I would like to donate this wonderful new F-150 to St. Cyril's and Father O'Connor." She looked at Reverend Jones, for BoomBoom was a staunch Lutheran, then kissed Father O'Connor as he came at her, beckoning for the keys.

"This is a small recompense for 1517," he said.

Most of the gathered knew that was when Martin Luther nailed the ninety-five theses on the doors of the cathedral at Wittenberg. Those who didn't were informed by their neighbors.

People laughed and cheered. Reverend Jones, never without his sense of decorum, strode up to Father O'Connor and shook his hand. Then the two men, priest and pastor, laughed.

Everyone who attended that evening's Christmas fund-raiser remembered it both for the party and for what happened later.

6

Her windshield wipers couldn't keep up with the snowfall. Deputy Cooper struggled in a police department SUV to reach a wreck on Garth Road. Her siren blared. If she was having troubles, she wondered how long it would take the ambulance to reach the scene of the accident.

Finally, just beyond the sign for Barracks Road Stables, she saw a new Explorer pulled off the road on the shoulder. She parked behind it, quickly got out. The young man who had pulled over and had made the 911 call got out of his old Corolla. He turned up his coat collar.

Cooper nodded to him, and he stayed behind her as she opened the door to the vehicle in front of his ancient Corolla.

"He was dead when I pulled over, ma'am."

Cooper noted that Pete Vavilov — dead in the driver's seat — wore his seatbelt. No blood. She closed the door, checked the skid marks that were rapidly fading. He just slid off the road. She also noticed another fading pair of tracks behind the Explorer.

"Did you see anyone else?"

"No, ma'am — I mean, no, Officer."

She looked around. No electric lights anywhere. The power died again.

"Let me take your information so you can go home. It's an evil night. If I have more questions, I'll find you. I know I will have some questions."

He handed her his driver's license. She wrote down his stats.

"You've got about nine miles of bad road." She used the old expression. "Think that car can make it?"

"I hope so."

"Here." She handed him her card. "That's my cell. If you get stuck, call me. I'll get you home in my SUV. Might take a while because we'll need to take care of this, but if I can't leave, I'll send another officer."

"Thank you." He opened his squeaky car door, grateful to be inside, and slowly drove away.

The temperature kept dropping, but Cooper wanted to investigate as much as she could. Already, the tracks of the young man's Corolla and whoever pulled up behind the Explorer were indistinguishable now.

She opened the door again. Felt Pete's neck. She knew he was dead, but if she felt his temperature, she'd have an idea of how long he'd been there. Not very long. Then she noticed that his right arm and hand hung down over the center console. The interior of the Explorer was black, otherwise she might have noticed this bizarre fact right away.

Pete Vavilov was missing his index and middle fingers.

7

Sunday, December 8, celebrated the Feast of the Immaculate Conception of the Blessed Virgin Mary. The Very Reverend Herbert Jones preached one of his famously rousing sermons. St. Luke's somewhat strayed from the Lutheran dogma that avoided saint's days. Reverend Jones felt those who had come before — leading exemplary lives, often lives of great sacrifice — should be remembered, whether Lutheran or Episcopalian, Baptist or Hindu. Anyway, so many saints suffered so exquisitely before the Catholic Church cracked open, it seemed churlish to Reverend Jones not to remember their holy devotion.

Harry, next to Fair, sat in a front pew in front of the lectern. She loved her pastor as a man, and she loved him as a servant of the Church.

His words on this day about the struggle of religion to honor and respect women struck a chord with her. Wisely, Reverend Jones did not dwell on the Immaculate Conception itself, for December 8 was the celebration of the conception of Mary, not the baby Jesus. How many Immaculate Conceptions can one have?

This thought occurred to Harry, followed by another in which she wondered how powerful men in the past wrote off outside children by a twist of logic — maybe not going so far as to claim an Immaculate Conception but some other twist of logic to wiggle out of an embarrassing situation.

As far as organized religion, Harry was devout in her own way, though she could never quite buy the whole bag of beans. For that matter, neither did many of her generation, among them her dear friends. They drew comfort and strength from their churches but shied away from dogma.

After the service, Reverend Jones stood at the rear of one wide church aisle to shake hands with the departing congregation. Waiting in the last pew and observing the passersby in all their Sunday finery were his Lutheran cats, Elocution, Cazenovia, and Lucy Fur.

"Good sermon. Poppy's voice just fills the church." Cazenovia had nestled next to Reverend Jones as he'd struggled to write

the sermon. She felt a big compliment was deserved.

"Poppy always tries to find a good balance. He was one of the first in the county to welcome female reverends. 'Course, the Episcopalians sent an ordained woman here as soon as they were accepted and Poppy personally greeted her. He thinks we all stand before God, even animals," said Lucy Fur.

"Yes," Elocution agreed, and while she loved Reverend Jones, Elo harbored feline suspicion about organized religions. She kept them to herself.

"Should, but he's talking to humans. They only want to hear about themselves, not the cat who kept mice away from the cradle or about any of us, really," Cazenovia shrewdly commented.

"He slips something in about animals now and then." Lucy Fur loved the Reverend.

Unaware of the kitty commentary, Harry and Fair shook Reverend Jones's hand, thanked him for his thoughts, and then walked into the foyer. Light from the huge floor-to-ceiling handblown windows flooded the room.

Slipping her arms into her coat held by her husband, Harry glanced out one of the windows. "They're early." There was still unloading to be done. " 'Tis the season of charitable projects."

Fair, seeing the few cars that he recognized, said, "You go to the meeting room, honey. I'll round up some of the boys and we'll knock this out in no time."

Harry stepped outside, the cold air bracing. She hurried down the beautiful stone arcade built right after the Revolutionary War to a two-story stone building at the end of this arcade. St. Luke's was built around a quad, with the back part open. Three sides had arcades, the church smack in the middle of the longest arcade. Two-story buildings anchored each end. The rear of all buildings looked into the quad. Front windows viewed the slightly rolling lawn at the front. The windows looking directly out the rear had an unbroken view down to the lovely old graveyard bound by a stone wall, which was the same stone as the buildings.

The trees, bushes, and plantings made over the centuries added to this spot's tranquility. Even with everything covered in snow, St. Luke's beckoned in the pale winter light.

Harry reached Jessica Hexham's car. Following Harry on foot were Susan, Boom-Boom, and Alicia. A bit farther back came Fair, with Ned and two other younger male parishioners.

The driveway to the rear of the meeting room building had been plowed. As Harry was in charge of the buildings and grounds, she always made sure everything was properly plowed in the winter. In spring she planted, she mowed in summer, and she raked in the fall. She knew the grounds and the condition of the buildings almost as intimately as the men who'd built St. Luke's more than two hundred years ago.

Brian Hexham drove their SUV. As everyone wore their church clothes, they stepped gingerly on the plowed macadam. Ice could be invisible.

Fair motioned for the two other cars and one truck to park next to the Hexhams, then he and the men began unloading box after box. Harry, Susan, BoomBoom, and Alicia carried the lighter ones, not because they couldn't handle the heavy ones — three of the four women did farm chores — but because all were in heels.

Once inside the church's meeting room, the tables were labeled: *clothes, shoes, outerwear, scarves and mittens, china and glassware, canned food, toys and video games, pet treats,* and *miscellaneous.*

Harry directed indoor traffic. Reverend Jones was still in his robe and vestments when he walked in, accompanied as usual by his cats.

"Look at all this." He thanked Jessica, who was head of the fundraising drive for St. Cyril's. "Jessica, this is wonderful."

"Everyone pitched in," Jessica replied.

"Anything that brings our various congregations closer is a blessing." Reverend Jones smiled.

Each Christmas, the churches in Crozet gathered necessities and gifts for those less fortunate. The various churches took turns storing the goods, sorting them, and wrapping them. On December 20, the boxes were delivered.

Over the last four years the drives had become so successful that the churches had to divvy up storage. The Episcopal and Methodist churches linked together, as did the Lutheran church and the Catholic church. Presbyterian, various Baptist churches, and the evangelical ones, too, all pitched in.

Apart from actual deliveries, the hardest task was determining to whom to give the gifts. The secretaries from each church's guild went to the county offices, sat with the people there to identify those in need. Also a big help was the sheriff's department. They saw what many other citizens did not. This year it was Deputy Cynthia Cooper who headed that effort.

Each year, more and more people slid onto the list for help. Rich as Albemarle County was and always will be, it, too, has people struggling.

"Look at that," Harry exclaimed when Brian tottered into the meeting room struggling under the weight of a huge carton.

Fair quickly grabbed the other end. "What's in here?"

"Wait until you see it." Brian and Fair edged the box onto the toy table, which was filling up.

Brian pulled open the cardboard top, plucking out a shiny model of an F-150 truck.

Ever excited by anything with wheels, including a toy, Harry hurried over to the box. "Wow! Who donated these?"

The box was filled with toy trucks, all Ford models from various years. It was a history lesson in Ford products.

"Peter and Charlene Vavilov," Jessica answered.

At the mention of Peter's name, a hush fell over the room. Reverend Jones walked over, lifted up a perfect truck, 1954. He opened a door on the toy.

"These are collector's items." He looked into the box again. "Beautiful, just beautiful. We haven't had time to talk about the terrible news about Cynthia finding poor Peter last night. That makes this gift even more special."

The cats, now on the table, also peered into the box. Being less impressed, they leapt over to the table with sweaters, each snuggling into one. As the humans were mesmerized by the toy trucks, they didn't notice.

"Charlene had mentioned she and Peter had put this together last week," Brian informed them. "Of course, she thought they'd deliver this together. This is so sad. I can't quite believe it."

Susan, voice low, said, "How can we ever thank her?"

"By handing out the toy trucks," Brian simply replied. "That's all I know to do."

Arden Higham walked over. "Somehow we've all got to focus on the task. After all, Peter was so happy last night."

Everyone seemed to talk at once. A few of the people had still not heard the horrible news of Pete's death, since it had just happened.

Leaving St. Luke's, Fair, in his vet truck, headed east toward Garth Road.

"Honey, I just need to check the de Jarnettes' gelding. Won't take a minute. We're halfway to their farm."

"Okay. I keep thinking about Pete. How terrible for Charlene. Christmas will always be a reminder."

"Yes, it will. You never know, do you?"

They drove on twisting roads, alongside fields glistening with fresh snow. Snow piled onto branches, the conifers bending under the weight, dark green peeping out against the white.

Ten minutes later, they entered through a tall, open, tremendously expensive wrought-iron gate. They drove up to a large new barn, also expensive looking. Lots of money was spent on show. The barn was functional, though, a relief to Fair, who dreaded working in barns with chandeliers, brass polished everywhere, yet the horses' stall floors were uneven. Things like that drove him crazy.

Fair returned to Harry waiting in the truck ten minutes later. He slid behind the wheel. "Doing fine."

Before he could drive around the circle, Max de Jarnette appeared on the house's porch, waving them over.

"Fair. Hello, Harry." After a brief acknowledgment of Pete's accident, the buff middle-aged man asked, "Fair, would you donate a free vet check for the youth riding program?"

"Sure. Max, go back inside. You'll freeze to death out here."

"Yeah. Well, I apologize for not asking at the Silver Linings event. Too much going on. I'm glad it was a great event. I'm glad Pete drove off happy."

"He surely did. The night was the most successful fund-raiser ever."

At last headed home, Harry sighed. "How do we get roped into these things?"

"I don't mind donating a vet check."

"I know, but I mean all the fund-raisers and parties we have to attend between now and New Year's."

"Honey, the only way I know to get out of them is death." Right away, he realized he'd said the wrong thing at the wrong time.

"Bite your tongue."

"You're right." He paused, hoping to lighten the mood. "How about a dread disease? Is that better?"

8

Gray skies dimmed the glare from the snow, which now sported a crust on top. Foxes, raccoons, and possums could walk on it without sinking into deep powder and struggling. Occasionally a small animal would hit a drift, fall in, and scramble out, but for the most part travel was easy, with the occasional slip here and there.

Having been holed up in their dens, or wherever they'd made a nest, everyone was hungry. The birds that hadn't flown south had built their nests with care in protected tree hollows. No one built a den or nest facing northwest, although the clever foxes might put an escape route in that direction.

Monday, December 9, was cloudy and cold. It would have been frigid if skies were clear.

Mrs. Murphy, Tucker, and a grumbling Pewter headed out from the barn. In the pastures, Tucker, being heavier than the cats, used deer trails. The three animals moved west toward the swift-running creek between Harry's farm and that of Reverend Herbert Jones. As St. Luke's offered beautiful living accommodations, Reverend Jones rented his old home place to Cynthia Cooper. Like so many Virginia farms, the clapboard house and small barn had been built to stand for centuries and did. The Jones place cornerstone, laid in 1811, had withstood two wars on Virginia territory, blizzards, sleet storms, hurricanes, a few small tornadoes, and, as always, the searing summer sun.

The three friends perched on a fallen tree trunk next to the creek. Although the trunk was snow-covered, it was a comfortable spot. One flat end on the ground was easy for the corgi.

Upstream, the edges of the ice-encased beaver dam glittered. The sides of the creek were also ragged with ice, testament to the frigid temperatures.

A little puff of breath rose up as Mrs. Murphy spoke. *"Beavers carry so much fat. I bet they never really feel the cold."*

"Just like Pewter," Tucker ungraciously replied.

Fat though she was, Pewter's reflexes were lightning fast. She whacked Tucker so hard the dog fell off the log and began sliding into the creek. The ice along the banks cracked, but the dog, with a mighty pull, managed to haul herself up.

Fangs bared, she threatened, *"I could grab you by the neck."*

"Ha." The gray butterball nonchalantly closed her eyes for a moment.

Watching a coyote, Mrs. Murphy suddenly shot off the log, heading east.

"What's gotten into her?" Pewter's eyes widened. Never one to miss any event if possible, the gray cat tore out after her friend, bits of snow flying off her claws.

The corgi followed, somewhat slowed down when she veered off to a deer path.

Now smelling the heavy scent of the coyote, Tucker barked loudly.

The unconcerned marauder loped off, carrying in his jaws the bones of an intact human arm from the elbow down. A bracelet hung at the wrist.

Pewter caught up with the tiger cat. *"Are you crazy, running after a coyote?"*

"He has a prize. He's not interested in me." Mrs. Murphy searched the snow, saw the shiny object that had caught her attention, and walked over. *"I saw the arm, saw something slide off."*

Pewter reached out to pat a gold bracelet:

a simple band of hammered gold with a small buckle.

Tucker plowed through the snow. *"Murph, don't you ever do that again!"* Seeing the bracelet, she put her nose on it. *"Nothing."*

"Considering it slid off bones, I doubt there'd be any scent." The tiger cat inspected the lovely gold object. *"Nothing else on it."*

"What would be on it?" Pewter was now intrigued, which held off any complaints about the cold.

"Oh, you know now how humans write all over stuff. 'Love Forever' or initials, silly stuff like that. This is gold and it's heavy. Expensive."

"Maybe that's why it fell off the bone. Heavy," Tucker opined. *"It was my barking that did it."*

The two cats humored her. *"Of course."*

The motion probably jostled the lovely gold bracelet off.

"Let's leave it here." Pewter's stomach growled.

"No." Mrs. Murphy considered its value. *"We'll hide it in the tack room. Someday it might prove useful."*

"Give it to Mom." Tucker knew Harry would like it. Their human admired simple, well-designed things.

"Not yet," said Mrs. Murphy. *"Let's hide it,*

then figure out how to give it to her for Christmas. She'll be shocked." Ever practical, Mrs. Murphy had already hit upon a use for the late-nineteenth-century bracelet.

"That's a good idea," the dog agreed. *"She likes jewelry. This looks like something good."*

"Then you two can take turns carrying it," grumbled Pewter. *"I'm not putting metal in my mouth in this cold."* She made for the barn, a half mile distant.

Tucker and Mrs. Murphy did just that, taking turns. Finally reaching the tack room, they considered hiding places.

"Can't put it behind the tack trunk — the mice will steal it." Pewter offered good advice, from her vantage point on the desk, for the mice would carry off anything they could.

"How about this pile of clean saddle pads?" Tucker walked over to the white square sheepskin pads.

"What if she pulls out a pad?" Mrs. Murphy could hear the mice scurrying behind the tack trunk. The tiger cat inclined her head toward the trunk.

Pewter jumped up, sweeping her right paw down behind it.

A mouse ducked in and a chorus of mice sang out, *"Fatty, fatty."*

"I'll kill you. I'll crush your skull!" Ever sensi-

tive to what she deemed fat-phobia, Pewter spat.

An old velvet-covered riding hard-hat helmet lay on its side on the floor, along with worn paddock boots and other items that Harry intended to repair or clean.

Mrs. Murphy carried the bracelet over, pulled the helmet lining out a bit with one long claw, dropped the bracelet inside, and released her claw. The bracelet had disappeared.

"That will do for now. You two remember where this is. We can fetch it Christmas Eve."

"What if she uses that helmet?" Tucker asked.

"The covering is all ripped to shreds," replied the tiger cat. *"She uses that helmet hanging on the peg. She's been talking about getting this recovered for a year."* Mrs. Murphy was confident she'd found the right hiding place.

Tucker smiled. *"This will be the best Christmas present."*

"What a surprise," Pewter added.

9

Tyler Higham shoveled food into his mouth at the breakfast table while his father watched, nostrils flared with disgust at his teenage son's eating habits.

"Slow down," Lou reprimanded Tyler as he folded the newspaper, quite forgetting what he himself was like at fourteen.

"Dad, I'll be late for school."

"I drive you to St. Anne's five days a week. You haven't been late yet."

Tyler did slow down but scraped his utensils loudly on the plate to irritate his father.

Lou picked up the paper again as his wife said from across the table, "Lou."

He paid no attention, so Arden raised her voice. "Lou."

Startled slightly, he set aside the paper before glancing at her. He jabbed at another waffle on the serving plate.

"Will you pick up the dry cleaning?" Arden asked.

"Yes, of course." Lou poured maple syrup on the waffles.

Tyler resumed speed-eating. Arden laid her hand on his forearm. He frowned but did slow down.

"This isn't a barnyard," she said and sighed.

Pushing away from the table, Tyler stomped out of the room.

"I can't win," she said resignedly.

"Give him sixteen years." Lou checked the large kitchen clock. "By the time he's thirty maybe he'll act like a man instead of a spoiled brat."

"If we live that long." Arden put down her fork.

Lou rose. "I don't know if that's a blessing or a curse. I'll tell you when I get there."

He walked into the hall, picked up the large artwork folder by the front door, and yelled, "Tyler."

Tyler thudded down the stairs, slamming the door as he left the house. It's doubtful he ever thought about it. He didn't think he was uncooperative, uncommunicative. He thought his parents were unreasonable and petty tyrants.

Arden heard the whine of the electric garage door as it opened, the whine and thud as it closed. She exhaled loudly. Like many mothers, she found herself in the middle between her husband and her son. Both drove her nuts.

After clearing the table, she loaded the dishwasher. Then she walked into the living room to pick up her iPad to check what still needed to be done for the St. Cyril's deliveries. The trees and the living room were all decorated in blue and silver, Lou's demand. It did look seasonal, but it didn't feel very Christmassy.

Father and son rode in silence in Lou's Acura MDX. Lou kept his eyes on the road. Tyler stared out the passenger window.

Lou finally said, "Homework done?"

"Yeah."

"You doing okay?"

"Yeah," came the unconvincing monosyllabic reply.

Silence followed, then Lou broke in. "If you want to talk about Pete's death, I can listen. I know he gave you a lot of attention on the soccer team. He was a good coach."

"If you say so."

"Life can be unfair, Son. If you'd take sports a little more seriously, things would go easier for you. You just bull through practices, head down."

"Coming from you, Dad, that's pretty funny, telling me life can be unfair."

"Why?"

"You're always at me. That's unfair."

"I just want you to be the best." Lou inhaled. "I'm here if you need me."

"Are you worried, Dad?"

"About you? You're no longer a little boy, after all."

"No, about you. You're getting old."

"Worried about me?" Lou's voice rose. A flash of anger reddened his face. He pulled into the line of cars at St. Anne's student drop-off point. Tyler didn't wait for Lou to creep up the line. He just opened the door, got out, and slammed it. Lou pulled out of line and headed to work at his advertising agency.

Meanwhile, Arden, laden with a food basket, walked up the shoveled stone path to Charlene Vavilov's front door.

Cars, SUVs, and one fifty-thousand-dollar truck lined the street in Ednam Forest subdivision. The Vavilovs' house was overflowing with people, testimony to the great affection felt by all for Charlene. And, of course, to the respect for Pete, who worked hard for many causes. Flowers filled the rooms; the long dining room table was

77

covered with food.

Jessica Hexham directed people. Since Pete's death, a lady from St. Cyril's was there from breakfast to the end of the day, to assist, offer comfort, be a friend. Jessica had organized the shifts. One woman was in charge of the door, another the telephone, another the kitchen, and three were in charge of cleanup.

Charlene stood in the living room, talking to everyone. Her two sons flanked her. It was obvious that mother and sons drew comfort from one another.

Harry, Susan, BoomBoom and Alicia, Miranda Hogendobber, the Sanburnes, the social powers in Crozet, all helped, too. Jessica also organized the St. Luke's ladies. Everything that could be done was done.

Harry and Susan carried out dishes and carried back clean ones laden with more food. BoomBoom ran the dishwasher and Alicia wiped down the glasses so they sparkled. Miranda cleaned coffee cups.

Arden stuck her head into the kitchen. "Need a hand?"

"We're running out of cups. People are guzzling the coffee and tea, I guess because it's cold outside."

"I'll run home and bring twelve more. Won't take me a minute. I'm close by."

Susan gratefully looked up as she had the refrigerator open. "Arden, that would be a godsend."

The old friends in the kitchen took a short breather.

"Any word from the pathologist?" Boom-Boom asked.

"Not yet," Susan answered. "Ned said everyone in hospitals are on overload because so many people die during the holidays."

"Really?" Miranda knelt down, looking under the sink for more dishwasher detergent. "Found it."

"Let me put that on a list," said Alicia. "Detergent lasts a day at the rate this is going." She scribbled on a pad affixed to the wall next to a large blackboard.

"That and suicides," said Susan. "Christmas pushes people right over the edge."

"Not Pete," Alicia piped up.

"No. Heart attack or stroke, I would think," BoomBoom said to her.

"Christmas would be a great time to get away with murder," Harry idly mentioned. "Just thinking. It would, you know." Harry shut up as Karen Turner, a St. Cyril's stalwart, tottered in carrying an enormous vase bursting with white lilies and red roses.

"Water."

79

Alicia took the heavy vase from the small woman. "You or the flowers."

Karen smiled. "Flowers! More just delivered. An interesting arrangement."

Jessica popped in. "Need reinforcements?" She noted the flowers and smiled. "What do you think, girls?"

"Gorgeous," came the unanimous response.

Jessica beamed, then hurried back out. She stuck her head in for one second. "Motrin?"

"I've got some." Alicia plucked her purse off a kitchen chair. "Be right out."

"Jessica sent those flowers, bet you." Harry was piling hot tiny cinnamon rolls onto a tray. "She has that incredible way of putting disparate things together."

As the friends talked and worked, Susan silently calculated how they would make up for lost time regarding St. Luke's food drive deliveries. So many people from both churches were here doing what they could.

What no one knew other than Charlene, law enforcement, and the funeral home was that two fingers were missing from Pete's hand. Sheriff Shaw had asked Charlene to keep the news to herself for now, not even to tell her sons.

For Charlene, all of this hoopla was surreal. Any minute, Pete would walk back through the door. But instead, Father O'Connor walked through the front door, and that's when it really hit her.

10

St. Cyril's was set back from Route 250. Quiet and beautiful, it invited congregants to worship by its peacefulness alone. The Victorian-style church, like all the churches and synagogues in Albemarle County, was a vital hub of community activity, and its priest, like his colleagues of different faiths, had insight into not just his congregants but to the community as a whole.

An alert member of the clergy would quickly know what was happening in the area, to whom and often why. The real question was: What does one do about it?

St. Cyril's, with a very mixed congregation — rich, poor, white, Asian, Hispanic, African American — was no exception. Clothing, toys, kitchenwares poured in for the holiday gift giving. Western Route 250, a ribbon of privilege, had residents who could give more, and many did. The labels in the clothing would have brought money from local resale boutiques. One might say, "Well, they can afford it." But how many who can, give?

Reverend Jones had been phoned by Father O'Connor, who assisted the aging parish priest. Father David O'Brien was slowing down, so these days Father O'Connor assumed more and more responsibility. The huge volume of donated goods this year was such that Susan Tucker arranged to begin distribution before December 20. Father O'Connor also told Reverend Jones that they had lost some valuable organizing time due to Pete's shocking death.

Susan borrowed a Suburban, as it could carry more than either her or Harry's station wagon, as goods continued to pour in. There was room in the vehicle for the animals, which the two ladies took along. In the past, they'd discovered that when they would call on houses with an elderly person living alone the animals made them so happy, often lowering their fear of who was at the door. Their cats and dogs also got the kids excited, and there were far more children in need than public officials realized. In rural areas, the poor are often invisible.

"Am I glad to see you." Father O'Connor beamed when Harry and Susan walked into

St. Cyril's. "We're working around the clock to get all these boxes packed."

"Oh, my God," Harry exclaimed, then realized where she was.

"Right place to say it." The attractive priest smiled. "I've said worse."

Neatly sorted and stacked, clothing filled every table, piled on the floor; even the walkways between the tables were clogged. There was even more here at St. Cyril's than there had been at St. Luke's.

Jan McGee had driven over from Manakin-Sabot to help. This lady could organize anything. Jessica and Arden had needed the help. Jan approached Susan and Harry, saying, "Isn't this something?"

"Yes, it is." Susan wormed her way through a narrow aisle to chat with Jan while Harry went over the delivery list with Father O'Connor.

"Susan, if the roads are treacherous off the main roads, put some bags of kitty litter in the back of the truck or SUV," Jan advised.

"I'll remember that. We will all start out with plenty of ballast. It's later, after we drop everything off, that I worry about."

"Kitty litter," Jan repeated. "I didn't grow up in Grundy, Virginia, for nothing."

Susan laughed, then thanked Jan for pitching in at the last minute.

"You know, Susan, it's not me. It's everyone." Jan was always happy to share praise. "In times like this we've got to pull together."

While those two caught up, Harry unfolded her county map. "The Dybecks are here, right?"

"Don't you have GPS?" asked Father O'Connor.

"Heavenly guidance of a technological sort?" Harry scoffed. "Why bother? Half the time, the directions take you miles out of your way. It's not that I don't know where these back roads are. I bet I know about every back road in this county, but I don't always know which house is which or exactly where. Some are pretty well hidden."

"I figure it depends on what they're growing." Father O'Connor chuckled.

"There is that," Harry agreed.

"A lot of the mailboxes have no names or numbers, and some of these people don't have mailboxes."

"You know, you have to have your number on your mailbox," Harry the ex-postmistress said. "But this is the country. If one is a federal employee you serve your people even if there are slight variations in the rules when doing so."

"Too many rules. Beyond the Ten Commandments, it's all just paperwork." Father O'Connor ran his hand over his clean-shaven face. "Okay, after the Dybecks, continue down to the base of the mountains to Mrs. Killigan. She's elderly and can't hear too well, so you'll have to make a racket."

He marked each delivery spot on the map with colored pens. Father O'Connor used a red marker if someone was hard of hearing, blue if their eyes were bad, black if they had a vicious dog, black and red if they were vicious. Sometimes folks went on a mean drunk. Best to know who. Drunks were marked with a wavy red line. A wavy blue line meant the person was a touch odd.

Both Father O'Connor and Jan helped the girls load up the vehicles. Being animal people, too, they petted the cats and Tucker and Owen, Susan's corgi, Tucker's brother.

By the last carry out, Father O'Connor was huffing and puffing. *"Whew,"* he said to Harry and Susan. "Thank you for this, for being at the Silver Linings fund-raiser, and for taking on so many extra deliveries while we pray for Charlene and her sons, as well as console the boys in Silver Linings."

"Father," Harry replied, "we all do what we can."

"How long is this going to take?" Pewter, leaning toward peevish, asked, as Harry and Susan shut the Suburban doors.

"Who knows?" Owen replied, always smiling.

"Long enough to get you crabby," Tucker teased the gray cannonball.

"Two seconds. You have two seconds to amend your attitude." Pewter unleashed the claws of her right paw.

Realizing the back of the SUV now allowed little room to hide or run around, Owen soothed the cat's feelings. *"Oh, Pewter, all Tucker wants is to be the center of your attention."*

After one hour, Harry and Susan had dropped off one quarter of the goods. The back roads — some plowed, some not — made for heavy going.

Harry checked the map. "We've got one delivery on that dirt road that runs east and west from Route 240 all the way back past Beaver Dam. No colors by this name. That's good."

"Jeez, I don't want to get stuck back there if there's ice on the road," said Susan.

"Know what you mean." Harry concentrated as Susan turned left, for they were heading north. "It doesn't always get plowed out and it's so darn twisty and narrow."

Susan drove slowly. The bare trees did improve vision back into the various hollows and meadows. "Coming up on Mr. Thompson," she said. "Haven't seen him in a long time."

As they swung round a tight twist, a small, once painted wooden dwelling sat between two majestic oaks, their dry brown leaves still attached.

Many oaks do not drop their old leaves, which are instead pushed off by the swelling buds in spring. So the oaks rustle from late fall until spring, creating a mournful sound, the sound of winter.

"Susan, just stop here," ordered Harry, sometimes bossy. "There's no way you can drive in there. Snow's too deep. It's not dug out. 'Course, Mr. Thompson's old and it's hard work."

"I can't leave the car in the middle of this road."

"Why not? You see any other traffic? You stay here. I'll carry in the box."

"It's heavy," Susan fretted.

"I'm a strong farm girl. If a car beeps at you, you just go on and turn around and come back for me when you can."

"All right, but I don't like this."

"I didn't say you'd like it." Harry opened the door, glad she had on snow boots. Opening the back of the big vehicle, she wiggled out a big box.

With a grunt, she hoisted it up, leaned it against her chest, and pushed through the snow. No path had been dug out to the door either. Tucker, ever mindful of her duties as Harry's dog, jumped out and followed. By the time Harry reached the screened door, hanging on one hinge, sweat rolled down her back. Once at the door, she put down the package and knocked. No response. Knocked again, harder.

At last, the door creaked open. A once handsome old man, now unshaven, smiled at her. "Harry Haristeen."

"Mr. Thompson. Merry Christmas from St. Cyril's."

"Come on in. It's cold out there," said her former eleventh-grade math teacher.

"Only for a minute, sir. Susan and I are making deliveries."

"Susan Bixby?"

"Tucker."

"She'll always be Bixby to me." He smiled at Harry. "Esther Mercier and I always said you two were good math students. So many girls weren't."

"That's kind of you to say. I liked solid geometry and trig. Once I got to college, I didn't like calculus."

"Calculus is the dividing line. Basic mathematics is practical, measurements, weight. But calculus opens the door to theory and, once mastered, that theory allows us to build guided missiles. What you can do with higher math, well, I don't think we even know the possibilities." He looked down at Tucker. "I have dog biscuits. My old dog, The Terminator, is sound asleep. Can't hear or see too good anymore, so he sleeps. He's in the kitchen by the wood-burning stove."

"Thank you. Tucker doesn't need treats. She's getting a little thick around the middle." Harry paused. "It was good to see you, Mr. Thompson. I'd better go."

"You tell Susan hello."

"I will, sir."

As Harry trudged back she considered the ravages of alcohol. Mr. Thompson had been such a good-looking man, and so bright. Each year he drank a little more until he started to sneak a drink at work and then two. Sometimes he didn't show up for class. Once fired, he worked at manual labor, but he became too unreliable. Good as his mind was, nice as he was, he couldn't stop with the booze.

"Mr. Thompson says hello," said Harry, climbing back in the vehicle.

"How's he look?"

"Like you'd expect. When's the last time you saw him?" Harry inquired.

"At the convenience store. I was coming the back way from Boonesville. Got thirsty. I was shocked when I saw him."

Harry, checking her map, said, "If you can find a turnaround, take it. Otherwise, we'll come out near Batesville."

"Used to be a covered bridge down there. That's what Dad said," Susan mused. "Tore so many down."

"Ever wonder what things will look like in one hundred years?" Harry pointed to a plowed-out private road. "Bet you can turn this big boat around there."

"If not, I hope you can push." Susan carefully began to negotiate the plowed private drive while backing partway into the narrow state road. "No, I haven't thought a century ahead. I'm not ready yet for tomorrow."

They bantered more as Susan, out now, headed toward a high ridge behind The Miller School.

Two hours later, they had just one delivery left, to a small tidy cottage near the Nelson County line. Pewter and Mrs. Murphy slept in the plush bed with sides that Susan had thoughtfully put in the car for Owen. The two dogs stared out the closed windows, observing everything.

The small cottage came into view as they slid around a bend in the old side road. The front walkway, framed by huge boxwoods covered in snow, was inviting. The door was painted bright red and drew one's eye right to it through the boxwoods.

They checked the list. There was a blue wavy line and neither remembered what that had meant.

Harry carried a box of foodstuffs while Susan carried a box of clothing.

Reaching the door, Harry put down the heavy carton, lifted the brass knocker, and gave two loud raps.

The door was flung open so quickly it took them all aback, even the dogs.

"Don't I know you? I'm Miss Rice."

Harry stared into bright blue eyes, an older woman of average height, wearing jeans and a clean sweater. With one arm she held a small dog, who also regarded the visitors suspiciously.

"We're from St. Cyril's."

"That tells me where you're from, not who you are," the woman correctly pointed out. "Sometimes my memory fogs up, but you all look familiar."

Harry introduced herself and Susan, as well as the dogs. The door opened, they stepped inside and set down the cartons.

"Of course." Flo Rice nodded.

"Ma'am, this one is heavy. Would you like me to carry it to the kitchen?" Harry asked.

"That would be nice." Miss Rice pointed Harry to the kitchen.

The house's interior was tidy but quite chilly. A fire in a fireplace tried to heat the front rooms. When Harry placed the carton on the kitchen table she smelled a strong odor, felt some warmth, then noticed a small kerosene heater tucked into an old fireplace.

Susan stood back in the living room, trying to make conversation.

"I'm not Catholic," said Miss Rice. "I was, once. I remember you all used to come to the stables," she said to Susan. "Mrs. Valencia's stables. I was a practicing Catholic then." She set down her dog and folded her arms across her chest. "I thank you and the church. Once they took Latin out of the church, I lost interest, really."

"Yes, ma'am," both women replied, although neither one really knew what to say.

"Gas is too expensive."

"Yes, ma'am."

"Everything is too expensive."

"Yes, ma'am."

Harry noticed a crucifix on one wall. That was it for anything that might be considered décor. Plain walls, plain floors, old furniture, but a bookcase filled with books, many with beautiful bindings.

"You two don't read Latin, do you? Took it out of the schools, too."

"Miss Rice, we both took four years of Latin in high school." Susan hoped this was a pleasing answer.

"Good. But no Latin in schools now."

"Miss Rice, I think private schools may offer it, but the state schools, maybe none."

"Enforced stupidity!" Flo clamped her lips together.

"You're right," said Susan. Agreeing with the old lady was the only route to take, but she did think it was unwise to remove Latin. "Some schools don't offer German either," she added.

Harry had her hand on the doorknob as the dogs barked outside. "Ma'am, we wish you a Merry Christmas."

"Are they wishing me a Merry Christmas, too?" A slight smile crossed her lips as the old lady regarded the menagerie. She picked up her little dog again.

"Miss Rice, I'm sure of it." Harry smiled big.

As the old lady opened the door, she said, *"Quo vadis?"*

This means "Where do you go?" or in more elegant form, "Wither thou goest?"

"Vale." The two said goodbye in Latin.

Before she closed her door, Flo said with some fierceness, "I know things."

On the way home, Susan sighed. "How terrible to live alone like Mr. Thompson or Miss Rice. I guess the blue wavy line meant oddball."

"Or worse. At least she has her dog. For some people it's the choices they made or the turn they missed in the road. They wind up weird and alone."

"I think some people are just too hard to get along with," said Susan. "Sends others running in the opposite direction." She paused. "I vaguely remember her when she worked for Mrs. Valencia at the stables. She didn't seem odd then."

"Time changes people." Harry simply shrugged.

11

Charlene Vavilov was staring into space.

Charlene kept herself busy, but from time to time she'd find she couldn't concentrate. Her mind would go blank or wander.

Fair Haristeen had stopped by the Ford dealership on his way back from a call Thursday in eastern Albemarle County.

He stood quietly outside the open door to her office, then cleared his throat.

The well-groomed middle-aged woman blinked, then forced a smile. "Fair, come in."

He brought with him a small grooming kit for horses, a red-and-green box with a long handle. He placed it on her desk. "For Salsa."

"Oh, he'll love it."

Charlene's kind Thoroughbred Salsa was one of Fair's patients. Charlene had grown up loving horses, but she also realized that in this part of the world, riding created opportunities. She had impressed this on her husband, Peter, but horses had scared him. Golf did not, however, and between these two sporting poles, the Vavilovs enhanced the Ford dealership. The number of F-250s and F-350s that horsemen bought to pull their rigs was the envy of the Ram and Silverado salespeople. Dodge and Chevy made good trucks, but Charlene showed up pulling her own rig with a Ford dually. And she was always ready to help another horseperson gain financing.

Peter invariably drove a Thunderbird or a new Ford SUV to the links.

Fair respected Charlene as a horsewoman and as a businesswoman. He had also respected Peter's ad campaigns, created by Lou Higham. It was a tough business.

"Let me know if there's anything I can do for Salsa." He paused. "Or you."

She swallowed, leveled her eyes, misting over at the tall man. "Fair, I know you mean that. I wish there was something you, anyone could do. All I know to do is to keep working, keep myself occupied."

"The showroom sparkles. And the decorations are wonderful."

"Good people work here. I don't know what I'd do without them. Your wife, Susan, all my friends, have been supportive. Arden has been a brick. She wanted to come into the showroom and work. I told her, 'It's almost Christmas. No. Go do stuff.' And Tyler needs her. Pete did what he could to interest Tyler in sports. Lou can be hard on him. So I said, 'Enjoy your boy while he's still a boy.' " She smiled. "Alexander and Jarrad have helped, too. I told them it's fine with me if they do things with their friends. They come here instead. Jarrad likes the accounting office." Her voice registered her pride in her sons. "Alex likes the garage. They've been a big help. They are growing up so fast."

"Charlene, you and Peter were good parents. And I don't know how you hung on, especially during the worst of the gas crisis." Fair prudently focused on business.

Despite the strange missing fingers, the initial autopsy report had declared Pete died of a heart attack. Happy to be able to talk about anything other than that verdict, she rose from behind the desk and sat next to Fair in an expensive Barcelona-leather-and-chrome chair.

"Ford sailed through some dreadful times," she said. "Finally, we got farsighted, gutsy leadership, and I think we will make a decent profit this year. Not taking the bailout money, going through those hard years before GM and Chrysler Motors tanked. It paid off for Ford and for the dealers who hung on."

"You always did have courage. Anyone that can ride Salsa when he's having one of his bad mood days is gutsy." Fair smiled.

She waved her hand. "Salsa's so funny, you know." She folded her hands, leaning toward Fair. "He knew. When I went into the stable after Peter died, he knew. He nuzzled me and put his head on my shoulder. I've tried to ride him a bit every day. I wouldn't tell that to too many people. I love that horse."

"He loves you."

This brought tears to her eyes as she nodded. "Love is more powerful than any of us realizes." She took a deep breath. "I'm a bit older than you, Fair. There's a time when a woman does think about the future without her husband. Nine times out of ten, you men go first. But I never thought it would happen so soon. Peter burst with fresh ideas and good health. This came out of the blue."

Fair reached over, taking her hand in his. "I'm sorry you have to think about it now."

She squeezed his hand, then withdrew hers to wipe away tears. "Arden says take it a day at a time. Good advice for life, no matter when."

"That's the truth." Fair's deep voice resonated.

"I've been thinking so much about Silver Linings. Pete loved working with young people. You know, what he really was focusing on was finding a building that could house the group. St. Cyril's is bursting at the seams. We have so many Hispanic members now. Pete wanted the kids to be somewhere relaxing and safe. Plus, St. Cyril's needs the space."

"Wonderful idea. And giving the truck for a raffle was so generous."

"We both loved doing that. We've been so fortunate. So many of those boys haven't. Pete always said, 'Give people a chance. Don't shut the door. Open it.' "

"Most people will go through the door." Fair agreed with Pete's philosophy.

"I've met so many of the new people through the church. Many are Hispanic, as I mentioned. It enrages me that the stereotype is an apple picker who can't speak English."

"Oh, Charlene, what would people do without stereotypes? What's the stereotype of a car dealer?"

This brought the relief of laughter. Someone was talking to her without a long face spouting platitudes about closure.

"Think I fit it?" She smiled. "Give me a cigar, and let's make a deal."

"That's not you."

Her son Alex popped his head in. Fair stood and shook his hand.

"Good to see you, Dr. Haristeen."

"You too, Alex. I know this is a difficult time. We're all glad you're working in the business over Christmas break."

"I like learning about the dealership." He acknowledged Fair's sympathetic words, then lifted his eyes to his mother. "Mom, the insurance claims adjuster is here to look at Dad's Explorer."

"Fine." She smiled. "If he wants it in the garage, have it towed in."

"Okay." Alex left.

Charlene turned to Fair. "Fixing a claim when you're a dealer is usually simple enough. We've had people total cars on test drives. Still, I never look forward to it. The paperwork is almost as bad as the accident."

"I can believe that." Fair's voice was soothing. "Don't you pay interest every day on cars on the lot?"

"You bet I do." Her eyes met his. "Owning a dealership is not for the fainthearted."

When Fair pulled up by the barn, it was already dark at 6:30. He cut the motor, sat in the cab and looked out at the frozen pastures, the deep night sky. Then he pulled the key, dropped it in the center tray. Inside, in the kitchen, he was greeted by his wife with a hug and a kiss.

Within minutes, both had provided recaps of their days.

"Glad Charlene looked good." Harry pulled out two cups. "Green tea?"

"No. I don't know what I want right now."

"While you're thinking about it, Susan and I saw Mr. Thompson. Our solid and trig teacher. Remember him?"

"Sure. I thought he was dead."

"Half dead. Pickled." She tipped back her head, swallowing an imaginary drink.

"There was a rumor of that when we were in school. Sorry."

"He has this deaf and mostly blind dog, lives alone. Has a wood-burning stove in the kitchen. All the paint's peeled from the house. It's funny. Our last stop, we also dropped things off to an older person, Miss Rice. House just the opposite. Neat as a pin."

"Rice." He pondered the name. "Little odd?"

"*Odd* doesn't cover it."

"She used to work for Diana Valencia, more money than God. Miss Rice worked in her barn office. I was starting out. She was nice, as I recall. Somewhat religious. As time went by, she rarely spoke to me anymore. Perfectly nice but introverted. I never knew how the Valencias got their money."

"When turn signals were first invented, the problems were with the wiring. In bad weather, a lot of them didn't work. Diana Valencia figured out how to solve the problem. This was way back when women were told they couldn't do mechanical or engineering things."

"Never knew that," said Fair, before adding, "Come to think of it, Miss Rice is Esther Mercier's older sister. I remember seeing Miss Mercier once at the barn. One thing about living in Virginia, your memory won't go bad."

"Why?" Harry asked.

"You need to use it constantly to remember who is related to whom." He laughed.

"Make up your mind yet?" She smiled.

"I am going to have a cup of green tea with a shot of scotch."

"That's original."

"Isn't that why you married me?" He grinned.

"There were other factors." She poured the hot water into his cup.

Listening in were the cats and dog all

curled up in their kitchen beds. They had beds everywhere.

Sipping their beverages, the husband and wife reviewed tomorrow's schedule.

"So you're going out again?" he asked.

"The response to the need for clothing has been overwhelming. Today we delivered stuff for St. Cyril's. St. Luke's is overflowing. More deliveries tomorrow."

"I thought December twentieth was supposed to be the big day."

"There will be plenty to do on that day, but we've got to disburse some of the canned goods and clothing. There's no way we can deliver everything in just one day. Also, we lost some days with Pete's death. Most of the St. Cyril's ladies were at the Vavilovs'. Us, too."

"I have a couple of old but good sweaters. I could root through my drawers."

"Honey, we have more than enough, plus all your clothing is covered in cat hair."

"No outfit is complete without it!" Pewter loudly proclaimed.

12

"What if I run out of the car?" Pewter maliciously considered this route in the back of the now almost empty Volvo. It had been a long, long day, with their human busy handing out food she could keep and nosing into other people's business.

"I'd chase you," Tucker solemnly vowed.

"Ha." Pewter swished her tail.

Nose-to-nose, Mrs. Murphy threatened her fellow feline, *"You aren't going anywhere. We're almost done with this run, and I want to go home."* The tiger cat then turned to Tucker. *"Don't set her off."*

Ears drooping, Tucker flopped down in the back of the Volvo station wagon.

Harry, by herself, had been dropping off food and clothing since eleven, the time she usually finished her farm chores. With one stop left, she peered upward out the windshield, then Harry reached over to pet Mrs. Murphy, who had come up to sit in the passenger seat.

The twisting road climbed toward the Blue Ridge Mountains. The sky threatened, charcoal gray. Harry turned left onto another snowpacked dirt road, followed the ridge, then turned right down a narrow drive that was at least plowed. She finished by 3:30.

At 3:30 Arden Higham labored in the small office at St. Cyril's. Friday was her regular bookkeeping day. With the end of the year looming, the demands escalated. Arden wanted to keep up with it all.

Jessica Hexham had the same idea. Walking in, she said, "It's a zoo out there. I'll be doing the church books until midnight."

"Lord, I hope not. If you'll be here to midnight, I'll be here until two in the morning. You're faster than I am." She twirled a pencil. "Traffic?"

"Yes, and it's snowing again. When is this going to end? Hardly any last winter, and now, *boom.*" Jessica shook her head.

Arden's cell rang. "Hello."

"Mom, where's Dad?" her son, Tyler, said. "I've been waiting forty-five minutes."

"Did you call him?" she asked, looking over at Jessica.

"Of course I called him."

"I'll be there as soon as I can. Jessica just walked in and said traffic is a problem."

Arden folded her phone, said to Jessica, "I've got to go. Lou didn't pick up Tyler. And he hasn't returned Tyler's calls. That's not like Lou, so he's held up somewhere where his cell isn't working."

"Sometimes the service goes down in weather like this." Jessica sat down.

"That it does. I'm afraid I'll have to come in tomorrow."

"Well, drive carefully. You never know what the other guy will do."

"Isn't that the truth?" Arden threw together her hat, coat, scarf. "You know, since Pete's death, Lou has been forgetful."

"Well, these things affect people different ways," Jessica sympathized. "I think it's harder for men — the death of a friend, someone they love. They can't fix it."

"As it is, Lou and Tyler pluck my last nerve. Lou can't get it through his thick skull that Tyler is not athletic —" At this thought, she stopped and wrapped the hand-knit scarf around her neck. "The holidays wear me down anyway. I feel like sending out invitations to my nervous breakdown."

"Hold on, girl." Jessica smiled at her.

"I will." As Arden sailed out of the room,

she looked at the large wall calendar.

Friday the thirteenth.

With her deliveries done, Harry walked to her barn as the first snowflake twirled down.

"Perfect timing."

The three animals and one human checked each stall, filled the water buckets, two to a stall, then Harry tightened her scarf, headed out the back of the barn, and started bringing in horses from the pastures. Night came so early, and this night would prove cold and long. The inside of the barn usually stayed warm enough for the water buckets not to freeze. Each horse wore a blanket, sized for him or her. However, Harry couldn't figure out how to keep them from pulling the straps off from one another's blankets. Horses loved this game, often accompanied by mock fighting, running about, and squealing. Though generally quiet animals, when they snorted, whinnied, and smacked their lips they did so with brio.

After half an hour, everyone was inside a deeply bedded stall, with clean water, an extra flake of hay to keep them busy. The big feeding came in the morning. If anyone needed a little help to keep the weight on, Harry also gave them grain at night.

By the time she'd put up Shortro, the last

one to come in and always a gentleman about it, a new thin white shroud already covered the existing snow.

Walking into the heated tack room, she unwound her scarf, hanging it over a saddle. Her Carhartt Detroit jacket she laid across a saddle rack. She sank into the chair behind the desk.

"I'm tired."

"Low pressure," Tucker informed her. The weather made the corgi tired, too.

On the saddle pads by the old riding helmet, Pewter was already asleep. Mrs. Murphy, curled up next to her, began to doze off. The wall clock read 5:50. The sun had set, darkness gathered. Flatface, a huge great horned owl, stirred in the cupola above the hayloft. The blacksnake Matilda hibernated in her special hay bale up there, and Simon the possum also woke up. He felt the snow coming, double-checked his treasures, for he hoarded everything from candy wrappers to broken tack. He waddled to the edge of the hayloft to see what Harry was doing in the tack room. She usually left treats. His bright eyes missed nothing, including the one lone mouse who zipped out from behind the hay bales stacked in the aisle for tomorrow's feeding.

"She's in there, you know," Simon warned,

but do mice ever listen to advice offered by possums?

"She won't hurt me." The little fellow stopped near a small hole the mice had made at the outside corner of the tack room. They had pathways between each of the stalls. Cleverly hidden behind a trunk inside the tack room was another door. All the mice could come and go as they pleased. It must have been mice that designed the glorious sewers of Paris. Who better to create tunnels?

"The cats are there," Simon warned.

Face upturned to him, the mouse simply replied, *"They're worthless,"* then wiggled into the hole.

Harry didn't know a small furry fellow walked by her boots under the desk, emerged on the other side, looked at the sleeping cats, then zipped for the back of the tack trunk.

Checking that day's delivery list, Harry thought that aside from her three pets, she was alone. One is never truly alone on a farm. If nothing else, there's always a spider within three feet of you.

Tucker raised her head, let out a low bark. *"Coop's here."*

This woke Pewter. *"Will you kindly shut up?"*

"It's my job to announce any person or

animal who comes onto this property."

"Yeah. Yeah."

Harry heard the motor cut off, then the barn door open. She stepped outside the tack room. "Damn, it's gotten even colder," she said.

Cooper entered and sat down. "Supposed to get into the teens tonight. Maybe a foot of snow."

"Everything okay at your place?" Harry inquired, making sure, for Cooper wasn't a country girl, although she was learning.

"Got the generator hooked up in case. The fireplaces help, too. I keep promising myself that I'm going to install a wood-burning stove in the basement like you have, but I never get around to it."

"Saves a boatload of money." Harry changed the subject. "I can make a pot of tea."

A nearby hotplate, rarely used, did work.

Cooper answered, "No, thank you. Harry, you know the Highams?"

"Socially. She plays cards with us. Why?"

"Arden Higham, sounding worried, reported that her husband, Lou, didn't pick up their son from school. He hasn't answered calls. She's called his friends and coworkers, and they said they hadn't heard from him. He left the office early to run

111

some errands and said he'd pick up Tyler. He wouldn't be back at the office. She's asked us to look for him."

"Like a missing person?"

"No one is using that terminology just yet. The man's only been gone for a few hours, and it is Christmastime and it is snowing."

"Right."

"Ever hear of any home trouble?"

Harry shook her head. "Like I said, I only know them socially, and things seem to be fine. The kid's at the gawky stage and just a whiz with computers. I can't imagine he'd run out on her and Tyler. Probably Lou's lost his cellphone or he's tied up somewhere."

"Yeah."

"Are you concerned? Do you know something I don't?"

Cooper teased her. "I know a lot you don't. I'm not concerned. Yet."

"Call me if I can help." Harry felt something run over her foot. She looked down in time to see a tail disappear. "A mouse."

Cooper reached inside her back pants pocket, rising to do so, retrieved a folded-over sheet of yellow paper, which she put on the desk in front of Harry. "A Christmas mouse. Here. Read my notes and tell me what you think."

Harry scanned the page. "Peter Vavilov. Well-off. Aggressive. Local. High school star athlete back in the late eighties. Community leader. Member of many nonprofits, such as Silver Linings, Red Cross, Cancer Fund, MS Foundation, et cetera. Church: St. Cyril's. Wife. Two sons. Well liked."

"Right?" Coop lifted her eyebrows.

"Right. He was a good fund-raiser." Harry then continued reading. "No mistresses. Especially concerned with sports and youth."

"No pretty young things on the side?"

Harry thought for a moment. "I rarely saw Peter around any woman other than Charlene or women at fund-raisers. Never heard any talk about Pete in that way."

"Can you think of anything else?"

"First, tell me what you mean by writing that he was aggressive."

Cooper crossed one leg over the other. "When I would question people, that word came up again and again. He was *aggressive* as a football player. He was *aggressive* in advertising Fords, competitive with other dealerships, especially other Ford dealerships, like in Richmond. Can you think of an old feud?" the police officer asked. "Maybe someone hated him?"

"No." Harry felt a tingling sensation at

the back of her neck. "I thought Pete died of a heart attack. Why these questions?"

"Curious." Cooper looked at the two cats. "So peaceful. Hey, that helmet has seen better days." She rose, picked up the riding helmet.

Tucker barked. *"Put that down. You don't really want it."*

The cats opened their eyes. Mrs. Murphy sat up.

Pewter, also now on her feet, reached up for the helmet but too late. Cooper turned it over and the buckle bracelet fell out.

"Good place to hide your jewelry. Who'd think to look?" The tall blonde woman bent over, picked up the golden object, handing it to Harry.

"Oh, no!" Mrs. Murphy wailed. *"There goes our Christmas gift."*

"I didn't put the bracelet there," Harry said, surprised. "It's not my bracelet." She studied the well-made piece. "Really pretty. Really expensive. It seems familiar somehow."

Leaning over Harry, Cooper commented, "My grandmother had one sort of like that. Way back when, lots of women wore buckle rings and buckle bracelets or ones with a simple golden knot."

"That's probably why it looks familiar.

How did it wind up in my old helmet?"

"Couldn't have been in the lining?"

"Coop, I would have felt it. It's good luck, a found treasure."

"Guess you would've noticed it in there. Well, it's yours now."

"I'll clean it up and wear it."

"Now what do we do?" Pewter asked.

Tucker sighed. *"The usual. Hope that Fair buys a present and puts our names on it."*

After Cooper left, Harry reviewed her friend's numerous questions. Something was most definitely amiss.

13

Outside, snow fell steadily as Mrs. Murphy sat in the hayloft with Simon the possum. Although it was early Saturday morning, the sky remained dark. The horses slept in their stalls. Tomahawk, the old gray Thoroughbred, sprawled on his side snoring, his blanket keeping him snug. The others slept standing up. When Harry opened the barn door, they'd open their eyes, whinny *"Hello,"* and begin banging their stalls. That sweet feed dumped into their buckets made every morning an exciting time.

The two friends sat side by side, Simon on his haunches as he played with a broken browbrand from a bridle.

"Doesn't it smell good?"

"Does." The cat knew to praise his treasures.

"I wish they made blankets for possums." Simon's obsidian eyes glittered. *"I can keep really warm in my nest, but I'm not going*

outside."

"Fortunately, you don't have to. There's enough dropped sweet feed in this barn to feed a mess of possums," the cat remarked.

"Wouldn't go out anyway. There's a coyote coming round, especially now that it's snowy and cold."

"A male? Medium-sized? Youngish?"

"You've seen him, too?" The gray fellow swung his rat tail around his feet.

"For the first time, almost a week ago. He was running across the far pastures. Had a human arm in his mouth. All bones. He didn't drop the bones, but a bracelet slipped off the wrist when some little bones broke off."

"All the coyote had to do was turn. He could have killed you all in a flash. And sometimes he comes in here," Simon added in a dark voice.

"Ah, so that's the smell. Tucker's mentioned it, but we weren't really sure and it doesn't seem to happen often. The scent." Mrs. Murphy thought about this. *"We've never had coyotes before."*

"We've got them now. I have to be very careful. They'll kill and eat anything."

"Does he try to get you?"

"No. He eats whatever's dropped on the center aisle. He can't get into the stalls, so he can't eat my pickings. He takes anything

118

Tucker drops, too. He only comes when the back door is open, so he won't be in here in the bitter cold."

"Have you ever talked to him?" the tiger cat asked.

"No. I just watch. He'll keep coming close until spring. Game is hard to find now, but he must be a successful hunter, because he's not ribby."

"Smart." The cat half closed her eyes. "Not as smart as a fox, but smart."

"Pewter ever make up with the fox in the west pasture?" Simon had heard from Pewter all about the torrent of insults the cat had endured last fall.

"Pewter hasn't even made up with Tucker." Mrs. Murphy laughed.

Simon, laughing as well, said, "Pewter always has to be the center of attention. Good or bad."

"Our very own diva."

Later, back in the house, everyone now awake, Mrs. Murphy told her two companions what Simon saw.

"Tucker, go over the garbage after breakfast, take anything that smells good, you know, like eggshells or a package meat has been in, especially if she makes sausages. That odor really carries."

"She'll pitch a fit." Tucker was not convinced.

"Well, don't do it when she's in the house." Pewter waited to hear what else Mrs. Murphy was thinking.

"I'll still get it because you all can't pull over the garbage cylinder," said Tucker. *"I can."*

The three animals eyed the cylindrical garbage can with the swinging lid.

"True," Mrs. Murphy agreed.

Harry put down their breakfast, which halted the conversation. She did indeed fry up sausages for herself and Fair along with eggs and corn bread. After the table was cleared, the two left for the barn.

"Okay, now! Knock it over," Mrs. Murphy urged the corgi.

"You still haven't told me why I should do this," Tucker balked.

"We're going to take whatever is best and put it behind the back barn doors, off to the side a little. It'll bring in that coyote. I want to talk to him."

"Murphy, he's not going to smell it from far away. It's too cold." Tucker sat immobile.

"No, but as he comes close to the barn he will. You canines have amazing powers that way."

"I don't know," Tucker stalled.

"Bother!" Pewter, on her hind legs, reached

up, just hooked her claws under the bottom of the swinging lid and hung on.

Mrs. Murphy jumped up and helped Pewter. The garbage can began to totter.

"I'll be blamed anyway!" the dog cried.

Mrs. Murphy raised her voice. *"Right. Help us out."*

Tucker reluctantly trotted over, stood on her hind legs to push over the can. It fell with a crash, the lid popping off.

"Pewter, you take the sausage package. Tucker, you and I will carry the eggshells. I can do two, I think."

The three animals wedged themselves out of the animal door in the kitchen door and the outside glassed-in porch door. Carting these treasures over the new fallen snow wasn't too bad, as the snow below had become hard.

"Here." Mrs. Murphy dropped her shells to the left of the big barn doors in the back.

Her two friends followed suit.

"I really don't see the point." Tucker again doubted Mrs. Murphy's plan.

"Trust me," advised the cat, fur fluffed out to help ward off the cold.

That night, December 14, the sky was clear. Three days from a full moon, the animals hurried to the barn, slipping through the

121

small animal door in the big barn doors. Tucker really had to squish and squeeze through.

The two cats climbed the ladder up to the hayloft while Tucker waited in the toasty tack room. Clever, both cats opened the hayloft's small doors just a crack. Usually Harry kept them open unless it was very cold, as she liked air to circulate over the stored hay. Horses need clean air, too. Building a too-tight barn was a typical mistake of someone who did not grow up with horses, the result being respiratory problems. Fair dealt with this all the time. He often felt that he was teaching Horse Care 101.

Simon snuggled in his nest, a tidy deep hole in a back hay bale.

"Here he comes," Mrs. Murphy whispered to Pewter. *"Go get Tucker."*

Excited at the espionage, Pewter climbed backward down the ladder, raced into the tack room, woke up the corgi, who then hurried to the back doors to listen while Pewter clawed her way back up the hayloft ladder.

Mrs. Murphy, eyes focused on the coyote, listened to the eggshells crack. She figured the young fellow must be about fifty pounds, quite a bit more than he would weigh if he were in Wyoming or Utah, anywhere in the West.

"Coyote," she called down.

Swallowing a pulverized eggshell, he looked up. *"Who are you?"*

"I could ask you the same thing. You're on my farm."

"Odin," came his reply.

"Mrs. Murphy."

"Pewter." The gray cat raised her voice.

"Who's the dog behind the door?" Odin could smell the corgi.

"Tucker. She can't get out that way. She's listening," the tiger cat said. *"We're the animals who chased you last week when you carried the bony human arm."*

"How'd you lose your tail?" Odin called mockingly at Tucker through the closed barn door.

Incensed, Tucker barked back, *"I didn't lose it. We're bred to herd cattle and we have no tails."*

Knowing he was safe, Odin asked, *"So you three live with the humans in the white house? I see them sometimes when I hunt here. They never see me."*

"Be grateful," Tucker warned.

Mrs. Murphy got to the point. *"Can you tell us where you found the arm?"*

"Up in the huge walnut grove, not too far. A tree blew over in that bad windstorm. The bones were buried under the tree. Now the skeleton is tangled in the roots. It's easy to see. No meat, but bones are good for you." Odin stood on his hind legs, front paws on the barn door. *"Been there a long, long time."*

"When Tucker and I chased you, a bracelet fell off." Mrs. Murphy leaned farther out the hayloft doors, opened a crack, and a blast of cold air hit her. *"Did you notice anything else, like a watch?"*

"Maybe there's stuff, but I wasn't looking. I just wanted bones to gnaw."

"If you leave the skeleton alone, we'll put out better bones, other stuff for you back here," Mrs. Murphy promised. *"We want to see the skeleton."*

"Snow's deeper up there. Can't get to it now. I won't bother it, but why do you want to see old bones?" Odin thought this very odd.

"A human buried outside a cemetery." Mrs. Murphy paused. *"Always means evil."*

"Not to you," the gray-coated fellow said.

"No, but I live with two humans. Bones upset them. We don't want them worried," Mrs. Murphy informed him as Tucker pressed her ear more tightly to the lower barn door.

Odin thought a bit. *"I don't understand it, but if you bring me food I promise I won't disturb the long dead."*

"*Deal,*" Mrs. Murphy swiftly replied.

"*Deal,*" Pewter echoed.

"*Deal,*" Tucker also agreed.

As Odin loped off, the two cats slid back the hayloft doors.

"*Thank goodness. That air is like a knife.*" Simon sighed, then said, "*I'd be careful if I were you.*"

"*We will,*" the two cats promised as they backed down the hayloft ladder to join up with Tucker, who was awaiting them.

The three rushed back to the house, eager for the kitchen's warmth.

Tucker shivered for a moment. "*Mrs. Murphy, there will be hell to pay.*"

"*Whoever is out there already paid it,*" the tiger cat replied.

14

Advent's music, as well as the vestments and church décor, always pleased Harry and put her in a holiday mood. She looked forward to this time of year, as did Lucy Fur, Elocution, and Cazenovia.

The candles, garlands in the hallways, the wonderful smell of Christmas, and the enormous tree in Reverend Jones's office were all a cat could ask for, but this year the overflow of goods in the meeting room down the hall made it the best Christmas ever.

Elocution had investigated every toy box, pulling out what moved or squeaked. Lucy Fur and Cazenovia, however, preferred to burrow deep into blankets, sweaters, even some especially plush towels.

This Sunday, December 15, after another good sermon preached, Reverend Jones, the cats, and the ladies in charge of the gifts to the poor wrapped toys after the service. The blankets and towels were tied up with red and green raffia, placed in clear plastic bags.

The door of the meeting room swung open, and the ladies from St. Cyril's came in.

Jessica Hexham walked up to Reverend Jones. "Have you all heard? Lou Higham is missing."

"No," Reverend Jones answered.

Jessica spoke louder. "Arden, who is a wreck, said he's been missing since Friday afternoon."

Harry, looking up from folding jackets, did not mention Cooper's stopping by the barn Friday afternoon, nor the deputy's being called in Saturday to help with the search.

BoomBoom wondered, "Why isn't it on the news?"

Jessica shook her head. "I don't know, but I bet it will be."

Reverend Jones put his arm around Jessica. "Let us know if we can help Arden if you hear of anything."

Looking around the room at all the boxes, Jessica said, "What we can do is make these deliveries until we hear otherwise. It's just so upsetting," she said to the others. "Well, I'm sure there will be a good explanation."

"Ladies," Susan called to the St. Cyril's

women, all talking, pouring through the door, "let's go over the list and you all can decide who takes what."

The Catholic women, Susan, and Boom-Boom huddled in a corner at a long table. Susan, ever organized, had maps that she had colored in Father O'Connor's unique code indicating drunkenness, et cetera.

"Better not take my toys." Elocution pushed a fuzzy ball on the floor.

"Get enough dirt on it and they'll leave it," Lucy Fur advised.

"Good idea." The fluffy cat hurriedly rolled the ball over wet footprints.

Harry kept on wrapping, hoping to be able to add more jackets to the boxes, which could use them.

The door opened again and Esther Mercier Toth walked in. "Girls, I'm late. Al and I had an argument over who would take the Explorer. Flipped a coin finally."

"That means you won." Jessica smiled at the older woman she barely knew.

Before Esther joined the St. Cyril's ladies auxiliary, she stopped by Harry. "Thank you for visiting Flo. I take care of her. I don't know how her name got on Father O'Connor's list, but Flo will enjoy a good Christmas now." She paused, thought for a moment. "How was she?"

129

"Uh." Harry struggled to find a way to frame the visit in the nicest way possible.

"Say no more." Esther smiled. "But she wasn't hostile, was she?"

"No, Miss Mercier, I mean Mrs. Toth."

This made them both smile.

"Old habits." The former math teacher smiled. "Flo, brighter than I, is really a good sort. You just have to work with her, know what I mean?"

"I think I do. Her house is immaculate, coldish, but very clean. And what a library."

"Yes, always the reader."

As Esther joined the others, Harry realized Esther had not heard about Lou. One by one, the news was passing through the volunteers.

Esther joined the others, all making notations on their own maps. No way you could write on your GPS.

Harry kept folding, but she wondered at the various ways people cope with pain, disappointment, crushed dreams. Most people feel terrible, tears are shed, their friends take them out or talk to them. Little by little, they reemerge. Some bounce right back. If anything, they seem strengthened by the setback. Others never recover. Maybe Flo fell into that group.

Harry figured she belonged in the middle

group. Noticing the women carrying boxes, she left off her task and began to tote box after box.

Once back inside, the women gabbed on as they worked.

BoomBoom closed up a box. "Lou better have a good story when he walks through the door."

"He can always claim amnesia." Esther picked up a light box to put in her car.

"If he's alive," Harry blurted out.

"Harry, that's awful. There are all kinds of reasons why he might not have called or gotten through." Esther had reached the door.

"You're right." After Esther had left the room, Harry said to Susan, BoomBoom, and Reverend Jones, "Since Friday afternoon? Something has to be wrong."

"Maybe he was in an accident and no one knows who he is?" Reverend Jones speculated. "No ID for some reason."

"He'd have to be a passenger in someone else's car and he would have to have left everything in his car," said Harry. "It is possible."

"Yeah, well, if he was in an accident, who was driving?" Susan's eyebrows shot upward.

The door opened and in walked Miranda.

The service at her church had just ended and she wanted to join the others here to help. Plus, she liked being with her younger friends.

"Good to see you, Miranda," said the Reverend. "Now that you're here, I can leave. The girls are, uh, being girls." He was glad to alter the drift of the conversation.

This made them laugh, but the cats protested.

"Don't go. Not yet." Elocution had indeed saved the now soggy ball.

"Come on, kitties." He knelt down and picked up Cazenovia. "Come on."

"The sacrifices I make!" Elocution trotted after him, as did Lucy Fur.

BoomBoom filled in Miranda on Lou, as well as Esther's conversation with Harry.

"Flo Rice tried to attend the Church of the Holy Light, but it wasn't for her," said Miranda. "She had a fit when her Catholic church dispensed with Latin." Miranda was more interested in Flo than in Lou, whom she didn't know.

The Church of the Holy Light, an evangelical church, was Miranda's church. She sang in the choir. Her magnificent voice brought people to services just to hear her. She had no ego about this gift at all.

"I knew Flo when she was young," said

Miranda. "We attended different schools, but Charlottesville, the county, so much smaller then, everybody knew everybody, or thought they did."

Susan got right to it. "Was she peculiar?"

"Not at all. She was vivacious, bright, popular. 'Course she had hot competition from Esther. They battled over everything, but sisters do."

"She's not vivacious and popular now," Susan said.

"She turned." Miranda used the old southern word for a big change in behavior.

"Do you know why?" Harry inquired of her former coworker, a dear friend of Harry's parents'.

"No, I was never that close to the Merciers. All I heard was she began to get snappy, quite irritable — oh, what, twenty-some years ago? Some people said her mother kept her in line, and when Mildred Mercier died, oh, 1990, Flo lost her restraining influence. I don't know. She offended her friends, her boss. That sort of thing. Never knew why."

"Do you think something like that could have happened to Louis Higham?"

"Harry, how in the world do you get from an older, highly odd lady to Lou Higham, Mr. Personality?" Susan threw up her hands. "And we don't even know if anything bad has happened to him."

"How do we know he didn't turn?" asked Harry. "People hide these things, families cover up. It's not so far-fetched. Nobody knows what happens behind closed doors."

Everyone in the room stared at Harry, then BoomBoom remarked, "She has a point."

15

On Monday, December 16, Deputy Cooper visited the Vavilovs' Ford dealership. Sheriff Rick Shaw had put another officer on the search for Lou, returning Cooper to the Vavilov case. The examiner had declared he died of a heart attack, but Cooper and Rick still wanted to know about Peter Vavilov's missing fingers. Both of them had been in law enforcement long enough to be very uneasy about this peculiar mutilation, which seemed to signify tremendous hatred.

In the car lot, looking again at Vavilov's Ford Explorer, Cooper realized she had not adequately inspected the vehicle. The insurance agent had gone over it, finding the Explorer salvageable. A bumper needed replacing, the driver's door and front left fender needed repair, but all in all, the car proved how tough it was.

Clouds slid over the mountains, light faded, Cooper used a high-powered flashlight as she checked the exterior. She had expected more damage, but heavy falling snow had obscured the vehicle when she reached the Explorer that night. Just reaching the accident after the report was called in took an hour. The snowplows couldn't keep up with the accumulation.

Satisfied with her notes on the car's outside, Cooper opened the driver's door. No seats had been jarred loose, the dashboard evidenced no damage at all, the windshield remained intact. The driver's-side window was cracked. Leaning over, her rear end in the cold air, she trained the flashlight on the back of the driver's seat, then the front of the seat. A small stain caught her attention, about a half-inch wide near the headrest. She couldn't identify it.

Closing the door, she walked around, got into the car, sat in the passenger seat, turned on the heater for both seats. She shined her light again on the small splotch. She'd been a law enforcement officer since graduating from college. At thirty-seven, Cooper well knew that any stain might yield potential clues. As to the half-inch stain, it appeared colorless, grease perhaps. Had she been Tucker, her nose would have picked up the remnant of an odor not easily identified but a whiff of something distinctive.

Turning, she shined light in the back of the Explorer. Then she exited the front, got into the back. Nothing there. Not even a gum wrapper.

Writing in her notebook, she stopped, leaned back, and cursed herself. She should have thoroughly investigated the car at the scene of the accident. The terrible weather, the removal of the body, knowing she and Rick had to call on Charlene: All those pressing matters had clouded her judgment.

Wedging her torso through the gap between the front bucket seats, she shined the light all over the passenger seat, looking for anything, a thread, a bit of wool from a sweater. If a clue was there, she missed it, but the forensic team would find it. She knew she had to call them in.

Cooper fell back into the rear seat, put her hand to her forehead. Then she got out, climbed into her squad car. The vehicles to be worked on or which were to be towed off sat in a lower lot behind the dealership. Rows of new vehicles not yet prepped were also at this location. The Vavilovs' lower lot had been plowed, but a thin veil of snow again covered everything.

Driving up the rise to the dealership office, Cooper composed herself. No point in letting anger at herself further cloud her judgment. She parked to the side, walked into the big showroom, smiling at the receptionist.

"Might I see Mrs. Vavilov for a moment? I know she's busy. I'll be quick."

The young lady, nicely turned out for her job of meeting the public, smiled and picked up the phone. She spoke to Charlene for a second, then looked up at Deputy Cooper. "Go right in."

Charlene stood up as the uniformed officer walked in. She liked Cooper. "Deputy, please sit down."

"Mrs. Vavilov, I won't take much of your time. I would just like to ask you to keep Pete's Explorer here."

"Of course. Can I help you with anything else? Would you like to see the invoice on it or have information about the four-wheel-drive capacities? Even four-wheel drive will slide off the highway."

"No, but thank you. I'd like a forensic team to go over the SUV."

A concerned look shadowed Charlene's face. "Of course. Is there something — well, you may not be able to tell me."

"I think we should have a closer look. I'm sorry to do this before Christmas."

Charlene looked down at her expensive, comfortable shoes. "The holiday doesn't really matter."

"Again, Mrs. Vavilov, I apologize."

"You're doing what's right. Would you like me to have the Explorer brought to the police station?"

"Oh, no. Just leave it on the lower lot. We don't want to draw attention to this."

"Thank you for that." Charlene reached out her hand.

Cooper shook it, then left. She hated even more that she'd been sloppy. Back at HQ she sought out Rick in his office and told him what she'd noticed.

Pulling a cigarette from his breast pocket, the sheriff put it in his mouth but didn't light up. You couldn't smoke in a county building, but the taste of the nicotine soothed him.

"Dammit."

"I'm sorry, boss," Cooper said, taking a seat across from him at his desk.

"Hell, I missed it, too. It was a filthy night and, well —" He waved the cigarette, now plucked from his mouth.

"Let's send a team to the accident site with rakes, whatever, to check the side of the road," said Cooper. "You never know."

"Right." He put the cigarette back in his mouth.

"Guys like Pete are well placed to generate illegal profits. I'm not saying he did, but we should bear it in mind."

"Overcharging for repairs can jack up a dealer's profits." Rick grunted. "Although I never heard of a complaint about that."

"Contraband could come in with those huge tractor trailers carrying new vehicles. Boss, I don't care what his death certificate says, I'm not buying a natural death."

Rick stood up and stretched, as sitting at his paper-strewn desk caused backache. "His wife didn't tell anyone about the missing fingers?"

"No." Cooper quickly added, "We told her not to."

Rick smiled, cracked his knuckles, cigarette still in his mouth, then sat back down. "Right, but did she ask you anything more about it?"

Cooper folded her hands over one knee. "I don't believe she wants to think about that."

Rick sighed. "Perhaps not, but we must."

He twirled his cigarette, changing the subject. "I don't mind going outside to smoke when the weather is cold, but it's hell on a day like today."

"It is." She had long since given up trying to get him to stop, as had his wife.

"I'm glad you went over there. You're a

good officer."

As Rick did not generally lavish his colleagues with compliments, Cooper simply replied, "Thank you."

"Ever think about the nature of crime?" Rick asked, playing with his cigarette. "Lately, I've been getting a bit philosophical and have thought of this a lot. In any culture, in any century, there are folks who live outside the law, others who live inside the law but break it, subvert it. There will always be people motivated by profit, and there will always be people who kill because of rage, revenge, greed, or other motives."

"Right."

"But what is a crime here in Virginia is not necessarily a crime in — say, Pakistan, or maybe even a country closer to our own ways, perhaps Sweden?"

"I think about that, especially our drug laws."

"Or laws about sex. There are still laws on the books in some of the original Thirteen Colonies that state you cannot kiss your wife in public on Sunday. It's crazy."

"This is Virginia. We confine ourselves to government-ordered probes for women seeking legal abortions."

"We're the laughingstock of the country. Jokes on late-night TV." He shook his head in disbelief. "Now, child prostitution and other abuse of children motivates me. Smuggling people across our borders to work for nothing, that motivates me. Everyone reacts to a mass murderer. I understand that. I react to it, too, but, Coop, it's the hidden crimes that irk me so: the hidden crimes by so-called respectable people, like keeping a maid from Asia who doesn't speak English and not paying her. It may not be as riveting as murder, but exploitation like that drives me wild."

"That I understand."

Rick, calmer now, and he was a man who rarely had an outburst, said, "I'm a pretty conservative guy. I think most law enforcement people are. I believe there's right and wrong, and maybe right and wrong is different in Cambodia than it is here, but I know what's right and wrong in America. What I don't know is why do we persist in what doesn't work?"

"Like what?" asked Cooper. The sheriff was really on a tear now. Best to just sit back and listen.

"Like thinking evil can be talked away. Sure, you can understand evil. Maybe you can understand the motivation of someone who commits evil. But you can't stop it. Only action stops it."

"Isn't that where we come in?" She half smiled.

"Yes, but lately I've been thinking that what we are really doing shields people from the failures of our society."

Cooper didn't have an answer for that, but her boss's frustrations haunted her as she headed home from work. She decided to pull into Harry's farm. The dog, the cats, the horses, Harry and Fair always made her feel better, even though sometimes she could just swat Harry for the dangerous risks her nosy neighbor sometimes took.

Tucker barked and Harry looked up as Cooper came through the kitchen door. "Perfect timing."

"What?" The tall woman smiled as she rubbed her hands together. She'd sprinted from the car without wearing a coat.

"Chicken corn soup. Made a huge pot, and it's fresh."

Inhaling deeply, Cooper smiled.

Harry pointed to the chair. "Sit down and be my guinea pig. You can tell me if I need more chicken, more egg, or more fresh parsley. I don't think I need more rice."

"I'm going to like this."

Tucker smelled the aroma. *"Grab the package the chicken was in, the little absorbent paper is still there."* The humans, distracted

143

by their conversation, paid no attention to Mrs. Murphy, who clamped her fangs down on the plastic, leapt off the counter, and hurried outside. She placed it behind the back barn doors.

The three animals returned, leaving wet pawprints on the random-width pine floor.

"We still need eggshells. She made eggs this morning and she put eggs in the soup," Pewter noted.

"We'll have to wait for them to leave the kitchen," Mrs. Murphy said.

Cooper dipped her spoon into the bowl again. "This is perfect."

"Not too salty?" asked Harry.

"No, you know I can't stand much salt. The parsley adds a lot to the flavor."

"It's my mother's recipe. She was like Miranda, could make anything from scratch."

Once finished, the two women repaired to the living room to sit by the fire. The animals took that opportunity to quickly fish out eggshells. When they knocked over the garbage can, Harry flew back into the kitchen, but the sneaky devils were already long gone. She righted the garbage can, then wiped the coffee grounds up from the floor.

Cooper knelt down and helped.

"I don't know what gets into them," Harry

complained. "Second time in two days. It's not like they're hungry."

Seeing the slight mark of coffee, which Harry scrubbed with a wet paper towel, Cooper blurted out, "Harry, I found a dot of something on Pete Vavilov's driver's headrest. I missed it at the scene of the accident." She caught herself. "I criticize you all the time for sticking your nose into our cases, and here I just blabbed something that I should have kept to myself. I'm just really upset with myself for missing it. You want to hear something else really strange? His index and middle fingers were missing."

Harry plucked the wet towel out of Cooper's hands, crumpled it with the one in her own, and tossed them in the righted garbage can, the lid swinging. "Don't beat up on yourself. Christmas adds to all this, too."

"Well, keep it to yourself."

"I will." Harry waited, then said in a strong voice, "It sounds like Pete wasn't alone in that Explorer."

16

The shopping centers in Charlottesville had cars circling in vain through the enormous parking lots looking for spaces. The snow, pushed up in piles, took up valuable parking. Tempers flared.

Looking for last-minute affordable gifts, Harry and Susan managed to find a parking place in the large Seminole Square center. The Office Depot drew their attention because here they could buy all manner of useful things. The two women, pushcart in front of them, trolled the aisles in search of stocking stuffers. Other shoppers hovered in the electronic section, buying far more expensive things than these two. After getting red and green paper clasps, colored paper clips, tablets with sparkly covers, and lots of ribbon spools, they stood in line, way back.

"Check your list again," Susan told her friend.

Harry fished the list out of her back jeans pocket and read it aloud.

Susan checked down in the cart. "Think we got it. Once we're out of here we should head over to Dover Saddlery."

"Susan, the place will be jam-packed and jelly tight."

"Listen, just endure it because we can pick up Farriers' Fix, saddle soap, vet wrap, all kinds of little gifts for BoomBoom, Alicia, Big Mim, and Little Mim. You know you always run out of vet wrap just when you need it." Susan referred to the useful thin wrap that would stick to itself.

"Okay," moaned Harry.

The line took forever. After Susan paid, the cashier asked her if she wanted her receipt sent to her computer.

"No, thank you."

As they left the big windowless store, Harry carried one bag, Susan the other. "Why would you want the receipt sent to your computer?" asked Harry.

"A lot of people do their accounting that way."

Harry was horrified. "Once your information is out there, anyone can steal it."

"Harry, it's out there anyway. People send pictures of their private parts before going on first dates."

Completely scandalized, Harry gasped. "You are making that up."

"I'm not. I have two twentysomethings."

"Your children don't . . ." Harry's voice trailed off.

"They showed me." Susan's eyebrows raised. "Danny called me over when he was last home. 'Mom, look at this.' I about died. He swore he never sent photos of himself, but he couldn't help but look. Well, then I couldn't help but take a gander at the girl. She was pretty but clearly had no sense."

"If a congressman from New York did this, why am I surprised?"

"Because in your own way, Sugar, you really are sweet and naïve. There is no shame anymore. Women send pictures of their bosoms and everything else."

"Dear God." Harry gasped as they reached Susan's Audi.

They tossed the Office Depot purchases in the back of the station wagon, then Susan pulled a vinyl cover over the goods. The cold air condensed their breath.

"We'd better walk over to Dover."

"Right," Harry agreed. "We'll never get a parking place."

Watching traffic since the holiday drivers were so distracted, a few inebriated as well, the women crossed the shopping center

148

highway, then hurried into the parking lot in front of Dover Saddlery.

Before they reached the store, they heard a loud voice to their left.

"Stop telling me what to do!" On the sidewalk, Flo Rice shook her finger at Esther Mercier.

"Calm down." Esther crossed her arms over her chest, her cap pulled down over her ears for warmth. "Calm down right now or I am not taking you into Dover."

"I'm the older sister," pouted Flo. "I'm supposed to tell you what to do. You leave me alone. I don't need you following me everywhere."

"Flo, I am not following you. I brought you here. You wanted to see Christmas decorations, the stores. Well, here we are, but you have to behave. And while you're thinking about being quiet, why did you put your name on the St. Cyril's need list? Al and I take care of you."

"You keep me from everyone."

"Flo, all you have to do is get in your car and visit old friends. Cletus Thompson doesn't live that far from you."

"I like him when he's not drunk, though he rarely is."

"All right. All right." Esther wearied.

"And I am not driving that ancient Toyota

anywhere. It makes me look poor."

"Flo, you are poor."

"You took all of Mother's money." Flo pushed her sister, not hard but hard enough that Esther had to step back.

"Dammit, Flo, I did not." Esther looked around to see if anyone overheard. She didn't spot Harry and Susan near the discarded shopping carts. "You aren't good with money. Don't blame it on me. And there are people who would like to see you. But this putting your name on a list of indigents, Flo, that was deeply embarrassing."

Neither Harry nor Susan moved. They didn't want to call attention to themselves.

Flo, however, scanned the packed parking lot, hoping to find an ally. "There you are!" She pointed straight at the two friends.

"Now what?" Susan whispered.

"We go over and pretend we haven't heard a thing." With a big smile, Harry walked over. "Esther, Merry Christmas. Miss Rice, Merry Christmas."

Susan followed suit.

"You didn't really remember me when you came to my house, but I remembered you. Sometimes I'd see you at the horse shows when I worked for Mrs. Valencia. I was nice to you. You didn't remember me." Flo indicated Harry.

150

"We were young." Harry tried to smile.

"I look different now. I'm older, and she" — Flo pointed at her sister — "treats me bad. She keeps me away from people."

On the thin edge of fury, Esther said through clenched teeth, "Flo, that is enough!"

Susan stepped between Flo and Esther. She engaged Flo while Harry moved Esther a slight distance from her very loud sister.

"Esther, can we help you?" Harry asked.

Esther's face crumpled in relief. "I don't know what to do. We were getting along pretty good. Flo wanted to do Christmas and —" She couldn't finish her sentence.

"Miss Mercier, why don't Susan and I try to get her in your car? I mean Mrs. Toth."

Esther's eyes misted over. "I'm afraid she'll jump out when I start driving."

"Let's try." Harry was thinking of alternatives if Esther's prediction came true.

She decided if worse came to worst she and Susan could drive Flo home.

Having greatly calmed Flo while exhausting herself, Susan was grateful as the other women approached her.

"Miss Rice." Harry used her brightest voice. "It will be dark soon, traffic is fearsome, we thought we'd go home, too. Just way too many people. Maybe you should

151

convince Miss, I mean, Esther to go, too."

A beady look crossed Flo's face. "Oh, she won't be happy until she spends tons of money."

"I promise I won't spend a thing." Esther managed a smile. "Harry's right, it's going to be a mess. If we leave now, we'll get home at a reasonable hour. If we wait, we'll sit in traffic."

"I don't know." Then a determined look came over Flo. "Don't talk to me anymore about Cletus Thompson."

Esther led the way across the parking lot to her car. "I won't. We'll talk about whatever you wish." She slid behind the wheel.

Harry opened the passenger door while Susan, quietly taking Flo's elbow, guided her in. Before the difficult woman ducked her head in, Flo whispered loudly, "She keeps me from everyone. Don't believe a word she says."

17

That same evening — still cold, with low clouds — Fair reached home an hour after sundown, early for him. Often when he'd cross the threshold, the man was so tired he'd gratefully sit down at the kitchen table. Harry usually knew when he would be arriving home. He was good about calling ahead, so oftentimes upon his arrival supper was on the table.

Harry never minded preparing meals alone, whether it was for her husband, the horses, the cats, or the dog. While not the superb cook that Miranda was, she excelled at the basics. In wintertime, one needed basics. As they ate, both discussed their days.

"Did you see the weather report?" Fair cut into a pork chop.

"Cold. Temperature won't break freezing maybe even until after Christmas. That's unusual."

"For us." He smiled. "Imagine living in Minnesota."

"I don't know how those northern states do it. The electric and heat bills alone would bankrupt you." Harry paid the monthly bills, and winter's bills skyrocketed.

"I guess they plan for it." He thought for a moment. "How can you plan for Mother Nature's revenge? Even with sophisticated weather predictions, they're often wrong and, boy, what a mess."

She switched the subject. "I can't get that episode in the parking lot out of my mind. It wasn't violent, nothing too grotesque was said, but how do you reason with someone who is unreasonable? Flo Rice was like a wizened child."

Fair folded his hands in his lap, leaned back a little. "You can't reason with the unreasonable. You try to manage them. With a horse, if I can get close enough I stick him with a tranquilizer. Can't really do that with a person unless you're in a hospital or some kind of home. Maybe not even then."

"You know, honey, that's the one thing that scares me the most, my mind unraveling."

He smiled at the woman he'd known all his life. "Harry, no one in your family has ever suffered from dementia or Alzheimer's.

You aren't going to be the first. You might drive me to it, but you'll be fine."

"You'll pay for that." She reached across the table as though to stab him with her fork.

"Yeah, yeah. I'm bigger."

"You have to sleep sometime."

This made them both laugh, then Fair said, "Something you reported made me wonder, though. Esther asking why her sister put her name on the needy list at St. Cyril's. And you heard Flo say she's being kept away from people? Maybe that's why she snuck her name on the list."

"She didn't say it exactly like that, but it was the sense of it. Flo doesn't go to St. Cyril's anymore. She says she left the church when they removed Latin from the service. That was one of the things she banged on about when Susan and I dropped off food and clothing."

"That is odd. Who knows what wires are getting crossed in her brain."

"I thought of that, too, Fair, and then I thought of a bit of history I was reading about the wife of Nixon's attorney general. Martha Mitchell told the truth and media painted her as a crazy alcoholic."

"It's done every day, especially now. But it doesn't seem to me there's anything Flo knows of import. No reason to keep her from people. If Esther took her out to see Christmas decorations, she's obviously not hiding her or keeping her hidden away."

"And Flo has a car, but there was something about that fuss in the parking lot that's bothering me and I don't know what."

"Honey, seeing anyone lose their clarity is unsettling."

"You're right, as usual."

"Oh, she can tell a fib!" Pewter called out from the floor.

"Not a fib. Managing your husband," Tucker sensibly replied.

"Rather manage him than her." Mrs. Murphy batted a small yellow ball with rattles inside to Pewter.

"Ha." Pewter whacked it across the kitchen.

The humans watched the cats chase the ball and each other.

"I often envy them." Harry admired the cats' delight.

"Me, too," said Fair.

"Still no news on Lou?" she asked.

"No. He truly is missing."

"I'd like to pay my respects to Arden, see if there's anything I can do, but I think I'd get in the way."

"Best to wait until we know something."

Harry shivered for a second, then said, "Someone walked over my grave."

"Let's not talk about graves."

Later, when their humans watched a movie, the cats retrieved the pork paper, the chop bones. Harry hadn't put them in the garbage yet. She'd put them in a Ziploc bag, dropping it in the sink. She figured she'd remove the enticing-smelling things later, and she was tired of cleaning up knocked-over garbage cans.

The animals took the food to the appointed place, slipped into the barn. It was not really warm but warm enough, and they waited.

Odin trotted across the back pastures about an hour later, happy for the pickings.

Mrs. Murphy, Pewter next to her, called down to the coyote from the hayloft, *"How you doing?"*

"Fine."

"If I go up the old farm trail in the walnut forest, how far before I reach the bones?" Mrs. Murphy asked.

Devouring another piece of corn bread, Odin swallowed again, then spoke, *"If you go about halfway up, there's another narrow trail, a deer trail that cuts across the old truck road. Go left on the deer trail, uh, quarter mile*

157

at most. You'll see the tree uprooted. You can't miss it." He waited, then smiled. *"I can take you there."*

"Odin, I appreciate that, but you'd eat me in a minute." Mrs. Murphy stared down.

"And ruin my nightly treats?" He grinned, revealing sharp fangs.

"Maybe, maybe not." The tiger cat grinned back at him. *"But I'm not taking a chance."*

As the coyote left, Tucker, listening at the back barn doors, trotted inside to the hayloft ladder.

Pewter backed down first, followed by Mrs. Murphy.

"Does Odin think you're stupid?" Tucker growled.

"No, but can't blame a guy for trying," the tiger cat replied. *"If we could get a break in the weather, some snow melt or tamp down, we could head up there in the daytime. Can't go at night."*

"We can see in the dark." Pewter puffed out her chest.

"Yeah, well, Odin doesn't do too bad in the dark either." Mrs. Murphy knew dogs had pretty good night vision — not as good as cats, but still.

"Even if Odin's not there, other hunters might be. A female bear lives up there." Pewter recalled the large animal since they'd

had unpleasant words one summer.

"*The bear won't hurt us.*" Tucker knew the habits of bears. "*I mean, not unless we provoke her, but if there's one coyote, you know there are more, and I'm not overfond of bobcats either.*"

"*Three sets of eyes, ears, and noses are better than one,*" the tiger cat proclaimed.

"*So you say,*" the corgi said noncommittally.

18

The next morning, Wednesday, Jessica arrived with Jan McGee at eight A.M. at St. Cyril's. Other cars, SUVs, and trucks already dotted the parking lot, as the ladies' auxiliary started early on the gifts for the needy.

Seeing Harry park in the lot, Jessica and Jan waited for her. "A lot of work to do." Jessica smiled. "I've come in to do the books, lots to organize. I'll have to come back Friday, too. And at the end of the month. End of the year," she said. "It's going to take all of us to get these things delivered by Christmas. A good sign, I think, but a lot of work."

Harry opened the door for the two women.

"A good sign." Jessica waved as they passed the room where the ladies worked. "We could all use a little good news. Visited Arden and Tyler yesterday." She lowered her voice. "A lot of stress, obviously. Tyler wants to comfort her but" — she held up her hands — "he doesn't know how with his dad missing. A lot of anger, worry. You can imagine."

Jan quietly said, "The trick is to keep Arden from imagining too much."

"You're right." Jessica nodded.

"My old church in Grundy burned to the ground. People's theories as to why ranged from faulty wiring, a disgruntled congregant, to Muslim revenge on Christians. Too much imagination." Always levelheaded, Jan knew many others who were not.

"Well, Jan, you know the gang in the meeting room," said Jessica. "Maybe you can help steer the conversation away from drama."

"Jan can do anything." Harry complimented the woman who had driven the hour from Manakin-Sabot to once again help.

Harry and Jan walked into the big room as Jessica continued down the hall. Despite all, she was determined to keep up with the books.

Opening the door into the tiny room, not all that warm itself, Jessica took off her coat but kept her scarf on. Once Father O'Connor came in, he'd open the door to his office, always warm, and that warmth would flow in.

Jessica sat down at the old heavy desk, pulled out the account book, studied it for a moment, then reached for a sharp pencil without looking.

The pencil felt quite cold as she bent over the books. Then she noticed before she touched the page that it wasn't a pencil. It was a human index finger.

Jessica let out a shriek.

The ladies heard it and ran to the room — Harry, the fastest, in the lead. Susan, who had recently arrived, was in the group, too.

Jessica, standing up, pointed to the finger.

Harry walked over, did not pick it up. The other women joined her. To their credit, no one fainted or threw up, but all of them were greatly distressed.

Susan took charge. "I'll call the sheriff. Ladies, I think we should all leave this room. Jessica, you come with us."

"I'll stay here." Harry's voice was firm. "Someone needs to guard the evidence."

"You think someone will come back for it — I mean, both of them?" Jessica now saw there was yet another finger in the large

mug containing pencils and ballpoint pens.

"We are taking no chances," said Harry. "You all stay in the big room. The sheriff's department will want to question us."

"Why, we didn't do it!" Anita Buckly, the president of the auxiliary, nearly shouted.

"Of course not." Harry tried to calm everyone, as people took shocks differently. "But someone might have seen something that seems inconsequential but isn't."

"This is a sick joke." Jessica's hand flew to her throat.

"It well may be, but we can't disturb anything and the sheriff or a deputy will want things as free of fingerprints as possible." Harry spoke like an expert on criminal investigations, which maybe she was.

Fortunately, Rick Shaw and Cynthia Cooper arrived within twenty minutes. Father O'Connor, now in his office, met them. Harry had informed the young priest of the events. Father O'Connor had called Father O'Brien and the old priest said he'd drive over to the church, but Father O'Connor told him to wait for the sheriff. Rick said he'd visit the priest later in his retirement home.

The two law enforcement officials inspected the fingers without touching them.

"They were kept on ice," Harry speculated.

"Or stuck in snow." Cooper looked around the room.

"No one was here other than Jessica," Father O'Connor burbled.

"Actually, Father, a lot of people have been through here," said the sheriff. "The ladies are wrapping gifts. Anyone could have slipped in and out, there's so much activity. Someone walking down the hall might not attract attention."

"Or someone came early." Cooper looked over at the shaken priest. "Your rooms are separate from this building, right?"

"The small house in the rear."

"Father, you can go," said Rick. "We'll call you if we need you." He was intent on doing as much as he could before more people trooped into St. Cyril's.

"My office is right here." Father O'Connor stepped through the door to the next room. "If you'll allow it, I'd like to go talk to the ladies. Perhaps I can help Jessica, the others."

"Fine," was all Rick said, as he was already scribbling furious notes. "Coop, we need forensics and maybe a forensic accountant."

"Before I make that call, let's make sure we take pictures." She pulled out her cell-

165

phone and began snapping shots of the desk, the position of the chair, the room as it was when the fingers were found.

Meanwhile, Rick studied everything.

"Would you like me to go?" Harry inquired.

"H-m-m. Yes. You didn't touch anything?" Rick flatly asked.

"No, like I told you, I sent the others into the big room, then stayed here to make sure no one disturbed the scene, including me. I walked into the office from that door" — she pointed to the hallway door — "over to the desk when I heard Jessica scream. The ladies hurried here. We stood at the front of the desk. Once they left, I didn't move."

"Coop, call someone to come pick up these fingers. We need to get someone to look over these books." He glanced at Cooper. "There has to be significance to them being in a pencil jar in the book-keeper's office."

19

"Kind of white, almost like freezer burn." Harry described the condition of the fingers to her husband.

She'd called him as soon as Sheriff Shaw and Deputy Cooper released her. Then she drove over to join him at Big Mim's stables.

Paul Diaz — the wealthy woman's stable manager, a good-looking man in his mid-thirties — held a mare for Fair.

"Gives new meaning to chicken fingers." Fair patted the broodmare Dinah on her hindquarters.

Paul laughed as Harry tried not to. "Fair!" she protested.

"Honey, it's all just too weird. Might as well laugh at it." He turned to the raven-haired Paul and waved at the horse. "She's fine. Is Big Mim thinking about breeding her in January?"

He nodded, adding, "She's not looking to

race the foal. She's more interested in a chaser."

"Dinah sure has the bloodlines for steeple-chasing." Harry knew the animal. "But you still want to put her under lights and all that to get her ready for January?"

"Or early February. It's to a Thorough-bred's advantage to be born as close to January as possible in the new year. December won't do you a bit of good." Fair stated a fact well known to racing people.

"Guess not." Harry sat on a tack trunk.

All Thoroughbred birthdays are registered at the Jockey Club as January 1, regardless of the month in which the animal was foaled. A Thoroughbred born in July would still be registered as being born January 1. So that fellow or filly would have to run against more mature horses foaled early in the year. The problem was that mares generally come into season with springtime, like most other mammals. The season had to be hormonally induced. This was time-consuming, expensive, but it had to be done.

The other wrinkle for Thoroughbreds is that the rules stated the stallion must cover the mare. No artificial insemination is al-lowed. This means vanning mares to the state in which the stallion stands. For Virginians, that usually meant Kentucky,

168

although West Virginia and Pennsylvania, thanks to legislatures that wanted the equine dollar, now stood some good stallions. Poor Maryland, once a powerhouse, had blown it. People flew out of that beautiful state, taking their horses with them. Politics destroyed a huge industry. Other states took notice.

The three people in Mim's barn — conversant with this, loving horses — wanted this mare to have a chance at a superior stallion.

As they chatted on, Harry slumped back against the wall, wrapping her arms around her, for the day was cold. "Ever think about how we breed horses with more care than we breed one another?"

"Yep," Paul replied.

"Seems unfair, doesn't it?" Harry continued in her line of thought. "If we were as responsible to ourselves as we are to Thoroughbreds, there'd be a lot less hungry, abused children."

"I give Silver Linings a lot of credit for reaching out to boys with problems." Fair wrote up his findings on a metal clipboard. "When you see cast-off kids, it hits you."

Returning from putting the mare in her stall, Paul said, "What's going to happen to Silver Linings now that Pete is dead? Didn't he pump a lot of money into that group?"

"He did," Fair answered. "The hope is some other people step up to the plate. Max de Jarnette has been generous, Coach Toth will call friends he has in the NFL. If he can get a big name attached to this, boy, that will really help."

"You're not a member, are you?" Paul asked.

"No. Harry and I go to the fund-raisers, but you can't do everything, and I am involved in so many equine and animal charities, including the riding for the returning veterans. I just don't have the time."

"That riding program is special." Paul smiled.

"Okay, here's Dinah's schedule. Put her under the lights. I'll check her regularly and we'll take it from there."

Fair and Harry walked outside to their respective trucks. Harry's cell rang.

"Hold on a minute, honey." She fished it out of her pocket. "Hello, Coop."

"Where are you?"

"Big Mim's."

"Stay put. I'll be there in five minutes."

Harry closed her phone, relayed the message to Fair.

"Well, I've got to get to my next call." Fair kissed her on the cheek.

"I am not telling her the crack you made about fingers."

"Good idea. I should be home by six. Maybe even earlier." As Fair drove out, he waved at Cooper driving in.

"What did I do now?" Harry asked as the lean officer climbed out of her car.

"Nothing." Cooper looked around. "Hey, get in my squad car. We found Lou Higham. His index and middle fingers are missing from his right hand."

20

A woman walking her golden retriever had found Lou Higham. The dog ran off, refusing to return to her. As Jake was an unusually obedient companion, his human followed her dog, trudging through deep snows. His incessant barking led her to Lou Higham's corpse.

He had died not far from home. His car had gone off an embankment, and had continued sliding into a narrow ravine. The continuing snowfall had blanketed the car. The treadmarks off the road were also covered.

Folded over the steering wheel, Lou was well preserved, thanks to the cold, although missing for five days. The weight of his head slightly stretched his neck. His lips were pulled back and his gums were white. His right hand showed two bloody stumps, frozen. His index and middle fingers were missing.

A plastic cup with a small slide for drinking remained wedged in the cup holder.

His contorted face bore testimony to the fact that he'd died in pain.

The TV news reported that the search for Lou Higham had ended. They did not announce details, such as the mutilated hand or his face's frightened expression.

Jessica Hexham immediately informed the delivery ladies of St. Cyril's while her husband called the men of Silver Linings. As they had done when Pete died, each adult male called five boys in the group.

Jessica also called Father O'Connor.

When these folks arrived at Arden's to help, they were surprised to see Charlene, Jarrad, and Alex already there.

Charlene simply stated, "We know how it feels."

The following morning, December 19, Fair and Harry prepared for their day. Last night, Harry had recapped the day's events to Fair. "Forgot to ask you," he said now. "How's Tyler?"

"Tyler's a mess," Harry replied.

Fair sympathetically said, "Dealing with your father's death is tough, especially at that age. Plus, he's not the easiest kid. I

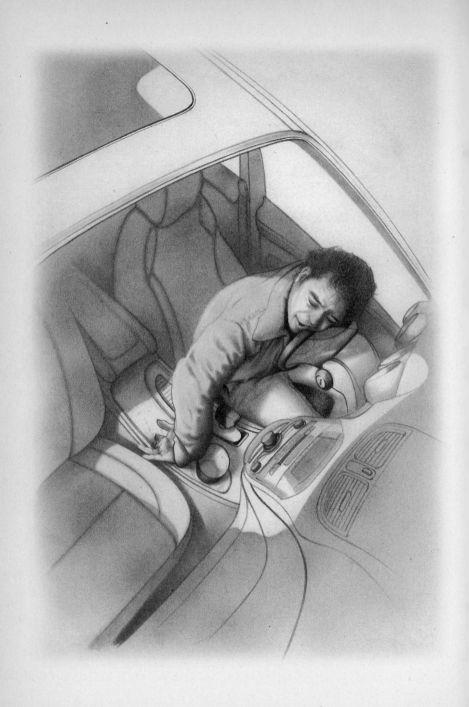

hope he can come through all this without being filled up with psychotropic drugs."

"Arden has enough to face right now," Harry replied. "But, really, Fair, maybe a temporary regime of calming drugs isn't so bad."

"Honey, I'm very suspicious of prescribing drugs to developing brains and bodies. But who will listen to a vet?" Then he added, "Let's count our blessings."

"I am a blessing, I am a big one." Pewter rubbed on Fair's legs.

"I think I'll throw up." Mrs. Murphy grimaced.

"Hairball," Pewter tormented her friend.

Mrs. Murphy lunged for the fat gray cat, who jumped sideways. They were off and running. Tucker sat tight. Everyone heard a smash.

"Damn them." Harry hurried in the direction of the noise. "Fair, help me."

Fair ran into the living room, where a lamp was in pieces, scattered over the rug. The Christmas tree swayed as though in a high wind. A very fat cat hung on at the top, bending the trunk over while, lower down, Mrs. Murphy, claws deep in the spruce tree, lashed out with one paw. Fragile Christmas balls swung.

Fair quickly reached into the tree, grabbing the trunk.

"You get out of there," Harry demanded.

"She has to back down first!" Pewter, eyes wide, shouted.

"Ha! I'll turn your fat butt into hamburger." Mrs. Murphy sank claws into the large target.

"She's killing me!" Pewter cried, ever the drama queen.

"You hold the tree up. I think I have the answer." Harry dashed into the kitchen, opened a cupboard, returned. She pried open the plastic lid on a small can of catnip. Then she held it up as far as she could. The fighting stopped. Mrs. Murphy backed down, jumped off, pine needles sprinkling over the rug as she did.

Harry crushed catnip in her fingers, away from the Christmas tree.

"Pig!" Pewter hollered from her perch.

"You can stay up there all day." Mrs. Murphy rolled in her herb. *"This is good stuff."*

"I hate her." Pewter cursed as she backed down, Fair still holding the tree, for there was a lot of cat. *"I hate her more than anything on this earth."*

As she jumped off, she knocked off a brilliant green ball, which Harry caught.

"Good save." Fair finally let go of the tree, after making sure it was secure.

176

"They are mental," said Harry. "Look at my china lamp. I really liked that lamp."

Fair knelt down beside her to pick up the pieces. "If I knew for one second what goes through a cat's mind, I'd be scared."

"That's an insult," a glassy-eyed Pewter managed to slur. The two cats now rolled in the catnip, purred, and batted at each other harmlessly.

Carefully depositing the broken lamp in a cardboard box, closing the top, Harry set it outside on the porch.

"Guess I know what to get you for Christmas," Fair said.

"You mean I'm not getting my pearl necklace from Keller and George?" For years, Harry had visited a lustrous pearl necklace, the pearls about nine millimeters big.

"When I win the lottery, you get your pearls." He smiled at her, but he did want to buy them for her.

Someday.

"Honey, what I want for Christmas is continued good health for both of us, laughter, work we enjoy, and time with our friends. The rest is fluff."

"It is. Before I forget, tomorrow is December twentieth — the big delivery day. Tell me tonight after checking with Susan how many of the husbands you need. I know all of the church ladies have had unexpected labors and have been delivering early, but I expect tomorrow will be over the top."

"It will. Susan has done a great job."

"She usually does." Fair, like everyone, recognized Susan Tucker's organizing abilities.

He kissed his wife on the cheek. "Thanks. I'll call in. Looks like an okay day."

"They always start that way." She watched as he walked out the door, thinking about the last time Arden and Charlene had seen their husbands, never dreaming they would never see them walk through the door again.

Once both humans left, Mrs. Murphy, coming to her senses after the catnip hit, said, *"It's daytime. Let's try and find those bones. We'll be safe. Coyotes usually hunt at night, and the snow has packed down. Let's do this before another snow."*

"I am not going out in the cold," said Pewter. *"And I don't care about human bones. They don't do us any good."*

"Speak for yourself," Tucker replied.

"You aren't going to chew on dried-out bones with dirt all over them. You live too good for that." The gray cat had a point.

"I'm going whether you come with me or

178

not," said Mrs. Murphy. *"That bracelet is expensive, it belonged to whoever is up there."* With that, she pushed through the animal door in the kitchen, followed by Tucker. Pewter pointedly did not move.

Following the farm road where the snow packed down in the ruts, the two loped past the back pastures, past the sunflower plots, the quarter acre of grapes, stakes and wire in place. Beyond that, another lone and wide pasture bordered the forest.

The snow crunched as they trotted over the pastures, the creek running strong on their left. With its beaver dam, this rocky creek divided Harry's land from the farm that Deputy Cooper rented.

The temperature at thirty-two degrees Fahrenheit felt as though it wouldn't budge throughout the day. The sun shone precariously through a light cloud cover that promised to thicken. The animals could smell heavier weather approaching.

Every now and then, one of them would blunder into a snowdrift. The crust disguised the snow depth. They'd flounder, then swim their way out.

Reaching the edge of the forest, the base of the eastern slope of the mountains, Tucker sat for a moment. *"Take a breath."*

Mrs. Murphy parked next to her. *"Odin*

179

said to go up the old farm road and where the deer trail crosses to turn left."

"The good thing about the trotting, and now the climb, is it will keep us warm."

"Right."

They started upward, the grade at first not terribly steep. Higher up, switchbacks had been cut into the side of the mountain to offset the steep grade. Onward, they puffed. About a half mile up, they hit the deer trail.

"This is farther up than that coyote said," said Tucker.

"It's hard to judge distance in this kind of terrain. Everything takes longer." The cat breathed in. "This huge old walnut stand, the black bark against the snow, it's almost spooky."

The hollies, dotted here and there, provided rich, glossy dark green color enlivened with bright red berries. Heading left on the deer trail, they traveled about two football fields in length. They now saw the uprooted tree.

Reaching it, both animals sat down. The skeleton had roots piercing the rib cage, one root snaked through an open jaw. The bones lifted out of the earth, suspended in the air, whitened with age. They were missing the left arm from the elbow down.

Tucker raised her head and sniffed. *"Coyote!"*

"Tucker, climb into the hole from the uprooted tree. The thick roots will protect you from him. We won't be able to outrun him. I'll climb up the tree."

Paws crunched on the snow and Odin appeared. He smiled, fangs prominent. *"Mrs. Murphy and the dog."*

"Tucker."

"You can come out of there. I won't eat you."

"I don't believe you." Tucker growled. *"Coyotes eat everything."*

On his haunches, the wild animal stared up at Mrs. Murphy now. *"You're just out of reach. I won't eat you either."*

Mrs. Murphy didn't budge. *"I'd like to believe that."*

"M-m-m." He didn't budge either.

"How many other coyotes live up here?" Tucker's nose stuck through the snow-covered roots.

"Two families. One at the edge of the high meadow. Another at the Pinnacles." Odin named the jutting rock outcropping near the spine of the mountain. *"I can walk down to the farm with you and keep anyone else away. Although I don't think they'll be down here."*

181

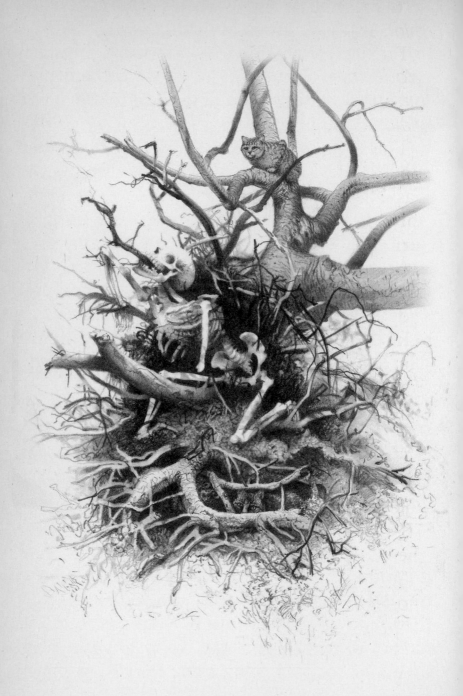

"Odin, you'd snap my neck in a skinny minute," Mrs. Murphy called down.

The coyote lay down, head on paws. *"You're going to get very cold. My fur is thicker than yours because I'm never in a really warm place."*

The three animals remained there as clouds moved in, the wind picked up. Hours passed. Tucker felt stiff, and Mrs. Murphy shivered. Odin watched them with his glittering yellow eyes.

As what little light there was shifted, the skeleton seemed to smile, then the light faded, the clouds turning Prussian blue.

In the far distance, Mrs. Murphy heard Harry's truck. Her uncommonly good ears would astonish a human being.

"Tucker, Mom's home. Start barking."

Tucker barked and barked.

Harry paid little attention, for the barking was far away. She walked into the house, laid packages on the kitchen table. She took off her coat, seeing only Pewter, thinking the other two were asleep.

"Mom, Murphy and Tucker are up on the mountain," said Pewter.

"You're chatty."

"This is serious," the cat screeched.

A half hour passed; Harry finally checked each room. No cat or dog. She threw on her coat, walked out to the barn. They weren't there either. Just then, Fair drove in, and as she was telling him, they both stopped. They heard their corgi barking.

"Tucker?" Fair wondered, then froze, for he heard Odin howl.

Harry hopped behind the wheel.

Fair did the same in the truck's passenger seat.

"Wait a minute." Fair quickly got out, opened his big vet truck door, then climbed back in. A .22 revolver rested on his lap. Ratshot could scare off animals.

Harry drove behind the barn on the farm road, keeping on it until the edge of the forest. She stopped, rolled down her window.

They listened intently. Again, they heard Tucker bark. Odin howled too, much closer now.

"This baby might be old, but she's four-wheel drive," said Harry. "You ready?" She looked at her husband.

"Yeah, I don't worry about my body bouncing around. It's my head hitting the roof."

"Get ready." She'd turned the small dials on the old hubcaps to drive through the snow when she came home.

Now she shifted into the lowest gear — the tires were winter tires — then hit the gas, and the rear end fishtailed. They climbed up the side of the mountain on the old road. It had deeper ruts than the farm road.

Each time the wheel slid into a rut, Harry gunned the motor to get out. Poor Fair bounced up, even with the seatbelt on. Finally, he put his hand on top of his head.

They reached a small turnaround.

"You'd better turn this around, keep her in gear, cut the motor. We can't risk going higher, especially now." Fair noticed snowflakes in the beams of the headlights.

She did as told, also yanking on the emergency brake. The turnaround was level enough, but she worried about sliding in the snow, even with the truck parked. It might give a little when they climbed out. Both of them, raised in the country, knew dumb things happen.

She cut the lights, pulled her scarf tighter around her neck. Fair stepped out, slid the revolver in his belt, pulled on his gloves.

Tucker was clearly close and to their left, so they walked through the walnuts, brushed by some hollies, tripped on uneven ground covered by the snow.

"We're here!" Mrs. Murphy yelled.

"Come on." Tucker yowled as she could see the flashlight swinging right and left.

185

Odin let out one howl before hurrying off into the darkness, calling over his shoulder, *"I wouldn't have eaten you. My call is louder than yours. I'll see you tomorrow at the barn."*

Neither animal knew whether or not to believe him. Tucker took no chances. She wasn't emerging until Harry and Fair reached them. The two animals had forgotten about the skeleton.

Close enough now for Tucker to smell her and Fair, Harry couldn't see much for the darkness.

Fair, beside her, shined the light right where Tucker still barked. The dog's eyes glowed in the flashlight. Fair flicked the light upward. There was Mrs. Murphy, whose eyes shone, too.

"What the —" Harry froze.

Fair now focused on the macabre sight.

Both just stood there as the cat backed down the tree and the dog lifted herself out from the roots, brushing by a dangling leg bone, which rattled.

Mrs. Murphy reached onto Harry's pants leg. Harry bent over and picked her up.

Tucker came next to Fair, who now shined the flashlight over the entire skeleton.

"I'm really cold," the dog whined as a snowflake landed on her nose.

"Me, too." Mrs. Murphy rested her face

186

against Harry's.

Already a half mile distant, Odin belted out one more howl, which added to the fright.

"Let's get back to the truck," Fair said.

Thicker now, the snow dropped onto bare tree limbs, making a soft noise as it did so.

They all got into the truck. Harry turned on the motor. The heater, already warm from the trip up, emitted welcome heat. "Do you have your cell?" she asked her husband.

He pulled it from his inside coat pocket and dialed Cooper's number. "No service up here."

"We're in a dead spot." Harry eased the vehicle back down the mountain road.

"Literally," quipped Fair.

Back at the farm, Harry flipped open her cellphone again. The snow fell harder. "I'm not getting anywhere. I'll use the landline."

Once in the kitchen, Mrs. Murphy and Tucker recounted everything to Pewter.

"See what you missed," Tucker gloated.

"Freezing my butt off, that's what I missed. You two are lucky to be alive. What if Odin called down other coyotes? They'd have dug you out. As for you, Murphy, you would have been trapped up there for days. And maybe

you wouldn't have lived either."

As the animals argued about whether Odin was or was not trustworthy, Harry dialed Cooper and the lights went out, the phone with it.

Fair pulled a flashlight from the drawer by the sink. "Bet someone ran off the road and hit a pole."

"I'm going to drive over."

"I'll come with you."

Tucker, Mrs. Murphy, and Pewter started for the door.

"Stay," Harry commanded.

"Bother," Pewter said and pouted.

Mrs. Murphy and Tucker, now really put out, as they were exhausted, crawled into their special fleece beds.

Fair drove this time. He had respect for bad driving conditions.

They reached Cooper's house within fifteen minutes, whereas it usually took five. A pinpoint of light shone from the living room window; smoke rose from the chimney, then flattened out.

Out of the truck, they walked to her back door and knocked. Within a few minutes, Cooper — holding a flashlight, as were Harry and Fair — opened the door.

"Come on in. It's the usual."

"Coop, I've been trying to call you on my cell, but the service isn't working."

"Come on into the living room. The fire helps. That and the fact that the power just went off, so it's not cold inside yet."

"Pain in the you-know-what." Harry followed her neighbor into the living room, as did Fair.

"Coop, let me get to the point," Fair said. "We found a skeleton up in the walnut grove."

Now on the edge of her chair, the blonde woman asked, "In what condition?"

"Bleached, tree roots growing through it," Harry matter-of-factly reported.

"It was missing the left arm from the elbow down, but that could be in the ground," said Fair. "Most of the skeleton is suspended," he added.

They told her how they heard the howls of Tucker and the coyote, of their shock at seeing the bones.

"This snow will complicate matters." Cooper checked the weather report on her Droid. "It will be mostly light, with a few heavy periods tapering off tomorrow afternoon." She looked up at her two friends. "And tomorrow is the big delivery day. I'm in charge for the department. Everyone off duty will be helping. 'Course, I really don't know who will be off duty tomorrow, thanks to finding Lou."

"A wonderful thought, but it is four days before Christmas." Fair lifted his feet to put them on the hassock, then thought better of it.

"Go ahead. I don't care if your boots are wet." Cooper didn't either. "I'll be at St. Luke's. Actually, the department is pretty well divided up among the churches. If someone attends a church, it made sense for them to help with deliveries that day. Tomorrow is going to be a long, long day, and there's no way we can get back up there without you two."

"True. GPS is no help." Fair nodded.

"Neither is the weather," said Harry. "The mountain road is treacherous even when it's dry. Plus, you can't reach the switch-backs."

"Why not?"

"Trees down." Harry knew the mountains. "Those fall windstorms, and now all this snow. You know, trees have to be blocking the switchbacks. They are closer to the top, more wind."

"It's good to have open access from a few directions, in case there's trouble," Cooper prudently mentioned. "Well, there's nothing we can do about it for now."

"The killer isn't coming back anytime soon, I expect," Harry flatly stated. "I mean, this has to be a murder victim. People don't get buried at the base of trees."

"I actually enjoy cold cases." Cooper inhaled the aroma of hardwood. "Makes me think."

"You've got so many more tools now," said Fair. "Things like DNA."

"DNA helps, but we'd need to find a living relative of the deceased to be sure. And if a body has been long buried and can't be identified, then you have a problem."

"Dental records?" Fair queried.

"We send out the information, pictures of the teeth and jaw, and hope local dentists will check their records. And we hope whoever the dentist was for the victim isn't retired or dead. Even today, there are unclaimed corpses in every morgue in every city. No one knows who they are. Some of those people most certainly have been murdered."

"No matter how bad it is here, imagine living in Argentina, years ago — all those people who just went *poof,*" said Harry. "Never to be found and no records." She thought this incredibly sad.

A flicker, and the lights came back on. The refrigerator hummed.

"That's a record." Fair grinned.

"It really is," Cooper agreed. "I'll call the boss. We'll get up there after tomorrow's delivery day, and once the weather cooperates. It's important, but it's not pressing. We will get up there, though, with your help."

"That skeleton isn't going anywhere," Harry remarked.

21

December 20, the snow continued but was light. However, the blustery wind demanded alert driving, especially on the back roads. As the plows first cleared the interstates, then the big state highways like Route 29, the back roads often piled up with snow. No one in their right mind would be out in anything but four-wheel drive.

At seven-thirty in the morning, cars lined up at all the churches, often a police squad SUV among them to pick up the cartons, the food, the toys.

At the door to the St. Luke's meeting room, Susan Tucker checked off people and cartons as they carried out boxes for delivery. Each table also had a St. Luke's person checking who took what box. If anything, Susan had overorganized, but she was determined not to overlook anyone in need. Even with all the early deliveries, everyone there knew this would go on until sundown.

They hoped not much beyond, but you never knew.

Susan had called her counterparts at the other churches. Managing her husband's campaign for the House of Delegates burnished her already formidable skills. Difficult as that was, this day was also a lot to handle, compressed by time.

Strong and willing, Harry helped carry out boxes for some of the other ladies. Fair did the same, along with Brian Hexham, who'd closed his office to help.

The clergy present — priest, pastors, reverends, rabbi — all were astonished at the labor and how many parishioners had closed offices or taken the day off, doing whatever they could to help the poor. Everyone understood that these were hard times, and everyone also understood that one day a year can't begin to address the problem. So they worked with full hearts and frustrated minds.

"Harry," Susan addressed her dearest friend as she came back into the meeting room for another load, "go out in the hall and bring in the extra dog and cat food and all the animal treats."

"Did we already load up all that we have in here?" Harry's eyebrows rose.

"We did." Susan showed her the clipboard

and then Harry looked at the back table.

"Okay. Everyone has to have a Christmas present."

By nine, everything was on its way — except for the last loads that Harry and Susan were taking. Fair had already left with an entire truckload of horse cookies, for the horses at the rehab centers and retirement places, many awaiting homes. There was little hope in the winter. He also carried some boxes for Almost Home Animal Shelter in Nelson County, as well as the sparkling, large Albemarle County SPCA.

Next to Susan, Harry rode shotgun in the Audi, list in her lap. "First stop, behind Miller School, and then we can work our way up Dick Woods Road, all those little side roads. And then —"

"Harry, I drew up the list."

"Right." Harry realized Susan had been putting out brush fires for weeks, each day more intense than the one before, and she was one minute away from cranky.

"I brought those nutrition bars you like. Want a chocolate one?"

"I would kill for chocolate." Susan held out her hand.

Harry reached into the small cooler at her feet, retrieved a bar, unwrapped it halfway, handed it to Susan. Then she launched into everything that had happened last night.

"I was going to call you last night, but I know how busy you are and it was getting late. You know I tell you everything." Harry finished the story.

"Most times." Susan smiled. "God knows it's bizarre. When the sheriff finally gets up there, call me, I'll come up, since it's on my land."

Susan's late uncle, a man who retired to a monastery, had willed her the huge acreage on the side of the mountain that abutted Harry's acreage. The difference was that Susan's side contained the large stand of black walnut, along with other hardwoods. One black walnut could fetch thousands of dollars. The market slid up and down, but one lone tree could add considerably to the comfort of one's bank account. Harry managed the timber, a job she loved. Anything involving timber, farming, or animal husbandry, and Harry reveled in her element.

"Seeing a human skeleton suspended, tree roots growing through it, it's awful, but at the same time I think, well, the body was put to good use," Harry said matter-of-factly.

"What do you mean?"

"What good does it do to put people in a box where decomposition doesn't enrich the soil, or if you put them out, wild animals could eat them? It really is wasteful."

Tension evaporating, Susan laughed. "Harry, only you."

Harry laughed, too. "Well —"

They chattered on about everything, the deaths of the two men, the skeleton, the fingers in the pencil cup, the bills currently on the floor of the House of Delegates, who was an idiot in Richmond and who was not.

After delivering a box, Susan hopped in the Audi, Harry closing the back door, and they rode toward the last of their drops. Susan returned to a never-ending fund of gossip, much of it about sex. "Ned says most of those guys in Richmond are cheating like mad and lying through their teeth. The more righteous they present themselves, the bigger the whoremaster — his words."

"Really?"

"Yeah, I think if you're a young woman and you want to rise in the world, go to work in a politician or lobbyist's office. You'll sleep your way to the top faster than in Hollywood."

"How stupid was I to go to work at the post office when I graduated from Smith?" Harry smacked her open hand on her forehead.

"Well, Sugar, there's still time."

Off and running, they blabbed about infidelity, Internet porn, non-porn people posting pictures of their genitals on same.

"You know, that's not a good idea." Harry wiped tears from her eyes, as she was laughing so hard. So much had gone wrong just lately, the laughter lifted their spirits.

"Last stop?" Harry turned around to double-check the back of the plush wagon.

"It is."

The young couple, trimming a tree they had cut themselves, welcomed the two inside. Harry picked up a baby crawling on the floor. While the two may not have had much in life, they were happy with each other, happy with the baby.

When leaving, Susan and Harry kissed the baby and hugged the parents.

Back in the wagon, Susan sighed. "I loved it when the kids were little."

"Babies are usually ugly — I mean, they are, but your two weren't."

"All babies are beautiful." Susan slowed as they were descending an old tertiary road.

"Hey, you aren't on the campaign trail with Ned," Harry teased her.

A pause, then Susan admitted, "Have you ever noticed that some babies look like old men or old women? You won't know what they will look like at fourteen, but you have a good guess at what they will look like at seventy, unless they've had plastic surgery."

"Same with foals. There's a brief period of time when you know what they'll look like in their prime. Then it disappears. Horses go through the same awkward phases humans do. Look how their backs sway when they get really old."

"Right. Hey, we're above St. Cyril's. Let me stop by for a moment. Here." She handed Harry her cellphone. "See if I have messages?"

"Wouldn't it make that noise? The message beep?"

"Yeah, but these last few days the phone hasn't been right. I keep losing power, then charge it up in the car."

"Couldn't call Coop last night on the cell. Most times they work, except for the hollows. Mountains are gorgeous, but they are the devil with electronic stuff."

Susan drove onto the plowed St. Cyril's lot, with cars parked and a few coming in and out. The sun had set.

The two women walked into the church.

Charlene Vavilov, her sons, and their teammates from football and baseball carried out the last of the boxes.

Susan called out, "Need a hand?"

Charlene fought to close the door as a gust hit it. "This is it."

"We're finished, too," said Susan. "I'll call everyone once I get back to St. Luke's to see how it's going, but I don't have any messages on the phone, so it must be okay. By the way, thank you for helping, given all that's happened lately."

"Arden was undone."

"Poor thing." Susan uttered the southern formula, but she did mean it.

"Susan, you did a great job with this Christmas drive, and I must say, the sheriff's department has been terrific," Charlene said, sounding tired.

"They have. Every year this grows."

"That's both a good sign and a bad sign," Charlene noted.

A loud voice was heard down the hall, coming closer. Harry and Susan looked at each other and then at Charlene.

Ahead of Esther, Flo Rice blasted into the room. Esther followed, out of breath.

"Where are the fingers?" squawked Flo. "I want to see the fingers. Were they bones, or did they have flesh on them?"

"Flo, that's enough." Esther, fit to be tied, came alongside her sister. "The fingers are gone."

"You lie! There are two fingers here. The

paper said so." Flo's lower lip jutted out in defiance.

In a soothing voice, Charlene said, "Flo, you're right. There were fingers here, but the sheriff took them away."

Flo thought this over, since she was more inclined to believe Charlene.

Esther handed Charlene an envelope. In a low voice, she said, "It's a small contribution. I'm sorry we couldn't help with deliveries."

Coats off, sleeves pushed up, Harry and Susan were ready to clean up and then go do the same at St. Luke's.

Charlene noticed. "Girls, don't bother. The boys will be back and, trust me, they can work harder and faster than we can."

This made everyone smile except Flo, who appeared fixated on Harry. "Where'd you get that?" She grabbed Harry's wrist, upon which was her found bracelet.

"Uh." Harry tried to gently remove Flo's hand, to no avail.

"Give it to me!"

"Flo, what's the matter with you? You can't take someone's jewelry." Esther pried her sister's hand from Harry's arm. "That's an old piece. Lovely."

"I want it. It belongs to me!" Flo screeched.

"Flo, you never had a bracelet like that." Esther was firm. "Now *stop* this this instant."

Esther forcibly propelled Flo from the room as the three women looked on.

"Give it to me! Give it to me!" Flo bellowed.

Even though the door had closed behind them, they could hear her as Esther shoved her down the hall. The three remained silent, then Charlene said, "What a pity. What a great pity!"

22

Marked for thousands of years by festivals, the longest night of the year retains its primitive power. All animals see the dying of the light, but only the human animal creates festivals of light to fight it off.

Wrapping gifts, Harry and Fair sat at the wiped-off kitchen table among wrapping paper, ribbons, and two pairs of scissors.

The horses were cared for. Everyone was in for the night, with fresh water, even treats put up in the loft for Simon, and Harry and Fair could concentrate on Christmas duties. They started snipping paper, curling ribbon, hand-making big bows.

"Your mother was good at this." Fair studied an antique level. He thought Blair, a young friend, would like the tool.

Married to Little Mim, Blair had become a new father, and everyone swamped them with baby gifts. Fair figured he'd find something just for Blair.

"Honey, the edges of that level are a little sharp. You need a heavier paper."

"Oh." Fair pointed to a thick paper dyed red. "That."

Harry picked it up. "Yeah, just be careful at the corners."

"Isn't this women's work?" he teased.

"Not this woman's." She took one arm of a scissors, ran it along ribbon off the big roll.

The gray cat ran with it, unspooling the ribbon.

"Hey! Hey!" Harry ran after the cat, who, naturally, dropped the ribbon and kept running.

"She's mental." Tucker believed this and pronounced judgment far too often.

"I remember Harry once saying that the mentally ill get worse at Christmas. More people get depressed. Lots of stress. More drinking." Mrs. Murphy, tempted by the ribbons and papers, resisted for now.

"That doesn't sound like much of a holiday," said Tucker. The sweet-natured dog gnawed on her play bone.

"Saturday. Remember when we lived for Saturdays?" Harry stood up to get a better angle on tying a ribbon.

"Usually I was recovering from getting knocked around on the football field."

"You did okay." She handed him green ribbon. "Goes better with that paper."

"Oh." He took the ribbon, changed the subject. "Sometimes I think about the days being named for the gods, mostly Norse gods. Of course, Saturday is named for Saturn, and he's an odd fellow, whether he's Saturn or uses the Greek name, Chronos. I wonder why he was honored and not, say, Poseidon or Neptune? Then I think about Jupiter or Zeus. It gets a little confusing."

"Yeah, we got Thor and Wōden's day." She twirled a big bow she'd made with a flourish. "Saturn is an odd choice, but it's a reminder. He brings harsh lessons, which I suppose we must learn."

"M-m-m. I loved it when we read the myths. Wasn't so happy when we had to read twentieth-century poetry."

"Fair, we read about four poems."

"And I didn't like a one." He smiled.

Harry rose again, walked to the kitchen window over the sink. "Boy, it's dark. No wonder there was Saturnalia, then Christmas, then Yule Girth — all those festivals from pre-Christian times to now. Can't really wipe them out so we co-opt them."

"And a lot else." He finished wrapping Blair's gift. "What do you think?"

"He'll pick it up and wonder what it is,

especially when he tips it and feels the level marker, that little roll of liquid."

"Think he'll like it?"

"Of course he'll like it, it isn't a pair of booties. People go overboard. The baby is too little to know about Christmas. Give to the parents. Actually, the best thing you can give them is a good night's sleep."

In the distance, they heard Odin call a long, high-pitched howl.

Harry heard an answer from another coyote. "How many of them do you think are out there?"

"If you see one, you know there's a family somewhere. They're established here now. We will never get rid of them." Fair picked up a GPS system for Reverend Jones to put in his truck.

"Fair, the new truck the church bought him has a screen in the dash."

"I know, but he can use this when he's out fishing." Fair grabbed shiny bright green metallic paper. "Honey, you were the one who suggested this, since he wanders about so when he goes fishing."

"Oh, yeah, I guess I did. I don't know, Fair. All this stuff that's happened. I'm forgetful. Preoccupied. I forgot to tell you that Rick, Cooper, and others from the department are going to try to get up the mountain Monday and look at our skeleton. Everyone needed this last weekend for shopping." She peered up at the sky, then over at the Chinaman's hat light at the edge of the barn roof. Below, the hayloft doors were shut tight, as were all the barn doors. "It's snowing again. This wasn't on The Weather Channel."

Fair got up, stood beside her. "Who can predict weather on mountainsides or on the top of mountains?"

"I predict we'll get socked."

Pewter sauntered back in the kitchen, leapt onto the table. Mrs. Murphy joined her. Tucker prudently took to her bed. You could never trust those cats around paper or ribbons. Tucker had seen them steal and shred stamps. They were obsessed with paper.

As the cats selected what they wanted to play with, the humans stared at the snow, which shimmered in the halo of the Chinaman's hat light. It wasn't heavy, but small flakes were coming down.

Odin howled again.

All the animals looked at one another. The cats leapt over to the kitchen counter. They, too, peered out the window.

Odin howled. *"Danger!"*

23

The last Sunday in Advent, a special Sunday in that wonderful season, used special hymns, special liturgy, and special vestments at St. Luke's, as well as at all the high churches, which is to say the Catholic and the Episcopal. The Baptists and evangelicals probably celebrated the most, but of course there were no vestments or other adornments. The Greek Orthodox church on Route 250 wouldn't be celebrating for two more weeks, as they were still on the Julian calendar.

After the church service, Harry, Susan, BoomBoom, Alicia, and the various husbands and helpers settled in the meeting room — which was now clean and shining, a few late boxes of donations on one table.

"What do we do with these?" Harry poked her nose inside.

Susan, who had gone through everything and organized the donations, replied, "I'll drop these off tomorrow. Cooper gave me a few more names."

"Have the other churches received late boxes, too — foodstuffs and whatnot?" asked Harry.

Susan nodded. "Cooper has given everyone extra names, dependent on where the church or parish is. She and the sheriff's department have been supportive, above and beyond."

While bending down to pet the three cats, Fair's deep voice rumbled, "Coop's been extra-busy."

BoomBoom picked up Lucy Fur, who felt any additional attention her due. "I believe you can judge any community by its police force," said BoomBoom.

"Why do you say that?" Fair wondered.

"If the sheriff's department or the police force are corrupt, I promise you the entire judiciary in that county is rotten. And trust me, there are places in Virginia that are still fiefdoms." BoomBoom kissed Lucy Fur.

Cazenovia and Elocution investigated the boxes, as the meeting room had been shut to them until now.

"Nothing we can shred," Elocution mumbled, disappointed.

"Or eat." Cazenovia popped out of the box.

"I expect it isn't just Virginia," said Alicia.

"There have to be fiefdoms throughout the country. The proverbial big mean fish in a small pond."

"Makes for a lot of misery in that small pond," BoomBoom agreed.

"On the other hand, maybe those places are well run even if undemocratic," Harry postulated. "In fact, they're well run because they aren't democratic."

"Aha, our dictator in training." Susan urged Elocution to come out of the box. Susan clapped her hands once. "This is it. We're done." She pointed at Harry. "Mussolini and I can take care of this. You all did so much. I am grateful."

BoomBoom answered, "Everyone did, Susan, but you had to organize it. We owe you."

Harry's phone beeped. She opened it, read the text. "What?"

All eyes riveted on her as the others watched her shocked expression.

"Honey, what?" asked Fair.

"Two more fingers showed up at St. Cyril's." Harry looked up from her Droid in disbelief.

"Who sent you that?"

"Jessica Hexham. Here." Harry handed the device to BoomBoom, Alicia reading over her shoulder.

"Hanging on the Christmas tree in the meeting room." Susan also read over Boom-Boom's shoulder. "Sick!"

Everyone started chattering at once. Harry wanted to tell the others about the skeleton, but she knew she shouldn't. She had told Susan to come over tomorrow, as the sheriff was going up to the mountain. After all, the remains were on Susan's timber tract. They could deliver the boxes after that.

"Body parts have significance," Alicia remarked. "Or maybe I made too many historical movies. Heads on pikes, that sort of thing."

"Fair and I have talked about what these missing fingers mean. We can't figure it out. You point with your index finger. You flip the bird with your middle finger." Harry absentmindedly stroked Cazenovia, who was sitting by the open box.

"I remember that piece of that Omar Khayyám poem," Alicia incorrectly recited. " 'The moving finger writes; and, having writ, not all your piety nor your wit can hasten back a word of it.' "

211

24

Trudging through the light flurries, Harry noticed that in the last few days perhaps four inches of snow had fallen on the mountain. Often clouds would pile up on the crest, snow on the ridge, slide down to fill lower meadows, pastures, and roads with snow. The eastern slope of the Blue Ridge didn't reduce rain, sleet, or snow's intensity. Nor did the wind blow right over your head. Rather, it, too, slid down the mountain like a great invisible toboggan.

Harry and Susan, Cooper and Rick parked at the turnaround. The animals traveled with Harry. She was glad to have them because she thought Tucker would keep them on course.

Her footprints and Fair's footprints had disappeared, but as they moved along she could see the great uprooted tree ahead.

"Come on." Mrs. Murphy ran as fast as she could, given the conditions. The other

two followed.

The humans arrived a few moments later.

Harry, astonished, raised her voice. "I swear this is the place."

No skeleton hung in the roots.

Cooper didn't doubt her friend and neighbor. Harry might stick her nose in the wrong place, but she was not given to illusions or telling lies.

Pewter, who had not been trapped up here by Odin, now paid close attention to everything. She carefully walked down into the hole, roots over her head.

As the gray cat looked around, the humans looked down.

Rick pointed. "Tracks. Can hardly make them out."

Cooper walked over, as did Harry. They began following the pair of human tracks, which led straight up. Had they followed them on foot, it would have taken an hour in good conditions.

"Harry, there's a footpath on the top, right?" Cooper spoke.

Susan said as Harry knelt down, "There are high meadows up there. If you travel four miles north you'll come to the monastery. The high meadows were used for cattle in the summer by farmers on both sides of the mountains. There are farm roads for that, but few roads down that a vehicle could use. The monastery rented them out, and Mary Pat," she named a long-deceased wealthy lady, "owned thousands of acres up here, which the government bought from her during the 1930s."

"Can a Jeep negotiate them?" Rick was following Cooper's line of thinking.

"With a good driver. The closest climb up the mountains from here zigzags up to the monastery. Switchbacks, but it can be done. The next one big enough is down by Royal Orchard." Harry cited a large, impressive private tract. "Miles away."

"Coyote tracks, mostly snow-covered." Tucker pointed them out.

Harry had enough sense to pay attention to her dog in this situation. She followed the tracks as they paralleled the remnants of the human tracks.

"Coop." Harry pointed them out.

"Is it possible coyotes took the bones?" Cooper wondered.

"They could have taken some, but there'd be dropped parts or we'd see a trace of drag marks," Harry replied.

The four people, along with Tucker, stood there, eyes lifting upward. Rick pulled out his phone, cursed, then put it back in his pocket.

Cooper stated the obvious. "No service."

"Let's get back down so I can call," said Rick. "I want a team up here and I want a team up top."

"Does anyone in the department know either of those routes to the top?" Harry inquired.

"The monastery route," said Rick. "Every now and then we'll get a call in the summer about a lost hiker. I want people up there coming down here and vice versa. And the light won't last that long." Rick started back.

"Wait —" Mrs. Murphy, now down in the pit with Pewter, called out.

Harry walked thirty yards back down to them. The two cats' pupils were huge.

Pewter, something in her mouth, was scrambling out with difficulty.

Balancing on a huge tree root, Mrs. Murphy climbed higher. They jumped onto the snow-covered earth.

Cooper knelt down. "Pewter. Kitty, kitty."

Pewter eyed her, didn't budge.

"Pewter, come on." Harry also knelt down.

Thrilled to be the center of attention, the gray cat simply glared back, jaw clamped tight.

"Pewter, that is of no worth to you," Mrs. Murphy scolded her.

"Boss, come back," Cooper called over her shoulder.

Rick turned, heading back.

Pewter finally released her prize just as Rick reached them.

Cooper, heavy gloves on, picked it up, held it in her palm.

Rick nearly shouted, "What the hell is this with fingers!"

Back in Harry's kitchen, Susan, Mrs. Murphy, Pewter, and Tucker warmed up before going out to deliver the last of the donation Christmas boxes.

"I took a chill up there." Susan wrapped her hands around hot chocolate Harry had made for her.

Susan sometimes even drank hot chocolate in summer, she loved the taste so much.

Harry joined her. The animals crowded in together in Tucker's bed, as it was bigger. They, too, wanted to warm up.

"Pewter" — Harry looked over at the gray cat, tail curled over her nose — "you get the gold star."

"Tuna," she said through her tail fur.

"What made you jump down there?" Mrs. Murphy asked.

"Remember when Odin ran across the back pasture with a part of the arm and the bracelet

fell off?" Pewter recalled. *"A few tiny pieces of bone fell off with the bracelet. I figured if someone moved that skeleton, bones might have fallen off then. All I had to do was dig around the fresh snow."*

"Smart." Tucker praised the cat who in general drove her crazy.

Mrs. Murphy joined the praise, which brought large, loud purrs from Pewter.

"I envy that." Susan smiled at the cats, too. "Owen is beside himself when I come home, happy with any toy, any attention. We want too much."

"Yes, we do," Harry agreed, took a delicious sip. "Not as good as Miranda's, but not bad."

"I think your hot chocolate is as good as hers. Apart from that, she's in a class by herself with anything creative, like gardening. Such an eye for proportion, color, balance. I think one is just born with something like that."

"Susan, so you think there are born killers?"

"Yes." Susan paused. "But I suspect most killings are circumstantial. You know, there's gain, revenge, or maybe even relief from pain."

"What do you mean?" Harry had never thought of it that way.

"A mother kills her husband, who beats the children."

A long, long silence followed this. "Personally, I think we should give her the gun."

"Don't say that publicly. Thousands, millions maybe, think violent people like an abusive husband can be taught not to be violent. I can almost understand all forms of violence except thrill killings, I guess, but harm a child or someone unable to fight back, I haven't a scrap of sympathy for whatever happens to that monster. But I can't say a word. I have a husband in the House of Delegates."

"All that's left of what Fair and I saw is a knucklebone, part of the forefinger attached to it. I have to believe that skeleton is a murder victim. As far as we know, there weren't serial killers around here back whenever. That happened — what, at least a decade, probably more? We'd remember." Harry paused. "We've had murders since, but once the perpetrator was caught, there was a twisted logic to what they did."

"What is the logic to hanging fingers on a Christmas tree?" Susan's lips began to get color back.

"It's logical to whoever cut them off. Both sets of fingers have shown up now. Sure, they have to do the DNA thing, but we all know those fingers belonged to Pete Vavilov and Lou Higham."

"Pete Vavilov?" Susan's voice grew loud.

"Oh, dammit!" Harry had let it slip.

"What do you mean Pete Vavilov? He died of a heart attack."

"Yes, it appears he did but —" Harry took a deep breath. "When the sheriff's people went to the site of the accident, the body was missing those fingers. They kept it from everyone."

"Why do that? I mean, it's so strange, they should have made it public. Maybe it would drive the worm out of the woodwork."

"They took the opposite gamble. Say nothing and hope someone trips up." Harry appreciated both approaches.

"Does Charlene know? Has she kept quiet, too? If so, she's one cool customer." Susan said this with admiration.

"She knows. Her sons don't."

"Someone is pointing the finger," Susan blurted out.

"Know what's being pointed out and you know your killer." Harry believed this. "It's grotesque but not horrible, like a beheading. You're right. Pointing the finger."

"Back to the skeleton caught up in the roots." Susan was worried. "Is it possible that murder is connected to these new killings? I'm so upset my mind is just making things worse." Susan sighed.

"It's possible, but whoever was buried by that tree was buried there so long ago that the roots grew through them. Pete and Lou were left for us — well, not us, but you know what I mean — to find. It seems to me that the tree murderer wanted the victim's memory to disappear along with the corpse. This killer wants to rub our noses in it, or the nose of whoever he is seeking to destroy."

"Harry, why not just kill whoever he or she wishes to destroy?"

"Maybe he can't."

"Well, I'm confused, but at least I'm warm now." Susan weakly smiled.

"Let's put all this out of our minds for Christmas Eve and Christmas," Harry offered.

"Coming from you, that's saying something."

"Yeah, well." Harry got up and retrieved the morning paper that she'd put on the kitchen counter but had no time to read. "Maybe there will be cheering news about the Santa Fund."

Each year the community raised monies through a Santa Fund, the daily total printed on the front page of the newspaper.

Harry unfolded the paper, gave Susan the front page while she took the local news section.

"Oh, no," Harry exclaimed.

Susan grabbed the section from her, read aloud, "A review by the sheriff's department found irregularities in the accounting for Silver Linings that have prompted a deeper investigation. The part-time bookkeeper, Arden Higham's lawyer, Dwayne Pellio, declares his client will fully cooperate. She has no statement to make at this time." Susan looked up at Harry. "Good Lord, could Arden have stolen from a church or the charity?"

"Never." Harry slapped the tabletop.

"Why?"

"Pointing the finger at herself. Forgive the pun. The fingers were in her pencil jar. Arden may not be the brightest bulb on the Christmas tree, but she's far from stupid."

Susan brought both hands to her cheeks, holding them there for an instant, then dropping them. "Don't they say some criminals want to get caught?"

"I don't know if I believe that."

"Nonetheless, Arden does the books for Silver Linings."

"Susan, there is no way Arden Higham stole money from a nonprofit."

"Stranger things have happened in this world."

"Strange, yes. This stupid, probably not."

25

Harry, Fair, Mrs. Murphy, Pewter, Tucker, the horses, and even the hayloft animals — Simon and Flatface, the great horned owl — didn't open their presents until Christmas morning. Matilda, the hibernating blacksnake, didn't receive fresh eggs until spring. Harry thought of that as an Easter present. While giving a snake eggs may seem strange, a blacksnake in one's barn does a world of good, cleaning out vermin.

The temperature climbed to thirty-eight by noon. Water rattled down gutters, flowed in ditches alongside roads. For all the melting, the snow wouldn't disappear unless a week of warm weather stayed over Central Virginia, and even then snow would pack in the crevices on the north side of the mountains or in deep, narrow ravines.

The robin's-egg-blue sky, the snow, the *drip, drip* of melting icicles, with sunshine passing through them pleased Harry to no end. Outside, doing her chores, she'd stop to listen to the music of the water.

"Boy, this will pack the snow down," she said to her crew as she swept out the center aisle.

"More snow is coming," Mrs. Murphy chatted as she walked alongside. *"I can feel it."*

"She can't." Pewter reposed on a center-aisle tack trunk bearing Harry's initials front and center.

"You don't think if she stood still outside, lifted her nose, she wouldn't smell the edge of the front?" Tucker could never understand diminished human senses.

"No!" Pewter declared.

"She'll feel it where she broke bones when it draws closer," said Mrs. Murphy. *"By tonight. But, Tucker, you know she can't smell much. You have to stick whatever it is right under her nose."*

"I can't imagine anything worse," the intrepid dog said.

"Simon's got a decent nose." Pewter liked the possum. *"But he's a night creature, and I think scent is stronger at night."*

"It most certainly is." Tucker was happy to discuss scent, a favorite subject. *"And that's why women should be careful how much and what type of perfume they put on at night. The scent is always stronger. Too strong and it*

makes my eyes water."

"That's why Harry spritzes her Amouage perfumes." Mrs. Murphy loved to sit on Harry's small makeup table. "Just a hint and it carries her through the evening. She's smart about some things, but then again, she spends a lot of time with us."

The high whine of an old four-cylinder engine sounded at the end of the long driveway.

Tucker rushed to the barn doors. "Stranger! Stranger!"

A beat-up old Toyota, a wire coat hanger twisted on for an aerial, skidded to a stop. No four-wheel drive and bald tires meant the driver was either poor, lazy, or just stupid.

Flo Rice crawled out, slamming the door. Poor seemed to be her category.

Seeing the dog in the open doors, then Harry, who stopped to turn around, she strode in.

"Give me that bracelet!"

"Miss Rice, I found that bracelet fair and square."

"I found it!" Pewter crowed.

"We found it!" Tucker corrected.

"Bother." The cat unsheathed her claws. She was on guard, thanks to Flo's behavior.

Mrs. Murphy had climbed up to the

hayloft. *"Pewter, get up here. If there's a problem, we can leap off and knock this lady off her feet."*

"I'll do the rest." At Harry's heels, Tucker raised the hackles on her ruff.

"Where'd you find it?" Flo eyed her suspiciously.

"In the tack room. I'll show you." Harry walked to the room, opened the door, and the two walked in, Harry first.

"Rats!" Mrs. Murphy exclaimed, hurrying to back down.

Pewter was thinking ahead. *"If we climb onto the highest saddle on the rack, we can still dive-bomb her."*

"Right." Mrs. Murphy blew through the tack room animal door.

"The upturned helmet was here," Harry explained. "My friend picked it up and out fell the bracelet. Finders keepers." She smiled, hoping to diminish Flo's anger.

"It's not yours."

"No. Is it yours?" Harry attempted her sweetest voice.

"No, no, but I should have it." Flo's voice quivered. "I worked hard. I should have something pretty."

"Would you like something to eat?" Harry frantically thought of things to distract Flo, and then she hoped to send her on her way.

"No." She paused. "Don't tell Esther I came over here, please. She hates me. She has always hated me."

"Oh, I hope not."

Pleased to be able to recount old disagreements, Flo nearly shouted, "You don't know. I was the pretty one. Esther hated me for that. I had more beaus. She'd try to steal my beaus. *Ha.* Never worked. Esther always wants what she can't have. Finally, when I went away to college, I thought I was rid of her."

"And?"

"She followed me to Mary Washington. She's like a giant tick! I hate her."

"Miss Rice, I am sorry."

"Give me the bracelet."

"No." Harry spoke with firmness.

Now downhearted, Flo started to cry. "I never get anything."

"Miss Rice, please. I am sorry you're upset. I'm sorry you feel your sister has been unfair to you."

"No, you're not. You have something that I should have for hard work. I never get anything. Esther promised me a car. Where is it? She wants me to die in a wreck in my old car." Flo headed for the open doors, the cold air flowing into the barn. "I'm going to see Cletus."

Harry, following Flo, knowing there could be more trouble, queried, "Cletus?"

"How many Cletuses do you know? Of course it's Mr. Thompson."

"He's a nice man. I'm sure you know Mr. Thompson has a drinking problem?"

Flo turned on her heel, put her face almost into Harry's as Tucker growled low. "How do you know he's not thirsty?" she asked. With that, she got into her car, turned the key.

The cats, now at Harry's feet, stepped back just a little.

"Let's pray she doesn't get stuck or we're stuck with her," Pewter said.

With the rear of the car sliding out, Flo took her foot off the gas for a moment and steered into the swerve. Her driving skills remained sharp.

She rolled down the window. "You'll be sorry," she warned Harry. "You shouldn't wear things that don't belong to you." She fishtailed out of the long driveway.

Harry walked back into the barn, closing the big doors behind her.

"People are crazy," Harry exclaimed.

"That one is," Pewter agreed as she, too, walked into the tack room. *"I'm exhausted. I don't know why that made me so tired."*

The cat, on the desk, had no answer.

Tucker did. *"When it's over, danger makes you tired."*

Harry opened the phone book. It seemed to grow larger every year. She found Al Toth's number and called.

"Mrs. Toth, it's Harry Haristeen."

"Harry, I'd know your voice anywhere," Esther warmly responded.

"I am sorry to trouble you on Christmas Eve, but your sister just left my farm and she was upset and angry."

"Flo? Angry at you?"

"Yes, ma'am. That old gold bracelet, she wants it. She said it doesn't belong to her but she should have it. She was very put out."

A brief silence followed this. "She's getting worse. I'm sorry she — well, really, this is my fault. I don't want to put her in some kind of assisted living. She's healthy, she can take care of her little place, but her mind just isn't what it should be. I'm the one who is in the wrong. I don't want to admit it. I don't want to put my sister away."

"Has she always seen you as a competitor?" Harry's curiosity got the better of her.

"Oh, what sisters don't fight? If it wasn't one thing, it was another, but for the most part we got along. This sullenness started in the late 1980s. I always thought it was her divorce and then Momma's death that started this."

"That's why she goes by Rice instead of Mercier?"

"I told her to take our name back, but she said she was tired of hearing people mispronounce a French name. She refused to be addressed as Mrs. Oh, I don't know. I'm not making much more sense than she is right now."

"This is upsetting news. And she's on her way to Cletus Thompson if her car can stay on that back road. Should be plowed out by now."

"Cletus Thompson? Good Lord." Esther sounded at her wit's end. "Well, I'd better drive over there and get her home. I really am so sorry you have to deal with this on Christmas Eve, and I thank you for telling me where she is."

"Despite all, Merry Christmas."

"Merry Christmas to you, too."

26

"*How long, O Lord, how long?*" Pewter dramatically complained as she sat under the fragrant Christmas tree, idly batting a glass ornament.

"*Another hour,*" Tucker guessed.

"*Or more,*" Mrs. Murphy said. "*They're used to rising with the sun, and it comes up so late now. That's why Mom sets her alarm clock.*"

"*Doesn't do any good. She rolls over and turns it off.*" Pewter turned her attention to a blue ball decorated with frosted snowflakes.

"*Not always.*" Tucker felt compelled to defend Harry.

"*Did you put more food out for Odin?*" Mrs. Murphy asked Tucker.

"*Good scraps, some cookies. We could go out and see if he's come by again.*"

"*Too cold!*" Pewter, on her back, batted everything she could reach.

"*Let's go back to sleep,*" Tucker suggested.

"We'll wake up when they do."

"M-m-m, catnip in some of these presents," Pewter mused. *"I can smell it. They put the toys in Ziploc bags, that's the nasty hint of plastic, but I can still smell the magic weed."* A candy-cane-striped small package had her full attention. *"Let's open it."*

"Better not," Mrs. Murphy advised.

"Oh, just one." Pewter sweetly tempted her friend before biting into a corner of the box.

"Those devils!" Harry exclaimed when she walked into the living room at 7:00 A.M.

Fair surveyed the damage, then burst out laughing. Every present bore teeth marks. Those promising catnip or dried-food treats had been shredded, the corners chewed off, the contents devoured. The crinkle of paper, the excitement of the gifts themselves had been just too thrilling. Colored paper, ribbons, bows lay strewn about. A few ribbons dangled from the lower branches.

The culprits who had desecrated most everything were nowhere to be seen.

Tucker, awakened, padded in from the kitchen. *"I told them not to do this."*

Hours later — gifts now opened, despite the claw marks, and the mess cleaned up — the cats appeared, strolling through the house as though nothing had happened.

They even went so far as to rub on the humans' legs.

"The gall." Harry had to smile.

"Merry Christmas," Pewter purred.

The kitchen phone rang.

"Merry Christmas," Cooper wished Harry when she picked up the phone. "Love my gardening tool set, and how you hid it in the shed I don't know. But when I opened your card, I followed the directions and found it. How clever. Thank you. You know I will write a proper thank-you."

"I will, too. Fair must have told you I needed a lamp."

"He did." Cooper then added, "Anyone who wanted a white Christmas got their wish this year."

"You sound a bit rushed or something." Though now and then she could miss things, Harry was sensitive to her friend most of the time.

"Oh, the dispatcher called. Not many people on duty today, so I was asked to help."

"What's up?"

"Flo Rice is missing."

Within fifteen minutes, Cooper showed up at their door, driving her Toyota Highlander. She'd gotten a good deal on a used one.

Fair, Harry, and the animals climbed into the cushy vehicle.

"You've got the full complement." Harry smiled.

"Flo might prove difficult if she's found," said Fair. "Anyway, if we all go out together maybe it will go faster. Then you can come to the house for Christmas dinner," Fair gallantly invited Cooper.

"Cooked the ham yesterday." Harry settled in next to Cooper. "And I took off the bracelet you found in my tack room. Sets Flo off. If we find her, that's the last thing we need."

The animals stayed in back with Fair.

Cooper had called in to headquarters to inform the dispatcher that her neighbors were helping her search for Flo Rice. As it was a holiday, and the department was on skeleton crew, the dispatcher offered no resistance. That was Rick's territory anyway. Why disturb him at home on the holiday?

"What did Esther say about Flo?" asked Harry. "I assume she's who declared her missing."

"Not much," Cooper replied, pushing out from the driveway. "She'd spoken to her sister last night, and apart from being surly, Flo didn't seem any worse than usual," Cooper replied.

"Think it's senile dementia?" Fair wondered.

"Who knows? They can be hard to handle," Cooper said. "Sometimes Alzheimer's patients can be difficult, too. They're confused, more are frightened, others become angry. Many of them resist, and the last thing you want to do is jack up some old person against the car. I've had them take a swing at me. Fortunately, their reflexes aren't that good. It's fairly easy to get out of the way."

At Flo's house, they found the door unlocked and her car gone. Her dog wasn't there either, and the fire in her fireplace had gone out. The place was cold.

"Let's restart a fire real quick," Fair said, on his knees by the fireplace. "Her pipes will freeze."

"Fair, she might not be coming home." Harry expressed a dark thought.

"Maybe so, but if she does, she ought to at least walk into a bit of warmth on Christmas."

Cooper looked through the rooms. "No tree. No cards. How sad."

Harry sighed. "That it is."

Fair quickly got the fire going, replaced the fire screen, and they left.

"Has anyone seen her car?" Harry asked.

"We put a call out, license plate number, but so few of us are on duty. Esther did mention that she told her sister to visit Cletus. She should say 'Merry Christmas' to someone. It may be that Esther hoped someone else would deal with Flo for a little bit."

"I know just where Cletus lives." Harry gave directions to Cooper, who didn't mind. "Fair and I were students of his in high school."

Fair rummaged through his pockets. "If we call on Mr. Thompson, shouldn't we give him something for the holiday?"

"Susan and I dropped by goods from the church. That will have to do." Harry turned to look at Fair sitting in the back.

"He'll see us. That's a treat," Pewter smugly answered.

When they reached Cletus Thompson's house, Harry noticed the drive had been shoveled out.

The three humans walked to the front door, cats and dog behind them. Fair knocked.

In a few moments, Cletus opened the door and smiled. "Harry, Fair, come on in."

Harry, ever mindful of her manners, introduced Cooper. "This is Mr. Thompson, Deputy Cooper. Mr. Thompson, she's our friend and neighbor."

"Come on, come on in." He motioned for them to step inside. "Dog and cats, too. My old dog, The Terminator, is asleep in the kitchen. They can go visit."

While the aroma of whiskey clung to Cletus's clothing, he seemed sober enough.

"Mr. Thompson —" Cooper began.

"Deputy, call me Cletus, and please sit down. Makes me nervous to see you all standing. Sit."

Tucker, on her way to the kitchen, sat, then realized the order was not for her. She rose and padded into the kitchen, warmer than the spare front room.

Cooper took a seat and started anew as the old wing chair wobbled a little. "We were wondering if you've seen Flo Rice."

"No. I hope she's all right."

"We do, too," Cooper continued. "She's just taken off. Her sister said they spoke last night. They haven't been getting along, and now she can't find Flo. She mentioned that you all were friends."

"I don't get to see enough of Flo, but she's a good girl. She and Esther haven't gotten on for years now. They used to be close, but" — he shrugged — "don't really know what happened. Once Esther got married, they drifted apart."

In the kitchen, the three animals spoke to the old dog. Half blind, mostly deaf, he lifted his age-spotted nose to sniff. Fortunately, he had a thick curly brown coat, which helped him stay warm.

"Who's there?"

"I'm Tucker," the corgi shouted. *"And I brought two cats with me, Mrs. Murphy and Pewter."*

"If you crawl on these old towels with me you can wiggle in and it's warmer," The Terminator offered.

"Thank you," Mrs. Murphy replied. *"We're only here for a short visit. Our humans are visiting yours."*

"That's good. Cletus is alone too much and I'm slowing down," the little dog forthrightly said. *"I'm not long for this world. I don't want him alone."*

"We hope you're wrong," Tucker shouted.

"Thank you, but I might as well accept it." His milky eyes looked out from under shaggy brows. *"See if you can't get your people to pay visits to him."*

"We will try," Mrs. Murphy replied. *"Was anyone here in the last day or so? Flo Rice?"*

"Not a soul."

"People think Flo is difficult, crazy," said Tucker. *"What do you think?"*

"Angry maybe, but I don't think she's crazy. At least when she comes here, she and Cletus talk about old times and current stuff."

"We hope we see you again." Mrs. Murphy listened as the adults stood up in the next room.

"My pleasure. It's nice to talk to someone who knows what you're saying." He chuckled.

Once back in the Highlander, Cooper called in to see if anyone had found Flo's car. No one had.

"Did anyone check the morgue?" Harry asked.

"I called them before I called Esther Toth. Let's pray she's still among the living."

Fair, Pewter on his lap, put his hand on the back of Harry's seat. "Have an idea. Go to the old Valencia farm."

"Where's that?"

"In Free Union. I'd tell you to go the back way, but I don't know about the roads being plowed out. Plus, there's that bridge construction."

They drove all the way round to Hunt Country Store, hung a left, and drove through rolling white acres, many fences wrapped with garlands, and almost every gate bore a boxwood wreath or evergreen with roses of red berries.

"Used to be hunt country. That's why the

240

store is called Hunt Country Store," Harry mused.

"Now it's Dollar Country." Fair laughed. "Give them credit, most of them buy a horse or two, but the land's all chopped up. Happening everywhere, really."

"Bet you can still find acreage at a bargain in Tornado Alley." Cooper was referring to that part of the Southwest and Midwest frequently slammed by the killer storms.

"Yeah." Fair leaned back in his seat, much to the comfort of Pewter. "Some wonderful country out there, good hay country, cattle, and good people, too."

"Never met anyone from those parts who's a lazy slug," Harry chimed in.

Cooper thought for a moment, then said, "You know, when people first move here they think southerners are lazy."

Harry and Fair laughed, then Harry said, "Well, so they do, until the first sticky, hot day they try to work the way they can, at their speed, up north. They drop like flies! No one can beat southern heat. You have to pace yourself and work with it."

"Hard to remember those sultry days now." Fair leaned forward again as the gray cat grumbled. "Slow down, Coop. Left at the fork. Two miles up ahead you'll see white fencing, river-stone gates with a big brass plaque set in front on the stone which reads 'River Run.' That's the old Valencia farm."

"The Watts estate." Cooper knew it by the current owner's name. "What a beautiful place."

"When Mrs. Valencia owned it she'd throw these great picnics," said Harry. "She'd invite everyone, workers, landowners, everyone from the hunt club, the churches, her children's playmates. What parties. What wonderful days those were. Maybe it's me, but I think people were more open then." She spied the stone gates ahead.

"Different times," said Fair. "Even if someone with Mrs. Valencia's resources displayed her kindness, lack of snobbery, threw parties, who would come? How many people have the time to enjoy themselves today like they did when we were kids?" Fair ran his forefinger under his nose, feeling the stubble, and he'd shaved that morning. "Everyone works all the time. I know I do."

"When you have the time, you don't have the money. When you have the money, you don't have the time," Harry succinctly put it.

Cooper drove up to River Run's grand main house. She was in uniform, so when Horace Watts opened the door, his expression quickly changed to one more welcoming. She explained herself. He nodded assent, then closed the door without so much as a holiday greeting.

"Mr. Comfort and Joy." Cooper grimaced once back in the car.

"He treats his horses well, but if anyone should be visited by the Ghost of Christmas Past I expect it's Horace Watts." Fair laughed.

"Honey, where do you want Coop to go?"

"Sorry. Drive to the stables, the one with the double cupolas. Lucky everything has been plowed. Park in front of the stables."

As softly as they could, the crew of three opened the main double doors — beautiful heavy oak doors, paned glass on top — and closed them behind them. The stable's interior was also heavy oak; brass fittings gleamed and a hand-laid brick floor added to the warm feel of the stable.

Harry's barn, also with a hand-laid brick aisle, had been built around the same time as River Run's stables but by her ancestors, people of more modest means. Fair walked to the tack room door, also half glass.

A little dog barked.

Tucker barked back.

"Hush," Harry whispered.

As Fair opened the door, Cooper stepped

through. "Miss Rice, you've given people a fright."

"I'm not doing anything," Flo defended herself, sitting in a chair with the farm's name embroidered on the back.

"Actually, ma'am, you're trespassing," Cooper informed her.

"I used to work here, you know. I could still run this place and I'm not using up Mr. Watts's money. I read by flashlight." She stayed in the chair.

"Ma'am, I can see that, and I bet it's warmer in here than at home, isn't it?"

"It is, but I didn't turn on his baseboard heat here. It was on, I guess so the pipes don't freeze in the bathroom. Honest. I didn't turn it on, and Mr. Watts doesn't even walk down to check."

Fair, hoping to jolly her along, said, "Bet you could run it, Miss Rice. You know all Mr. Watts's horses are in Camden, South Carolina, for the winter. Still, a place needs running."

"Does," she answered as Buster, her dog, leapt onto her lap.

Cooper asked, "Where is your car?"

"What's it to you?" Flo sassed.

"Miss Rice, we're trying to help," said Cooper.

"I'm not telling."

"Well, you can't stay here, so I'll have to take you home in my car. How will you get around? Maybe your sister will come pick up your car if you won't tell us, but you have to leave." Cooper's voice was nice but firm.

"My sister! Ha."

"Miss Rice, Deputy Cooper is right," said Harry. "You are trespassing. You don't want Mr. Watts to press charges."

"Watts, what does he know? I worked for Mrs. Valencia when this place was grand. Mrs. Valencia never cut a corner or a person. She was gracious. These new people don't know how to act. They don't know what's expected of them. You take care of the people who work for you. You buy one of the old Virginia places, you have to come up to the mark."

Fair smiled at her. "Miss Rice, you're right."

Pleased at this, she petted Buster. He was interested in the three animals and vice versa.

Cooper wasn't letting up. "Ma'am, gather up your things."

"I don't have anything. A toothbrush."

"Miss Rice, please don't force Deputy Cooper to call in more officers because you're uncooperative," Harry cajoled. "If you cooperate, things will be fine."

"Right." Fair beamed at Flo. "Now, where's your car?"

She wiggled in her seat for a moment, then looked up at the tall, powerfully built man. "Next barn. The breeding shed. I drove it right in. No one's there at all."

"May I have the key?" he asked.

"In the ignition," she replied.

"All right. I'll follow you girls" — he looked at Flo when he said "girls" — "and I'll meet you at your house. I'll take good care of your car."

"My house is so cold." Flo made a face. "It's old. I'm old."

Cooper stepped toward her, holding out a hand. Flo took it and was pulled up, Buster under one arm.

"I built a fire before we drove over here," said Fair. "I'll stoke it when we get to your home." He smiled.

"What if I don't go?" She hesitated for a moment.

"I'll have to call backup and we'll have to hold you for an appraisal of your condition," said Cooper. "And then I must put you in a cell."

Flo raised her voice to the officer. "No! You all won't let me keep Buster."

"I will personally take him to the Albemarle County SPCA. He will receive good care. Now, what will it be, ma'am?"

Buster whimpered, *"Don't take me away."*

Tucker comforted the small dog. *"Don't worry. Cooper's bluffing. She doesn't want to do any of this. Make your human see reason."*

Buster licked Flo's face.

Flo announced, "I'll go back home."

"Good. Your sister is worried about you," Cooper said.

"She wants to kill me."

27

Christmas underscored Arden and Tyler's misery. She did her best to wrap gifts, place them under the silver tree with the blue lights, balls, and silver garlands that Lou adored.

While Flo resisted Cooper and the Haristeens before finally coming around, the Highams sat in silence. Tyler fiddled with his iPad.

Finally Arden said, "I don't really like an all-silver-and-blue tree. What about you?"

"I don't care. Dad always had to be different."

Lou's ashes, in the urn, wrapped in silver and blue ribbons, matched the tree.

"He did. But if you gave in on the little things like silver and blue, you often won on the big things. Not that we argued all that much."

"He saved that for me," Tyler sullenly replied.

Arden put her feet up on the hassock. "He wanted the best and, like most fathers, he thought if he kept pounding away on the same note, you'd hear the music."

Tyler glowered. "He didn't think I was smart enough to be a doctor. Said I'd fail organic chemistry. I'm not even in my junior year and I've read the eleventh-grade chemistry book. Done some of the experiments. I'll pass organic chemistry. Just wait."

"Honey, organic chemistry is a long way away. You are a smart young man. The chemistry teacher at St. Anne's certainly thinks so. That's why he tutors you."

He returned his attention to his iPad, then said, "We do cool things in the lab."

She firmly said, "By the time you reach your junior year, St. Anne's will have to send you to chemistry classes at UVA."

"Mom, I'll bet Cal Tech has a great chemistry department." A flash of enthusiasm crossed his face.

She smiled, for one moment seeing his excitement. Cal Tech was years away.

"Do you want me to drive you anywhere today?" she asked. "Maybe stop in and visit some friends?"

"No."

"Another year and a half and you'll get your license."

"Dad said he'd buy me a car. He wanted to buy me an old Volvo because he kept saying they're safe. They're ugly."

"Let's see where we are in a year and a half."

Tyler's eyes flashed. "Mom, I need a car."

"I didn't say you didn't need a car, but it's a ways off."

"Why can't I have Dad's car?"

"Never." She heated up. "You are not driving that car, you're not driving his car."

"The Acura dealer cleaned it up."

"Tyler, for God's sake. I'm selling the car. I don't want to look at it. We'll talk about this when the time comes."

"You're the one who says time flies."

"It does. And I hope next Christmas is easier than this one."

"Mom, all Dad cared about was his business. When was he ever even home? I wasn't what he wanted. He wanted me to be like Mrs. Vavilov's sons. You know, football players. He didn't care about me."

"That's not true. Tyler, whatever his failings, he was your father."

"Yeah." He sank farther into the cushy chair.

"I miss him." Her eyes filled with tears.

"I don't. I don't have to hear about how lucky I am. I don't have to hear about what kids at Silver Linings go through or what a good athlete Dad was. I hate sports. He would spy on me. He'd ask me weird questions like do I like boys. I'm glad he's dead."

"Tyler, you don't mean that."

"I do. Mom, he'd get the old jocks at Silver Linings to work with me. His words — 'work with me.' That meant the weight room or throwing the football. All I want is my computer. I can do a lot more than those dumb jocks." He raised his voice, then lowered it. "And I don't like boys."

She glared at him, but there was an element of truth to her son's accusations. Everyone loved Lou — Mr. Energy and Ideas — but he was never home.

"Tyler, I never once thought you were gay, not that it matters. I love you. Your father had a narrow definition of manhood. He made so much of it, I wonder if he was afraid he wasn't really a man despite appearances. He was hard on you, but he loved you."

Tyler sprang up, strode to the fireplace. He grabbed the urn off the mantel and threw it into the fire.

"He can burn in hell."

That Christmas night, finally home, Harry asked her husband, "How hungry are you?"

251

"I could eat a whole ham," Pewter volunteered.

"Not very," said Fair. "I'd be happy with a sandwich. I told Coop to come by, but she's on overload."

"Oh, it's Christmas night. I'll warm up the sweet potatoes and a few slices of ham. Just seems more like the holiday. Actually, I'm not too hungry either."

"I am."

"Pewter, pipe down." Harry tapped the cat's rear end with her toe.

"Brutality!" Pewter could have been a student at The American Academy of Dramatic Arts. *"How can I survive winter with such insensitivity, without lots of calories to ward off the cold?"*

"Quite nicely, I think." Tucker couldn't hold it back.

Whap! Pewter smacked the corgi hard on the shoulder.

"Don't you dare." Harry raised her voice and the wooden spoon in her hand, which provoked the gray cat to hold her tail high and sashay away from the dog. "No fighting."

Still, Pewter hissed.

"Sometimes these critters wear me out." Harry watched the cat's performance.

"Imagine if she were as big as a horse."

"Fair, what an awful thought."

As the food warmed up, the aroma filled the kitchen. At least it smelled like Christmas.

Pewter's snit vanished when Harry cut ham into cubes, putting it in the three separate bowls.

As she put food for herself and Fair on the table, she sat down. "Honey, thank you for going along with Cooper. I sort of dragged you into it."

"Didn't mind a bit. She had to work at short notice. Cooper puts in a lot of hours, and on holidays, too."

"Her boyfriend is in Oregon. Maybe when he comes back, she'll have some time. The department ought to give her time off. Really."

"How's that going with Barry?" Fair inquired about Barry Betz, the new UVA batting coach Cooper had been dating for three months.

"Okay. She put a framed photo of him on her desk at home. Always a good sign." Harry scooped out some sweet potatoes. "Sad about Flo Rice, isn't it? She acted mad as a hatter, but I can't be angry with her. She really is sad. How many lonely people are out there on Christmas? It breaks my heart."

"You'd think that her sister and Coach could get someone to live with her." Fair, too, was relishing his sweet potatoes.

"Might be difficult. I mean, Flo might be difficult."

"Right. But I don't see how they can leave her as she is. What if she keeps running away and her house stays cold? Seems well built enough. Poor Mr. Thompson's is falling apart. Boy, he was tough when I had him for math senior year."

"Yes, he was. I took that class the next year and I had to work at it. He was a good teacher. I had him for eleventh and twelfth grade. That's another person that could use some help."

"Yes. What's sad about him is he was a brilliant teacher," Fair said.

"At least they both have dogs, and who knows, maybe Flo will settle down. Christmas triggers a lot of emotions, you know."

"Does for me. I think of my parents, their friends, my grandparents. People seemed happier then, or maybe as a child and then a young person I couldn't look beneath the surface."

"I don't know. The past is always golden, isn't it?" Harry thought for a moment. "Well, maybe not. I wouldn't have wanted to live through Henry the Eighth's Dissolution. Being Catholic may or may not be easy, depending upon which country you live in, right?"

Fair looked at his wife. "Harry, there's a thought, but St. Cyril's is doing fine. Then again, we've had since 1607 to figure out religious differences."

"Oh, don't give us credit. What we had was Maryland. The Catholics could go there. Religious intolerance certainly played a role in our beginnings."

The sweet ham melted in his mouth. "It's your glaze that makes it so good."

"My secret is a little orange juice. But remember, it's a secret."

He laughed.

Later, the humans by the fire, Fair's arm around Harry's shoulders, the three animals slipped out to the barn.

Odin came by, thrilled with the rich scraps.

The two cats looked down as he looked up.

"I've never tasted anything so good."

From the other side of the barn door, Tucker said, *"It's Christmas."*

Pewter, filled with ham and importance, called down, *"Yes, they found this baby in the bulrushes, put him in a cradle and lit torches*

255

and stuff to fight off the long winter night."

"When was this?" the coyote asked.

"Over two thousand years ago," Pewter said.

"Pewter, it was Moses in the bulrushes. Jesus was born in a stable. There were cats," Mrs. Murphy corrected her.

"There had to be a dog," said Tucker. "I know it. How can Joseph be a shepherd without dogs? Think about it!" Tucker was adamant.

Odin did. "Any festival is a good festival. Coyotes follow the moon goddess. She's young, and she hunts, too. But a god born in a barn is close to animals."

Pewter said to Mrs. Murphy, "Odin's not a Christian."

"Isn't there an Egyptian god who has the head of a coyote?" Tucker puzzled.

"Odin, you're named for a Norse god. Our humans read all the time. So we know," Pewter called down. Then she said as an aside to Mrs. Murphy, "He's kind of ignorant, and really, Murphy, he's not a Christian."

"What are you saying up there?" Odin swept his ears forward.

Pewter opened her mouth and Mrs. Murphy said low, "He's also bigger than us." She stared down at the golden eyes looking up at her. *"She's wishing you a Merry Christmas, Odin, as do I."*

28

"I hate this." Harry threw grosgrain rolled ribbons, a tape measure, Scotch tape, old ballpoint pens onto the counter as she rummaged through the catchall drawer in the kitchen.

"She's making so much noise," Pewter complained, watching from the kitchen chair. *"My delicate ears."*

"Keys," Mrs. Murphy said.

"The keys aren't in the drawer. They're in the station wagon." Tucker also observed the fuss.

"Aha." Triumphant, Harry plucked the metallic key ring, and the key to the storage unit dangling from it, from between the pages of the phone book, where it had migrated.

"If she'd buy a key holder, screw it beside the door, this would never happen," the dog posited.

"Too logical." The tiger cat moved toward

258

the door.

Pausing a moment, Harry plucked the gold buckle bracelet out of the oversized shot glass where she had dropped it yesterday. She had grown to love that bracelet. She moved to the door, lifted her winter work coat off a hook, slipped it on, wrapped a scarf around her neck, checked the pockets for gloves, opened the door.

Pewter surprised everyone by shooting past Harry. *"You can't go without me."*

Happy in the back seat of the vehicle, the animals remained on the warm seat cover made for animals on the ride to the grocery store.

"Hope she buys chicken." Pewter watched the human trudge toward the large supermarket after parking the wagon. *"I'd like roast chicken."*

"What about tuna?" the dog inquired, as she'd heard enough about the wonders of tuna in their life together.

"Time for a change," the gray cat replied.

The supermarket was jammed with people running out of food for the holiday. Harry checked her list, hoping she could make short work of it.

Being a farmer, she marveled at the fresh produce. Here, in the dead of winter, crisp lettuce, carrots, endive, squash, and all kinds of fruits were displayed. It often crossed her mind how rich Americans were and how much we take for granted. She bagged some potatoes, lettuce, then headed for the meat department. She actually was going to buy a capon. If Pewter had accompanied her, the cat would have jumped into the case and tried to steal everything. Pewter believed "Never steal anything small."

"Harry." Esther Toth rolled her shopping cart next to Harry's. She stared at the beautiful bracelet, then looked directly into Harry's eyes. "I hope you had a happy Christmas. You certainly made ours one." She smiled. "You, Fair, and that nice Deputy Cooper, all the trouble you went to to find my sister. I can't thank you enough."

"We wanted to find her," said Harry. "She found a warm place. I think that was a lot of the motivation of her taking off." She smiled back.

"Well, Al and I didn't know if she was sick or injured. We couldn't reach her by phone." She took a deep breath. "Flo's means are slender, but I want you to know that Al and I don't want her sitting there with only a fireplace and a small heater to keep heat in the house. We are more than willing to install a new furnace. She won't hear of it."

"Maybe she'll come around now. It's a cold, cold winter."

"I hope so. Sorrowful, in a way, that she hid at the old Valencia place. So many fond memories for Flo, I guess, and, well, Mrs. Valencia was such a kind person."

"She was. I can't decide if more people were nicer then or if they were kind because I was young."

"Maybe a bit of both," Esther replied. "My sister has her odd moments, but she is clever, really. She knew the stable wouldn't be too patrolled. I hear that Watts has as much or more money than Mrs. Valencia. Not much of a social person, though. Well, it's a beautiful place. Al and I drove down once."

"Yes, it is," Harry agreed. "Is Flo all right today? She didn't want to leave the tack room at River Run."

"Let's say she's composed." Esther tightly smiled. "One day she's fine and the next day she runs off or accuses me of keeping her from seeing people. I just don't know."

"Could those mood swings be a sign of dementia?"

Esther took a long time, then said, "Yes. But I don't think someone has to have senile dementia or Alzheimer's to be angry. Maybe it's fury at your own body, your mind slip-

261

ping. I don't think Flo is ill exactly. Or maybe I don't want to face it."

As Esther and Flo were close in age, Harry wanted to say, "But you aren't failing," but she thought better of it. "Maybe she'll snap out of it."

"Take some advice from your old teacher: Stay involved in things and with people. I really believe that's Flo's problem. She's not involved with the church anymore. Occasionally she'll visit Cletus Thompson, but she really doesn't have friends, and she used to have a circle of pals. No stimulation other than Buster. I truly think that's the problem, and I can't pull her out of it, nor can Al. She gets along with Al better than with me, but that makes sense."

"Maybe she wants to be alone. Some people are solitary by nature, or life makes them so."

"True, but Harry, you didn't know my sister when she was young. By the time you met her, she was already middle-aged. Flo was pretty, outgoing. I don't think she missed a party within a fifty-mile radius when we were young." Esther smiled. "Well, you don't need my trip down Memory Lane. Again, I do thank you."

29

That Thursday, the day after Christmas, Cooper sat across from Arden in her peach-colored living room. Somehow the blue and silver Christmas decorations clashed with the peach. The women had been talking a bit, Cooper easing Arden into the more pointed questions.

"So you never brought the Silver Linings books home?"

"No," Arden stated. "As you know, Jessica does the church books. I do Silver Linings. We thought it best to have two different people keep track of things, even though we're both involved in many of the same activities. Also, this way, if we run into a snag, we can check each other."

"The drawer of the desk is unlocked?"

Arden nodded. "We both use the big double bottom drawer. I expect it will be locked from now on."

"Anyone can walk into the office?"

"No. The door to the hall is locked when no one is in the room, but the door between the office and Father O'Connor's usually isn't."

"When you're in the office, do you open the door to the hall?"

"Usually."

"Are you and Jessica ever there together?"

"When we can. The work seems to go faster if we are. I'd say half the time." She shrugged. "I'm not being very precise. I'm sorry."

"Mom." Tyler walked into the room, saw Cooper in uniform. "Are you here to arrest me?"

With a wry smile, she answered, "Not yet."

He smiled in return. "Mom, Mark Turner's mom will pick us up and take us to the shooting range."

"When?"

"Half an hour."

"When will you be back?"

"I don't know. Come on, Mom, let me go."

"Will Mrs. Turner stay there?"

"Mom, she's one of the best shots in the place."

"Tyler, that doesn't answer my question."

He handed her his cellphone as he punched in the Turner number.

Looking at Cooper, Arden apologized. "Hello, Karen. Tyler tells me you're willing to pick him up and take the boys to the range. Will you be there?" A pause. "Fine. Thank you for including Tyler." She handed his cellphone back. "You can go."

"Mom, can I have some money?"

Arden looked apologetically at Cooper again. "Go get my purse. It's in the hall."

He returned, she opened her expensive Bottega Veneta bag, plucked out a fifty-dollar bill. "You take Mrs. Turner and Mark to lunch."

Shoving the bill in his pocket, he beamed. "Thanks, Mom." He left the room.

"Deputy, think twice before you have children."

Cooper laughed. "I need to get married first."

"Think twice about that, too," she said. "Would you like something to drink? Something hot, perhaps?"

"No, thank you." Cooper returned to business. "You come to the church on days other than Fridays?"

"Not too often. I usually do Silver Linings's books once a week, unless there is a special need, then I go in. The end of the month takes an extra day. The end of the year, more than that. So much paperwork.

The officers of the organization can see the books any time they wish, but they cannot issue a check. All checks are under my signature because years ago before I came on board there was an officer who drew money from the account. He replaced it, but, well, this seemed a better way."

"Yes, I can imagine." Cooper shifted in her seat. "Do you know or suspect that any Silver Linings officer is in financial trouble?"

"No. Given the downturn, some people's businesses are doing better than others, but no. No one's on food stamps." She tossed her long, well-groomed hair.

"Right." She scribbled in her notebook. "Did your husband or does Tyler accompany you to the office?"

"Occasionally Tyler comes with me. Lou drove his Acura. He didn't like my car, but then he rarely had to haul groceries. Sometimes I would be in the office during Silver Linings meetings. Jessica, too, since Brian is president. We would try to be there. It was easier for me to talk to the officers since everyone has such full schedules. Just being able to grab someone if I have a question is a plus. But no matter what, the checks must go out by the end of the week."

"I see. How many people know your routine?"

"Oh, uh, Father O'Connor, my late husband, Tyler, I suppose, if he thinks about it, the Silver Linings officers, my girlfriends. A lot of people."

"Correct me if I'm wrong, but isn't it the usual practice if someone is going to steal checks they take them from the back of the book?"

"It is." Arden, like all bookkeepers, knew that and from time to time would flip through the large checkbook to make sure all was in order.

"Yet these missing checks were pulled from the front. You couldn't help but spot the theft once you returned to the office."

"That's why I think they were taken by an amateur."

"They're still not cashed."

"I don't understand any of this." She looked at the tree then back at Cooper. "The fingers in my pen cup. Were they Lou's? I really should know and I would think there's been enough time to . . . to identify them."

"That's one of the reasons I've called on you: to tell you that they are your husband's forefinger and middle finger."

She grimaced slightly. "Whose fingers hung from the Christmas tree?"

"I can't tell you that."

"Deputy." Arden's voice was sharp. "What is this about?"

"I don't know yet, but I will." Cooper slowly asked, "Did Lou have heart trouble?"

"No."

"I assume he went for annual checkups."

Arden exhaled through her nose. "A fight. Always a fight."

"But eventually he would go?"

"Yes, and I would double-check to see that he kept the appointment. Honestly, Deputy, Tyler is more mature about doctor's appointments than Lou. How difficult is a checkup?"

"Well, if he learned he had a condition, say prediabetes, do you think he would have told you?"

"That's the real question." Arden ran her tongue over her lower lip. "No. Truthfully, no. I'd have to worm information out of him, but I could often tell when he was hiding something. Usually about money. At least I thought I could."

"Would it be easy for him to hide medication from you?"

Arden tilted her chin upward. "He could keep it in his office or even in the car. Neither of us scanned the other's papers, calls, emails. Sometimes, Deputy, you don't want to know."

"Would his doctor tell you?"

"No. He would let me know if Lou kept an appointment but nothing else. I guess they have to be private that way, same as priests in confession."

"Yes." Cooper took a breath. "Mrs. Higham, your husband died from taking too much Coumadin."

"The blood thinner?" Arden's voice raised up.

"Yes."

"But that's rat poison. Really, Coumadin is rat poison." Her voice was high and loud now.

"I'm sorry to have to tell you this." Cooper kept her voice low.

"How could that happen? How?"

"I don't know."

"Rat poison." Arden's eyes widened. "Rat poison. Lou bled to death!"

Cooper did not reveal that she had interviewed Lou's physician, who had prescribed Coumadin. He wanted to try low doses, look for improvement, and if not, then he would discuss a bypass operation. The doctor felt certain there would be future heart problems if Lou did not take action now.

Cooper also said nothing about Pete Vavilov's disfigurement. Both men had played football for Coach Toth in the late

1980s. Both worshipped at St. Cyril's, giving generously to the church as well as to Silver Linings. Two successful men, well regarded, fathers of sons, and both in seemingly strong marriages. They were community leaders, and both died in their cars.

There was the remote possibility that Lou had committed suicide. No possibility that Pete had done so.

The missing fingers were the link. Cooper knew that.

Then again, so did Harry.

30

Tree branches moaned as they rubbed against one another. Bending low in the wind, the conifers added a whooshing sound to the dolorous moan. The wind slashed down the eastern slopes of the Blue Ridge Mountains.

With her scarf wrapped tightly around her neck, Harry stood at the base of the up-rooted tree. Ugly as the morning was, she had driven the old truck to the turnaround spot, then walked to the site. Bits of snow flying off the branches stung her face.

Mrs. Murphy and Pewter carefully picked their way into the cavity, roots icy but protected in the hole. Tucker moved to the opposite side so the wind lifted up her fur. Harry also turned her back to the wind, then came round, felt it full in the face. She wanted to study the spot as it was when she first saw the skeleton.

She circled the edge of the cavity. Kneeling down, she took her penknife out of her pocket, opened it, and stuck it into the snow. She wanted to gauge the depth. The knife disappeared in the snow. She fished it out, wiped it on her coat, closed it, and stuck it back in her pocket, guessing the snow was about eight inches at that one spot.

"*Let's dig,*" Mrs. Murphy urged Pewter.

Snow flew beneath their paws like white rooster tails.

"*All I do is get hung up in more tree roots.*" Pewter complained but kept at it.

"*Me, too.*"

Tucker called down, "*Murphy, something flew up behind you.*"

The tiger cat turned around. A silvery rounded button, the Scottish thistle imprinted on it, stood out against the snow.

"*Look,*" Mrs. Murphy loudly meowed.

The three animals sang a chorus so Harry finally knelt down again, spied the button next to the tiger cat. She placed one foot onto a thick root to balance herself, held on to another tree root. Despite her efforts, she slid into the cavity.

"*At least you're out of the wind,*" said Pewter, which was her idea of consolation.

Harry felt the snow creep into her boots. She picked up the button, studying it, before putting it in her pocket.

A chill gave her the creeps as she realized she was in the hole where the body had been buried. The roots had grown through whomever it was, and for a moment Harry imagined them grabbing her, too.

She reached up for a thick root, wiggled one foot out, had a time freeing the other one, then, with all her might, she pulled herself up and out.

"Winter clothing sure adds the pounds," she wheezed once topside.

Tucker was ready to say something about Pewter and pounds but shut her mouth as Mrs. Murphy gave her a look. The crack would have been too easy.

The two cats, claws sinking into cold roots, popped out of the hole with more ease than the human.

Harry noticed old coyote tracks as she moved a bit away from the tree. The wind stiffened, roaring now.

"Let's get out of this weather." Harry put her head down.

Once in the truck, she turned on the ignition, waited for the heater, as her feet were now cold. Pulling off her heavy gloves, she held her hands to the vent to warm up faster. Once warm, she pulled the pretty button out of her pocket.

"Whoever it was was Scottish or perhaps wanted to be," said Harry. "Such a distinctive national symbol."

"Mom, get out of here. The truck's rocking from the wind," Pewter advised.

Finally home, the animals sat before the fire while Harry called Cooper to tell her of her find.

"We found it," said Harry, and Pewter, surprisingly, did not try to steal the credit.

Hanging up, Harry dropped the button in the catchall drawer in the oversized shot glass.

As Harry was closing her kitchen drawer, Arden Higham sat with Jessica Hexham in the church office, books laid out before them.

"It's odd to be using these books after they've been dusted for prints." Arden turned over pages. "People think I stole those three checks."

"No one thinks any such thing," Jessica told her. "And, really, Arden, you don't have to do this. Take a break."

"I don't want a break. It makes it worse." Arden was argumentative. "And, of course, people think I took them. I do the books."

"Well, I certainly hope not, and the checks

274

haven't been cashed."

"Jessica, how do you know that?"

"Deputy Cooper questioned me, and I questioned her back. As best I could. They never tell you everything. I guess they hope you'll blurt something out if you're the guilty party."

Arden's face reddened. "Just makes me crazy. People thinking I'm guilty." She changed the subject. "Listen to that wind."

"It's already been a ferocious winter, hasn't it, and there's still three long months to go." Jessica pulled the arm on the tabulator.

Both women liked to see the numbers on the roll of paper. They also used a small computer to double-check everything.

"I can't concentrate. I'll take a little walk and be back."

"Arden, go home. Or take your mind off things. Go to a movie."

"No. I will do my job. I just need a walk."

To save money, the office buildings were kept at a low temperature, sixty-five degrees Fahrenheit. Given the howl of the wind, the windows and doors rattling, it seemed even colder. Arden wrapped her arms around her torso as she walked down the hall, up and back a few times. Then she went downstairs to the rec room. The large meeting room felt even colder. She pulled a tattered throw off the sofa, cushions sagging, and dropped into a fairly well-upholstered wing chair. She pulled the throw over her, picked up a newspaper, a few days old, off the table next to the chair. She'd hardly got any reading done before she fell asleep. When she awoke, she checked her watch. She'd dozed off for forty minutes. Rising, she fluffed the cushion, replaced the throw, brushed off her sweater, as she didn't think the throw was too clean.

As she replaced the paper on the table, out of curiosity she opened the drawer.

Inside was a cheap tin about five and a half inches by three inches and one quarter of an inch high. It was a good size for pins, buttons, paper clips. Opening it, she picked up shredded bits of one check.

Pencil behind her ear, Jessica looked up. "Almost done. Good walk?"

"You won't believe what I found in the rec room."

"Yes?" Jessica's eyebrows raised, she took the pencil from behind her ear.

"A shredded check. One of the stolen ones." She dropped the tatters on Jessica's desk.

Jessica paused, pursed her lips, then said, "Oh, Arden, this isn't good."

"Where are the other two?"

Arden dropped into her chair. "This is all too much. Dear God."

"Prayer might be in order." Jessica, disturbed, pieced the paper bits together. "Arden, let me talk to Brian about this. Really. There's been enough — well, we all need some calm right now."

"I have to call Deputy Cooper." Arden put her palms on her cheeks, then dropped them.

Jessica made a note in a small notebook, lifted the long paper from the tabulator, and neatly stapled the note to the numbers. "All in order. That's some good news, and yes, you do need to inform Cooper. I'll leave these check pieces on my desk."

"Good."

Jessica had gone over Silver Linings's books while Arden slept, and she wrote out checks for Arden to sign. The women often helped each other going over the books, but this was a special favor. She slid the big checkbook over to Arden.

"Sign."

"You did all this?"

"What are friends for? You sign them, we'll stick them in envelopes, stamp them, and toss them in the mail with all the St. Cyril's checks."

"Oh, Jessica." Arden swallowed, tears filled her eyes.

"Come on, girl. Sign. Can't sign if you're crying."

This brought a rueful smile, and Arden began signing the checks. "You balanced the books, too."

"Apart from the now two missing checks, not a penny missing." Jessica smiled. "Has it occurred to you that whoever took and tore one up downstairs is dumb as a sack of hammers?" she said, using the old southern expression.

"Perhaps I should be grateful."

31

Blue snow reflected twilight. The sunset, brilliant against a winter sky, held Harry's attention as she finished up her outdoor chores. She observed the flaming sky — reds, golds, and hot oranges — as it was infiltrated by dark fingers of encroaching clouds. She shut the back barn doors, which she'd left open to freshen the air. The temperature, mid-forties, dropped with the sun. Sweet-smelling hay, the tang of fresh water in the bucket, the rich, comforting odor of the horses themselves made her barn the one place in the world where Harry always felt better no matter what. Walking the aisle, she checked and double-checked. Everyone's blankets stayed on properly, a miracle, given the hijinks in the pastures that afternoon. Lots of kicking forward with forelegs, snow flying off their hooves, the crystals like tiny little rainbows shooting through the clear air.

Earlier, seeing Harry leaning on the fence watching had encouraged the horses to play harder until finally they'd raced up to the fence as though they were going to blast through. At the last minute, the boys stopped, turning sharply left or right, hollering like banshees as they did so.

The girls, in their large pasture, took no part in the gelding foolishness.

"Just wait, Tomahawk is going to rip Shortro's blanket," the oldest broodmare snorted.

"Oh, Pots, that will make Harry furious," Silver Cups replied to Pot O'Gold's prediction.

Just as Pots said, Tomahawk lunged out with his long Thoroughbred neck (he was a good 16.2) and grabbed the side of Shortro's blanket. The rip had resounded through the pastures. Even Harry heard it.

Now, as Shortro munched away in his stall, she investigated that rip. The side of his wonderful Rambo blanket bore a ragged scar, testimony to the force of the effort and Tomahawk's teeth. Ripping a Rambo takes real strength.

"Well, after I repair it with duct tape, this will get us through the winter, but I'll have to get it sewn up after the last frost. You all live to make me spend money."

Shortro lifted his head, his deep brown

eyes utterly sympathetic. *"He did it."*

"Wimp," the old Thoroughbred called from his stall.

Above in the loft, Mrs. Murphy, Pewter, and Simon listened and laughed.

Tucker, already sitting at the tack room door, knew the routine. Harry would go inside, check the barn phone for messages, sit for a moment, pull out her notebook, make notes on horsefeed and behavior, then shove the notebook back in the middle drawer of the desk.

Next, she'd lean over and double-check the large wall calendar. She'd scribbled in the big squares. Tucker never interfered with this ritual, but she couldn't understand why Harry would curse and throw pencils or ballpoint pens in the trash. This often happened when she'd write on the calendar.

Why did she aggravate herself? Tucker didn't see the logic of it.

"Let's go down and get in there." Mrs. Murphy headed for the ladder.

"You first," Pewter said.

"Such good manners!" said a surprised Mrs. Murphy, for it was right that Pewter, younger, show deference.

"I like to keep you off guard." The gray cat swept her considerable whiskers forward, then she said to Simon, *"We'll be out later, I*

281

think. Need to drag out some food for Odin."

"He's been coming around regularly just lately," the possum noted.

"Winter's hard, even on as good a hunter as a coyote," Mrs. Murphy called as she backed down the ladder.

"Luckily, I have Harry," said Simon. "She even unwrapped some Jolly Ranchers for me. Yum. Watermelon." The marsupial salivated at the thought of the hard candy he especially favored.

"How can you eat that junk?" Pewter headed after Mrs. Murphy.

"It's so delicious. Every color is a different taste. I like them even more than jellybeans."

"More than molasses?" Mrs. Murphy called from the aisle.

"Nothing is better than molasses," came a firm reply.

The cats shot through the animal door to the tack room, the deep fragrance of leather filling their nostrils.

"We miss anything?" Mrs. Murphy asked.

"She's been writing notes," Tucker replied. "Lots of good it does her."

Harry finished with the notebook and dialed Susan. "Do you need anything for tonight's meeting?"

"No. I don't think it will take that long. The Christmas drive was a tremendous success, due to everyone's hard work."

"Especially yours. Not even a bottle of wine, something like that?"

"No. I'm good. Your husband is picking up mine, I'm sure you know. Going to the movies. Ned says he's not going to be in the house with a bunch of churchwomen. So I asked him, would he prefer a bunch of hookers?"

Harry chuckled. Indeed, it seems politicians in general had a penchant for working girls. Birds of a feather, Harry supposed. "And?"

"A big smile. Ned said if it got ex-Governor Spitzer a TV show, maybe it would get him one. We could use the money."

"How thoughtful."

"Yes, that's what I said." Susan laughed. "See you at six."

Harry left the barn, walked into the house, saw Fair at the kitchen table reading the newspaper. She relayed Ned's conversation with Susan.

"Ha!" was his reply.

"I'll leave you to your thoughts. I'm taking a shower, then heading out for the meeting. Pasta's in the fridge. Just heat it up."

"Thanks, honey. Ned and I are going to eat on the mall. I made him promise not to talk about politics. Actually, with the topic of hookers to discuss instead, that might be easier than I thought."

Harry threw up her hands, said nothing, hurried back to her shower.

Once cleaned up, wearing a plaid wrap-around skirt and white blouse, a sweater tied around her neck, she walked into the kitchen. He looked up. "You look good."

"Thank you."

"Don't your legs get cold?"

"Sometimes. The high socks help, and I guess there aren't as many nerve endings in your legs as elsewhere."

"Maybe women have less than men, because my legs would be blue. But you look like a college girl. Really."

"Hold that thought." She kissed him. "I really hope this meeting won't drag on. I'm shooting to be home by nine-thirty."

"I should be back around then, too."

By the time Harry reached Susan's house, all the girls were there from St. Luke's and St. Cyril's. Jan McGee sat at the dining room table, too. The other paired-off churches also had meetings on this night, Sunday, December 29. They wanted to review the deliveries while memories were fresh. Then the heads of each church's food drive would meet in a week, and any new suggestions for improvement would be thrown on the table. The system worked quite well, for each year they did better. Pressure stayed high, however, for each year the numbers of those in need rose, and this provoked a lively discussion from all. Charlene Vavilov, Arden Higham, and Jessica Hexham tried to help Susan in keeping the meeting moving. Charlene and Arden, it seemed, just wanted to be with friends, anything other than being home at dark without their husbands. While Harry thought their attendance at the meeting was perhaps too early to be out in public, she wasn't scandalized, as her mother's generation would have been. The old rules had a logic to them, but some folks needed to find their own way.

Owen, Susan's corgi, was sleeping through this vigorous meeting. Food would have kept him awake.

BoomBoom rapped her pencil on the table. "Why can't we keep tabs on the needy throughout the year?"

Cooper, who was in charge of the sheriff's department group, was also present, especially since she was close to the St. Luke's group. "BoomBoom, that's an enormous amount of work."

"I don't doubt that, but why can't we have a liaison with Human Services and each month go over those who are new to the list of needy and those who have gotten jobs or improved?"

Charlene stepped in. "We do use Human Services. The county's been very helpful, but BoomBoom, a lot of our information is word of mouth through the church or friends."

"Well, can't we figure out a way to sweep up information from a variety of sources?" BoomBoom persisted.

Alicia, a good long-range thinker, had heard all about this before from Boom-Boom, who'd taken the bit between her teeth. She wanted to support her partner without appearing to disagree with others. BoomBoom could sometimes forget to smooth feathers.

"First, we have to identify the sources." Alicia quietly put forward the obvious. "It may be as easy as setting up a website or using email or whatever comes next. We can't have meeting after meeting. Technology can speed the process."

"BoomBoom has come up with an idea that will help us more accurately predict need so we can go back to our churches and ask for specific items apart from food."

Harry liked the idea. "I don't see why email won't work with one person in charge."

"We need to get this idea out to the other churches. We don't want to look as though we're running the show," Arden sensibly suggested.

"The only woman who could take on this job if anyone wanted it would be someone who is retired," Jan said. "Once you get into this, it will take a lot of time. Email is one thing. You need to talk to people face-to-face. I'd add to BoomBoom's idea that it wouldn't be amiss to sometimes visit the people throughout the year. The other thought I had is talk to the doctors in your congregations. As you know, Frank, my husband, is a doctor. He often knows who is in financial distress as well as physical. People can't pay their bills."

"Good idea." Susan nodded.

Jessica had brought a detailed county map, which she flattened out on the long mahogany table. "If you look at where we made deliveries, the areas of greatest need jumps out at you."

Susan spoke up. "Who is behind on their property taxes is another clue. Kind of the same thing as Jan's suggestion about medical bills."

"I'd never thought of that," Harry exclaimed.

"It's often the first sign that there's trouble. So many people are sliding downhill." Susan peered at the large map.

Also studying the detailed map, Harry noticed the fire road on the spine of the Blue Ridge Mountains and the switchbacks down those slopes. Lumber and farm roads were not marked, but even without them she could see how easy it had been for someone to hide a body up above her house. Her mind kept wandering to the skeleton in the tree roots. A long time ago or at least however long it took to turn a corpse into bleached bone, someone had carried a body along that ridge, then dropped down to bury it. Getting on that line was easier than she thought. Curious as she was about the deaths and severing of Pete and Lou's fingers, she'd seen that skeleton dangling. The smile of the skeleton haunted her.

Leaning over to Cooper, she whispered, "After the meeting, look at this map with me."

The lively meeting moved along, thanks to Susan. All agreed BoomBoom had a solid idea, and Susan volunteered, with Jessica, to contact the other drive chairs at the various churches.

"I move we adjourn the meeting," Alicia said.

"I second the motion." Cooper smiled.

"All agreed say aye." Susan could do *Robert's Rules of Order* in her sleep.

The ayes were unanimous.

"Jessica, may we borrow that map for a moment?" Cooper asked.

"Of course." Jessica rose, heading to the already crowded bar.

Harry and Cooper bent over the folded-out paper, Harry tracing the route with her forefinger.

"Whoever carried that body brought it *down* the mountain. It would be too, too hard to carry it up."

"Harry, why couldn't someone drive up like we did?"

"Because they'd have to drive past my barn."

Cooper smiled. "Yes, but those bones might be fifty years old, older. You weren't always at the barn."

"Yes, but" — Harry took a deep breath — "you can find out the approximate age of bones. I know, I know — this isn't on the front burner. You certainly have more pressing cases, but still, I found a skeleton, which is now missing. That's pretty curious, wouldn't you say?"

"I would." Cooper nodded. "Okay. So what if you're right? The body was carried down or even slid down, like on a canvas. Doesn't prove who did it."

"But it might prove useful information sometime."

"Right." Cooper looked over to the bar. "Come on. A cup of cheer will do us good."

Harry folded up the map and joined the ladies at the bar. Handing the map to Charlene, she said, "Thanks."

Emotions unrestrained, Arden blabbed about the torn check at St. Cyril's, even though Jessica had advised against it.

Jessica winced but did not admonish her, instead saying, "I spoke to Brian about that. Arden said she'd call Cooper. Who knows who put the torn check in that little drawer? Best we don't jump to conclusions."

Everyone started talking at once.

Finally, Charlene said, "Shouldn't someone tell Father O'Connor?"

"No," Alicia forcefully replied, surprising everyone.

"Why not?" Arden's voice rose.

"It's better to find out if he knew," Alicia evenly answered.

"Really?" Arden knocked back another glass of white wine.

Jessica knew she'd better stop her from

guzzling a third.

Alicia continued on. "Best not to stir things up. This is a job for the sheriff's department. We will only muddy the water."

BoomBoom was instantly alert. "What are you saying?"

"What if it's an inside job? It certainly looks like one." Alicia leaned against the bar.

"But the checks haven't been cashed." Arden really shouldn't have spilled the beans. Too much wine. Too much emotion.

"How awful," Arden said.

"Theft is a loaded issue, especially with two leaders of Silver Linings recently dead," Harry calmly spoke.

Jessica looked into her glass, set it on the bar counter. "Since no monies are missing, it's possible this is a bad prank. Brian operates on the assumption that boys will be boys."

"I guess it's not the boys we're worried about." Harry crumpled her cocktail napkin. "First, this distracts attention from the loss of two powerhouses in our community. Secondly, who is to say the checks won't be cashed at a later date? Leaving one behind is a surefire way to confuse people. We just might be dealing with someone smarter than we think."

"Oh, I hope not." Arden burst into tears.

The women comforted her. The discussion stopped while Harry's mind roared forward, not to good places. For the second time, the first being when she saw the skeleton, Harry felt the chill of fear.

32

"Father, I appreciate the time you have given me." Cooper smiled as she spoke, although Father O'Connor knew the police officer was in his office for a reason.

Flummoxed for a moment, the priest queried, "You're here about the torn check, I assume."

"With any luck, Father, we might lift a print when the check is reconstructed. I mean, other than Arden's or Jessica's."

"Yes. Yes. We can hope." His eyebrows knitted together.

"If there is one, our team will find it, but real police work isn't necessarily like TV. Rarely do we get an instant answer or shall I say person of interest in a case like this. This will take time, and much of it painstaking," she honestly reported. "Let me ask you, have you ever noticed special friendships between the boys or certain adults and boys?"

He rubbed his temples. "Deputy Cooper, that's difficult to answer. Naturally, there is affection. Building relationships and providing possible role models is rather the point of Silver Linings. Some boys like some adults better than others. I believe the adults try not to show favoritism. I have never worried. It seems natural to me."

"I see."

He paused, choosing his words carefully. "Deputy, you know the Church has been under attack." He raised his hand, palm outward. "We have to clean house. There is no doubt about the terrible covered-up abuses, but the media seems to enjoy fanning the flames of any story in which we are portrayed in a bad light. Lawsuits have drained the finances of U.S. churches. Worldwide, the Church may be rich, but I would have to say that here in the States we are struggling. Fewer and fewer men enter the priesthood. Rome appears to lack interest in us, preferring areas of the world where fewer questions are asked. However, the hard truth is we need to ask questions."

"So if you spoke out against a position from Rome that you felt outmoded or unsuited to your flock, would you lose funding?"

"What I would lose is my parish." He

sighed. "Rebellious priests are never in fashion."

"A few make a great difference."

"Deputy, I never expected you to be interested in the Church. I'm grateful that you are. And yes, a few priests have made differences, but they are better at public relations. I'm a simple parish priest and I tend to my flock as best I can. If I have a disagreement with dogma, and I'm not saying that I do, I keep it to myself. The time is not right, and it may never be right for me. I don't know. But I don't think I will do my people any good if I speak out on such issues. In fact, I think I would cause harm, divisiveness, and confusion."

"I understand that." She nodded. "Law enforcement can be rigid and difficult, too. I'm not suggesting it's the same, only that I understand the conflict between obedience and speaking out for reform."

"It's a volatile time, isn't it?" He sighed.

"Yes, it is. You have lost two of your mainstays, and I am sure that Peter Vavilov and Lou Higham offered generous support to the Church, as well as to Silver Linings. And now there's the publicity about the missing checks."

"I could always count on Pete and Lou. They would be so valuable at a time like this. Solid, smart advice."

"Father O'Connor, did anyone ever come to you and report inappropriate behavior about Pete and Lou?"

"None." He answered readily, but the question unnerved him. "I would have been shocked. I'm shocked to even think of those two in such a light. They were mainstays."

"I'm sorry to ask these things, but I must. I have to consider every possibility, no matter how distressful. Did anyone ever complain about Silver Linings; perhaps they felt the boys were engaging in wrongful activities?"

"Yes. Some reports of drinking on the premises, also smoking pot. Brian Hexham looked into it and talked to the boys who had indeed drunk or smoked. And then when Brian gave his lecture on how one's body changes — sexual desire and responsibility — that drew fire from some of the boys' parents. I handled that." He blinked. "It may seem odd to you that a celibate priest can or should speak to such matters, but I think we are bound to do so. We sacrifice our sexuality, if you will, to the Church, to the community. A married man will not put the flock first, he will put his family first, as he should. I am bound to the Church, to Christ. I realize this is a vow few would wish to make and even fewer understand."

"What happened?"

"Some parents were upset, but the young men were grateful for the information. We forget how tough adolescence is. At that difficult time, you don't even understand your own body, and there's so much pressure to conform. To condense what I said, I told the few parents — three mothers and one married couple; most of these boys are from broken families — that if we don't clearly and honestly address the realities of these boys' lives, we will have more children out of wedlock, more heartache. Obviously, I believe in abstinence, and just as obviously I know that isn't going to work for every teenage boy. Everywhere these young people turn, it's sexual imagery, lyrics in the songs. So while I preach abstinence, I allow Brian to discuss birth control. It's a bit of a cheat." He blushed slightly. "But we must protect our boys as well as the girls. And if there's one thing I emphasize and Silver Linings emphasizes, it's respect for women." He threw up his hands. "We're struggling against the whole culture."

"Yes, you are," Cooper agreed. "I'll give you a break and not ask how you feel about women becoming priests."

He exhaled. "Thank you."

"As to the matter of Silver Linings's finances, the good news is, despite missing three checks, the forensic accountant who works with our office said the books are in order." She paused, then again said with sympathy, "Father, I regret having to ask you some of these questions, but there is a great deal at stake. For one thing, I don't want another murder."

His hand flew to his heart. "Do you think —"

"I strongly believe both men were killed. Very slight evidence, but I've learned to trust my gut feelings. You have your calling, Father, and I have mine. It's one thing to solve a murder, it's another to prevent one."

As Cooper spoke to Father O'Connor, Father O'Brien was sitting in the confessional booth. He gave Mass twice a week and offered confession twice a week.

Father O'Brien's feet were cold. He was wrapped in a heavy shawl and he kept looking at his watch. One more hour.

Someone entered. A woman's voice, low, said, "Bless me, Father, for I have sinned."

"Go on, my child."

"I am an accessory to murder."

33

Low clouds covered the stars. The sparkling winter sky, obscured, deepened the night, but the cloud cover did keep the temperature a bit warmer. The mercury hung at thirty-one degrees Fahrenheit.

"I hate New Year's Eve." At the kitchen table Harry wrapped a gift in silver paper, finishing it with a white ribbon.

"I don't hate it, but as I've gotten older I can't say that I look forward to it like I did at twenty-five." Fair sorted through the mail.

"I did that already, honey."

"I know, but I like to check and see the dates on the bills."

"Have you noticed that the credit card bills are now due in three weeks, not a month? Everything is compressed, pushed forward. It's like the entire world is trying to squeeze operating capital out of us."

He leaned back in the kitchen chair, tidying the bills. "Yep. Some magazines send you renewal notices early or they offer you a deal if you renew early. You know, like a twenty-five percent savings. Then I get confused because I don't remember when my annual renewal date really is."

"It's a racket," she said. "The date is usually in fine print somewhere on the renewal notice. Sometimes I think I'll just let everything run out."

"Me, too. Then again, I know in time I'd miss something." He stood up, walked to the sink, stared out the window. "Did you look at the weather report?"

"No. I'll pull it up." She plucked the Droid off the counter, opened it up, touched the weather icon. "Below freezing tonight, cloud cover, cloudy tomorrow and chance of snow on New Year's Eve." She looked up. "We really do have to go to that party, don't we?"

"Fund-raiser," he flatly stated.

Harry opened her mouth, stopped before she spoke, for a long, high-pitched coyote yowl captured her attention. "God, that's a mournful sound."

Fair peered out the window again. "Yes, it is. Sounds like he's up in the walnut grove."

"Danger," Odin called loudly.

The animals listened intently. They'd heard his warning before. Mrs. Murphy finally asked, *"Danger to him or to us?"*

"Do we have to find out?" Pewter asked.

"If we don't, it might find us," Tucker prudently stated.

"Hush your mouth," Pewter immediately replied.

"I'm going to the hayloft," the tiger cat announced. *"I can see better up there. Maybe Odin will come down and enlighten us."*

Tucker said, *"We put out what's left of the T-bones, plus some cooked rice. Harry threw out half a pot in a Baggie."* The corgi thought this a pretty good haul.

Aroused at the talk of food, Pewter chirped, *"I'll go with you, Murph. It's not so cold up there in the hayloft, especially if we wait in a hollowed-out hay bale."*

"I'll come, too," Tucker said, headed out the kitchen animal door.

The two cats hurried after her, the door flap slapping as they bolted through.

"What's gotten into them?" Harry wondered.

"You never know." Fair smiled. "Predators work harder in winter. A lot of wildlife moves around. And that was probably a hungry coyote."

That hungry coyote loped down from the timber, across the back pastures, as the cats watched through the slightly opened upper hayloft doors.

"He's headed our way," Pewter called down to Tucker.

"Okay." Tucker pressed against the huge ground-level doors, listening.

Odin covered a lot of ground at an easy gait, reaching the outside of the barn within minutes of the cats spying him at the back open meadow. He quickly gobbled up the rice, then lay down to chew the delicious steak bones.

Mrs. Murphy looked down at him. *"Odin, what's this talk of danger? Whatever is going on up there?"*

He swallowed before answering, *"Two humans moved down from the top of the ridge. Their faces were wrapped up. One had a full pullover mask on, with eyeholes and a slit for the mouth. The other had a scarf across her face. I'm sure it was a her. Smelled like a female."*

"How'd the other one smell?" asked Tucker from behind the door.

"The wind shifted; plus, I wasn't close. One thing's for sure, I don't trust either of them. I thought they might have guns and take a shot at me. So I don't know how the one with the mask smelled."

"How did they move?" Pewter asked. *"Old, young? Damaged?"*

Looking up at Pewter, Odin shook himself for a moment. *"They moved like two cold humans struggling in the snow. Slipping and sliding, but no one was stooped. I don't think they were really young, though. And another thing, one had binoculars around her neck."*

"Why did you call out danger?" Mrs. Murphy wondered.

"Because they were watching down here. Not moving. Watching like a predator."

"And they came down from the ridge?" Tucker wanted to make sure she understood.

"Yes. That's difficult for humans, impaired as they are," Odin remarked. *"Going down in bad footing is harder than going up. That's why I called out to you. They want something here."*

The three domesticated animals were silent for a moment, then Pewter called down, *"Were they by the uprooted tree?"*

"They weren't far from it. I didn't follow them back up because I wanted food. But I'd be careful."

"Did they see you?" Tucker inquired.

Odin laughed. *"Of course not. I can be six feet from a human if the cover is good. They haven't a clue."*

"When the weather is better, do you see a lot of humans on the ridge or walking paths

down the side of the mountains?" Pewter asked.

"Not much. Most humans walk on the Appalachian Trail. They don't wander onto private lands, and we steer clear of them. If hikers see us, you know they'll call other humans and some of those humans might come to shoot us or trap us. We stay away." Odin polished off the one bone, picked up the other.

"So these two know the trails and probably not just down to our farm," Mrs. Murphy said. "Odin, did you see any guns?"

"No, just the binoculars," he said, crunching another bone in his powerful jaws.

34

Cletus Thompson awoke early on the last day of the old year. He tended the fire, petted his dog, opened a can of spaghetti that had been in the Christmas basket from the church and ate that. A cup of hot coffee helped warm him up from the inside out. As his stove was gas and he paid the bill, no matter what, he always could make hot coffee. Sometimes he might scrounge up the money by shoveling a driveway or taking on other odd jobs that the convenience store owner allowed him to do. Cletus's neighbors sometimes helped, but an alcoholic loses friends as trees drop leaves in the fall. Even if the drinker does not cause scenes or turn nasty, the inevitable unreliability destroys friendships. Still, Cletus was always loyal and good to The Terminator, ancient as the creature was. Even if Cletus didn't eat, his dog did.

Despite the years of alcohol abuse, the

former math teacher had a strong constitution. Had he not, he would have been dead long ago.

He felt in his bones more snow was on its way, so he thought he'd dig out his driveway in advance. Whatever came down would still need to be removed, but this would make that future task easier. Coat and gloves on, cap, too, he opened his front door.

"What the —" He walked over to Flo's car.

She was asleep inside, with her dog, Buster, in her lap.

Rapping on the window, he startled her. She sat up straight, staring up at Cletus doing the tapping. Buster barked.

"Flo, are you all right?"

She rolled down her window. "I was so tired I fell asleep."

"Come on in the house. It's warmer than out here, and I have a pot of coffee on the stove. Bring the dog. My fellow sleeps most of the time."

"Okay."

"Unlock the door." He turned his back on her, knowing that would do the trick.

Sure enough, she stepped outside, her dog in her arms, following him into his house. Flo hated to be left behind.

After using the bathroom and brushing

her teeth (as she carried a small bag with a toothbrush, toothpaste, and some aspirin in it), she joined her unruffled host in his kitchen.

"Sit down," he said kindly. "Milk? Sugar?"

"Sugar."

Two heaping teaspoons dumped into the liquid pleased Flo, who gulped it right down.

"Flo, all I have to eat are some canned goods the church left me. In fact, it was brought over by Harry and Susan, my old students. You remember them?"

"They left me things, too," she said, wrinkling her nose. The warm coffee felt wonderful. "Your house is warmer than mine."

"In winter, I mostly sit in the kitchen or by the fireplace. No reason to run up the bill. It's warm in the kitchen. I don't need much." Once he thought she might be relaxed, he got to the point. "What brings you out here?"

"I've been avoiding Esther." She breathed deeply a few times. "I'm afraid of my sister. She wants to kill me."

"Esther?" Cletus was taking all this in with a grain of salt.

"She's not the same person you knew when you all taught together. Oh, Esther

307

was always looking for the main chance, I can tell you that, but she kept on track."

"Why ever would Esther want to kill you? I would think she's happy. Married. Enough money to live good in retirement."

"Ha!" came the derisive response. "She tells people I'm the one with mental problems, but it's her. She was jealous of the fact that I was more popular than she was when we were kids, and then when she fell in love with Al Toth that took her right round the bend. It was all she could think about, talk about. Esther was always trying to get me to help her attract men, especially Al."

"Well" — Cletus paused — "I knew, of course, that Esther was wild about him. We all did, but she didn't run her mouth. Naturally, she would to you, you're her sister. She got him in the end."

"I hate her for all that and more," said Flo. "He didn't make her happy. It's not Al. He's okay. It's her. She can't stand that I know who and what she really is. She scared me so much I hid at the Valencia farm and then Deputy Cooper found me. Fair Haristeen was with her, and Harry too. They were the ones who figured out where I was. They thought they were helping. Esther had everyone in an uproar."

Cletus wanted to say that it was Flo who appeared to have everyone in an uproar, but instead he said, "Did Esther threaten you?"

"She says if I don't behave she's going to put me away. A lot, she says it a lot."

"That's a mean thing for her to say." He poured himself another cup of coffee and one for Flo, too. "Look, your little fellow is curled up next to mine."

"They can keep each other warm." Flo smiled, a rare event.

"Why did you come here?"

"We always got on, you and me. Sometimes I'd stop by and we'd remember the old days, the days before everything went haywire. I thought you'd hear me out."

"You want to stay here?" His eyebrows and voice raised.

Flo nodded. "If you help me hide my car when she drives by, I should be safe."

Cletus didn't answer that straight up. "We never had bad words, Esther and I. But she's like everyone else, doesn't want to waste time on a drunk."

"She doesn't want to waste time or money on me either. She doesn't need me anymore. Tonight, I'll prove to you that Esther wants to kill me. You'll understand everything then. We'll need to go out, but not far."

"Supposed to snow."

"I know." Flo held the coffee cup in her hands. "You have to promise me not to drink."

He shrugged. "Easy promise. I'm all out of hooch."

"And whatever I eat, I'll replace. I have money." She pulled forty dollars from her pocket, slapping it on the table. "I can't go out and buy food because someone might see me. I don't think Esther knows I'm gone yet. She calls in and checks every day. If I don't call back after a couple of hours, she drives over."

He put his hands in his lap. "Keep your money. We can get by on the canned food."

"Well, I'll pay when I go, which will be tomorrow at the latest because when you see what I have, I'll be in the right. I can go up against Esther before she finds me. She will eventually. She'll call the sheriff's department again. The fact that it's New Year's Eve helps. Everyone's busy. Take the money now."

"No. I'll buy bourbon. I don't trust myself. I'll want to buy food for both of us, but I don't trust myself. Especially on New Year's Eve."

"Then I'll give you the money later."

"Flo, don't worry about it. Let's go hide your car. First, I have to move my truck.

You drive your car. I'll push if you get stuck."

"Where are we going to hide it?"

"Only place I really have is behind the woodshed."

Going slow, Flo steered her dilapidated vehicle around the back of the house, the domicile's curl of smoke from its chimney the one sign of habitation. Behind her, Cletus kept his hands on the car's trunk. Once she did slide out a bit. The right rear wheel spun, but he gave a hard push and the car straightened out. Cletus made Flo drive around so the car nosed out the way it had come, just in case. Then he moved his truck back in place in the driveway.

From the state road, a person wouldn't see the tracks to the side of the house unless they looked carefully. And if it did snow, that would somewhat cover them. The woodshed behind the house did the rest.

Back in the house, they stomped their feet. Both dogs woke up. The Terminator barked. Buster followed suit, but neither dog moved off the pile of old towels they'd burrowed into.

Back in the kitchen, Flo bent down to pet her dog and Cletus did the same. He opened a can of soup, poured it in a saucepan.

"Made me hungry, and I know you are, too."

She didn't deny it. "Cletus, you've tried to stop drinking. I didn't help in the past, bringing a bottle. I thought I was being sociable."

He nodded. "Longest I went was a year. I stopped and then I don't know. Just started up again. No reason."

"Does it make you feel good?"

"Used to. I crave it sometimes. Can't explain it. Then I'll take a drink, next it's two and I don't know. When I wake up, the bottle's empty."

"So you get these cravings, the booze doesn't make you feel good anymore, but you still drink it?"

He thought a long time as he stirred the soup in the saucepan. "Well, kills the pain."

"Maybe I should try it."

"Don't."

35

Standing in her cowboy boots at the fund-
raiser, Harry felt the hot flush of embarrassment creep onto her cheeks. The usual:
She'd spoken before thinking, or as Susan
would put it, "No edit button."

"How can I ask her that?" Father O'Connor, also in cowboy boots as well as his
clerical collar, demurred.

"Well, I hadn't gotten that far yet," Harry
stammered.

In front of them, on the other side of the
solid low wall, people danced on a raised
wooden floor built specially for tonight's
event.

Financed by the de Jarnettes, the affair for
the Youth Riding charity was held in their
indoor riding arena. The arena, heated at
God knows what cost, was filled with
people, all in western wear, dancing to a
country and western band. So many people
attended at $150 a pop that latecomers

would have to sit in the bleachers. And while $150 per person paled before the $10,000- and $100,000-a-plate political campaign dinners, it meant a married couple needed to cough up $300. For many, that wasn't easy.

However, unless one moved in only UVA circles, a resident of Albemarle County sooner or later had to attend some form of equine activity. If nothing else, it eased social life, and in this and other cases, it raised monies for worthy causes.

"I'm sorry, Father, I know you've been under great stress," Harry apologized. "I'm trying to find answers and am not doing a good job."

Placing his hand under her elbow, he escorted Harry to a quieter place, which meant the enormous feed room. There was a covered walkway between the barn and the indoor arena so Darlene and students could ride from the barn into the huge arena without facing bad weather.

Placed at the corner of the barn, the feed room was filled with sweet feed, crimped oats, dried molasses. It smelled heavenly.

Father O'Connor hit the light switch. "I don't think Max and Dar will worry that we're stealing feed."

"No." Harry wondered why he had taken

her away.

"You suggested the missing checks were taken to throw law enforcement off the track. I can't say I've thought of that, Harry, but you may not be far wrong. Since the Silver Linings checks haven't been cashed, it seems to me they were taken by someone who had no intention of cashing them. It's puzzling, disquieting, especially given the deaths of two of the church's most generous members."

She took a deep breath, then launched into her theories. "Father, I don't think it's just the checks. I think it's a message, someone who can't speak up out of fear."

He leaned against a large built-in feed bin. "But I can't imagine where uncashed missing checks would lead."

"Tyler knows his mother's schedule. If she left him in the office for a time, she wouldn't worry about him stealing."

"What could Tyler fear that he couldn't tell his mother?"

"What if he has a good idea about how his father really died? And then there's the ugly reality of those fingers."

Father O'Connor whitened. "Yes, yes, of course. Harry." He reached out and took her hand. "Perhaps we both might call on Deputy Cooper. Tomorrow."

"Usually she tells me not to be so nosy." Harry grimaced slightly.

They heard footfalls by the feed room, which had a large window in the door.

Esther and Al were walking through the beautiful stable, headed back to the dance floor in the arena.

Noticing that Father O'Connor held Harry's hand, Al good-naturedly opened the door and said, "None of that."

Esther slid in behind him, took Harry's hand away from the young priest, her own hand covering the found gold bracelet on Harry's wrist. "Now, Al."

The genial coach slapped the priest on the back. "All in good fun, Father. Happy New Year."

As he turned, Esther squeezed Harry's wrist. "Happy New Year."

Harry didn't think a thing about it. She'd pay for that.

Light snow fell as Flo and Cletus drove in his old but serviceable four-wheel-drive Dodge truck, bought a year before he was fired from the school district in 1994.

"Go beyond the storage unit, go down the road, then turn to where the three abandoned schools are — you know, Random Row?"

"Okay. Flo, how long is this going to take, because this snow is going to come down harder."

"Not long." She held a powerful flashlight in her lap.

They turned on the snow-covered gravel road, reached the three old lovely school-houses: white-frame buildings with almost two-story floor-to-ceiling paned windows.

"Turn into the parking lot of the schools."

Cletus did just that. He parked the truck and pocketed the key because he found if his elbow hit the door the wrong way he could lock himself out, shutting the door as he heard the click too late.

Flashlight on, Flo highlighted the snow-flakes. Outside she slipped, as the lot hadn't been plowed since the storms started. Numerous times the snows had melted a bit, and more snow packed on top. Flo pushed along, picking her feet up with care.

Cletus followed. Catching up, he walked beside her. She led him to a small shed at the back of the buildings.

Opening the door, she shined the flashlight on a skeleton, laid out, one arm missing from the elbow down.

"Flo, we need to go to the sheriff's department."

"No, Esther's got everyone thinking I'm

crazy. If they do believe us enough to come out here, she'll blame this on me."

He considered this. "I imagine you're right, Flo. Al will back Esther up so it will be two against one. Does he know about this?"

Flo vigorously shook her head. "No."

"Is it who I think it is?"

"Yes." Tears rolled down Flo's cheeks. "I didn't kill Margaret, Cletus. I had nothing against her." She took a shuddery breath. "But I helped Esther bury her body. I should have gone to the sheriff, but I just couldn't. I couldn't turn on my sister, but now, now she's turned on me."

"Is this when you started to drift away? You know?"

She nodded. "Help me."

"In for a penny, in for a pound." He turned up the collar of his threadbare coat.

"I have a plan," Flo quietly said.

That New Year's Eve, Margaret Donleavey made yet another journey. Covering the bones in an old tarp and coat, Flo and Cletus drove her to Harry's farm. They propped her up against the barn door, the Chinaman's hat shining over her. Flo arranged the loose bones as best she could.

Then Flo returned with Cletus to his house to hide out. She figured she could call Cooper tomorrow. Yes, the deputy would eventually speak to Esther, but if Flo could just state her case, all might be well.

For the first time in twenty-five years, Margaret Donleavey was aboveground — a social occasion of sorts.

36

"I thought we'd never get out of there." Harry stretched her legs as far as she could in the Volvo station wagon.

With the windshield wipers on high speed, Fair drove at thirty-five miles an hour. "If we'd stayed until midnight and rung in the New Year, we'd have been there until three in the morning. For one thing, people trying to get out of the parking lot, loaded as they would be, we'd never make it. We'd be stuck." He half laughed. "There were some happy people."

"I swear, some of it is the relief that the holidays are over." She peered into the darkness, snow falling harder. "We'll be home right about midnight. No way you can drive fast in this stuff, and no way the road plows can keep up with it."

"I just want to get home before someone else knocks over a telephone pole." He checked the gas gauge. "We're half full.

Hours sitting at idle will wipe that out."

"True." She smiled. "What do you think of Father O'Connor?"

"I like him."

"If he or Father O'Brien heard a confession from a killer or the killer, would he keep it to himself?"

"Yes. They have to, honey." He squinted into the darkness ahead. "Do you think he knows more than he indicated to you?"

"I hope not, but I believe the root problem is at St. Cyril's."

"That's a depressing thought." He slowed for a curve. "Rats."

Harry leaned forward as she saw the flashing lights. "Looks like we can eventually get by."

That eventuality took a half hour. A car had slid off the road. Half was in one lane, and while there wasn't much traffic, cars began to form a longer line waiting for the police cars to get out of the way. By the time the Haristeens chugged down their driveway, it was 12:30. They'd heard the bells, whistles, and firecrackers earlier while waiting in the car.

"It's going to be a good year," Fair wished.

"Don't we hope that every year?" Harry smiled as they approached the barn, and the headlights flashed on a gruesome sight.

"Fair, what's that?"

Harry jumped out of the car as soon as Fair came to a stop. As she wore her cowboy boots, she slid in the snow, her feet moving in opposite directions. Down she went.

Fair reached her as she managed to get on all fours. Putting his hand under her armpit, he hauled her up.

The two of them approached the barn doors.

Margaret's eye sockets, filled with snow, stared back at husband and wife.

"It's the skeleton from the tree!" Harry felt the cold enveloping her feet.

"Missing part of an arm." Fair brushed snow from his eyelids. "I never thought we'd see this again. I never wanted to."

Tucker charged out of the house. *"Flo and Cletus. Old truck. We came out. I barked."*

Surfing through the ever-deepening snow, Mrs. Murphy joined her corgi friend. *"They didn't touch anything, go anywhere. Just leaned these bones against the door."*

"Let's go inside, honey." Fair, hand still under Harry's arm, walked his wife to the porch, animals stepping in their prints.

"Fair, shouldn't we move that person inside?" Harry fretted.

"No. Whoever that is can't feel a thing. Let Cooper handle this. We can enter the

barn through the back doors if she can't get here until later tomorrow."

Inside, good coats off, Harry sat down to remove her cowboy boots. Her throbbing feet were cold and wet from the snow. The boots weren't made for this weather.

One eye open, Pewter called from her bed, *"It's almost one o'clock in the morning. What-ever and whoever is out there, nothing you can do about it now."*

"Fair, I should call Cooper despite the late hour. We don't want a repeat of last time, when someone took the skeleton."

He dropped in a chair. "All right."

Harry called Cooper, who had just crawled into bed after a long day and night. "Harry, are you all right?"

"I am. Cooper, I'm so sorry to call you, but the skeleton is back, leaning against my barn door."

"I'll be right over."

Fifteen minutes later, the animals rose from their beds as they heard the tires of Cooper's Highlander crunching on the snow. Harry and Fair, knowing the keen senses of their friends, pulled on snow boots, heavier coats, hurried out to greet the weary deputy.

Tucker accompanied Harry and Fair. Mrs. Murphy walked to the back of the barn, lifting her paws high after each step.

The glow of the Chinaman's light and the falling snow created a surreal scene.

"This is no way to start the New Year," the tall officer said and sighed.

As Cooper investigated the bones without disturbing them, Mrs. Murphy checked to see if Odin had eaten the latest leftovers. He had. Trotting back to the front of the barn, she sat under the eave, a bit out of the falling snow, watching.

"Let's go inside," Cooper suggested.

Once there, she called in to the dispatcher, herself half asleep. "I know no one can get out here now, but put it on record that I called you at quarter to two, January first. Have someone call me on my cell when a team can get out here. We don't want to lose this evidence one more time." She ended the call, looked at her friends. "In my head, I keep hearing that song, 'How Bizarre.' Great song." She rubbed her eyes.

"What can we do to help you?" Fair asked.

"Let me sleep on your couch. If anyone comes down your drive, Tucker will tell me."

"I will. I will," the dog promised.

Pewter turned up her nose. *"Tucker, you're so obsequious."*

"You think I don't know what that means?" Tucker cocked her head.

Noticing the glares and raised hackles, Harry stepped in. "Don't you dare. Both of you."

Fair, sheets and blanket in his arms, walked into the living room.

"I'll do that," said Harry. "You stir up the fire." She smiled at her thoughtful spouse, then focused on Cooper. "I'll bring you a robe. I really hope whoever did this doesn't come back."

As Harry finished up making a bed on the sofa, she reminded Cooper she could stay in the guest room.

"I know, but it's at the back of the house. Short of sleeping in the barn, I want to be as close as I can. Just in case."

Tucker settled down near the fire, Mrs. Murphy curled up next to her. Pewter remained in her cushy bed in the kitchen. Why go too far from her crunchies?

"Good night, Cooper." Fair headed down the hall.

"Night and thank you," she replied.

"See you in the morning." Harry paused for a moment. "No matter what, Happy New Year."

"Happy New Year to you, too. All signs point to an exciting one!"

37

The dawn of a new day and a new year provided no respite from the snow. When the sun rose, the clouds obscured most of the light. By 9:00, it was still coming down steady, snowplows working overtime. There was hope that by nightfall this would end. People stayed inside. It was a holiday, a hangover holiday.

Outside by the barn with the three-person retrieval team, Cooper wore plastic gloves, as not to compromise the evidence.

"You know, I shouldn't really worry about fingerprints or blood." She couldn't help herself and laughed. "This defines a cold case."

Dabny, another officer she liked, fired back, "Cold, yes. Snow, yes. But, Coop, you never know."

Her cell rang. "Cooper." Listening, she looked at the small crew, working on a holiday, too.

Walking back to the house, Cooper, head down, pushed open the kitchen door. "Flo Rice is missing again. Her sister is having a fit that she's frozen."

Harry was making coffee for everyone as Fair was frying up eggs and bacon. She said, "Not again."

"Another five minutes," said Fair. "What about you?"

"Coffee's just about ready," said Harry. "I'll set the table. Would do everyone good to come inside for a bit. The cold seeps into your bones."

"This isn't exactly how I thought we would ring in the new year," Fair said. He put the bacon on paper towels to soak up the grease.

"Don't do that," Pewter yowled. *"Pour it on my crunchies."*

Hearing the cat, Fair looked at the other two animals. He saved the grease, pouring it in a china cup. "I'll let that cool."

"Heaven!" Pewter purred loudly.

"It's not on your crunchies yet." Tucker enjoyed pricking her dream.

"Wonder if Flo ran back to River Run?" Harry folded napkins.

"If that's where she headed, let's hope she got there," said Fair. "Tricky roads."

"Yeah. She's been a pain, rude, you name

328

it, but I feel sorry for her."

"I do, too."

Flo had ample occasion to feel sorry for herself as Esther drove into Cletus's driveway that morning.

After two long strides to the front window, Cletus ordered, "Hide! It's Esther."

Flo ran into his bedroom, which was cold as ice. She prayed her sister hadn't spotted her car behind the shed.

Cletus opened the door and acted as though this was a common occurrence, Esther at his front door during a snowstorm. "Esther, how are you?"

"Cletus, have you seen Flo?"

"No. Come on in out of the snow."

Esther stepped inside the front door. "What a winter this has been! We have winters with no snow and then winters with lots of snow. I don't understand it."

"Me neither."

"I've called the sheriff's department. I'm so worried about Flo. She's been wandering lately and gets so angry. I hate to think of her out in a storm. I thought she might have stopped by here. I remembered once she told me she'd drop by here to sit and talk."

"No. Should I call you if I see her?"

"Better to call the sheriff's department."

Hearing Esther's voice, Buster clambered out of the crunched-up towels and barked.

"Terminator, that's enough." Cletus knew it was Buster.

"Do you still have that adorable dog? Oh, I must see him."

"He's in the kitchen. You go in and I'll be right behind you, if you will excuse me for just one minute."

As she stepped into the kitchen, Cletus opened the bedroom door and grabbed Flo by the wrist. They shot out the front door just as Esther bent down to look at The Terminator and also beheld Buster.

"Buster!"

As Esther shouted the dog's name, Cletus skidded behind the wheel of Esther's sturdy SUV, Flo already in the passenger seat. Esther had pulled in the driveway behind his truck. He had the presence of mind to notice she did not come to the front door carrying a purse and did not have keys in her hand. He took the chance that she'd left her keys in the ignition. Luckily, he was right.

Turning on the heavy vehicle, he gunned it out of the driveway just as Esther stepped from the house, shaking her fist. "Stop!"

"Crank up the heat," Cletus ordered Flo.

Frightened of her sister, she was also

brimming with admiration for Cletus. "What are we going to do?" she asked.

"We're going back to Margaret and pray, and I mean pray, Flo, that we get there before the cops get us."

"Why would they get us?" Flo rubbed her upper arms as the heat was flowing out of the vents.

"Because your sister is on the phone right now calling the sheriff, declaring we stole her car. My wall phone is hard to miss. The second call she'll make is for Al to pick her up."

He was right.

As Esther calmly explained to the police about the drunk and her crazy sister who stole her Lexus, citing the license plate, Buster shouted to The Terminator. He had to bark loudly at the deaf old dog, *"Have you had your rabies shots?"*

Nodding his head, ears forward, The Terminator replied, *"Yes."*

"Damn," Buster cursed.

"Why?" the ancient dog asked.

"You could bite her."

This made the old boy laugh, then Buster joined in. Esther, fuming, thought they were snuffling.

A wary Cletus slowed down while driving the back roads, most of them gravel. The car would shimmy out now and then, but he'd steer it back on track. "Do you have a cellphone?" he asked.

"Cletus, I don't have squat."

"Well, what good are you?" He half laughed.

"Good enough to give you the most exciting New Year's Day you've had in years."

He thought for a moment, then grinned. "Got that right, girl."

Carefully, they hugged the back roads, alert for state troopers and sheriff's department vehicles. Fortunately, most of them were working the major highways and interstates today.

At long last, Cletus turned down Harry's snow-covered road, as she hadn't had time to plow the new fallen snow.

"Traffic. Look at the tire marks," he noted.

"Reckon she called the sheriff about Margaret?"

"Flo, what the hell would you do if you came home and found a skeleton sitting under a light in front of your barn doors?"

"You're right. I don't remember you being quite so forceful, Cletus."

"Get used to it," he barked. "Now, this is what I want you to do. You find the highest-ranking officer, tell him your story. I'll back you up. They probably won't believe you. And if they don't know already, they will soon enough that this is Esther's stolen Lexus. So you will be put in jail."

"No." Flo turned the door handle, and he grabbed her left arm.

"Flo, do what I tell you and everything may turn out okay. Tell them everything. *Everything.*"

"Oh, it's so horrid. So very horrid."

"Flo!" He leveled his gaze at her. For a second, she glimpsed the man he once was.

"I will."

"They'll still lock you up. I'll do what I can. The first people I will ask to help us are Fair and Harry. They were good kids. I expect they're still good. I'll do my best for you."

"Cletus, you already have." Flo's eyes were getting watery, but she brushed them clear.

He pulled up next to one of the squad cars. Everyone was in the kitchen eating. Margaret remained in front of the barn doors.

Tucker barked, *"Intruders."*

Harry walked to the back door, looked

out the glassed-in porch. "It's Flo and Cletus. Dear God, who next? The Rockettes?"

Cooper stood up. "I'll bring them in."

"I'll put more food out," said Harry. "Whatever they've been up to, they'll be hungry. I've seen how they live."

Cooper stepped outside. "Come on in."

Neither Cletus nor Flo wore a coat. Still, they were apprehensive about coming in.

"Come on, Flo. Your sister reported you missing and her car pinched. You can have breakfast before we deal with that."

"She tell you I stole her car?"

"I took that call a half hour ago," said Cooper. "She called the department."

Dabny stood up, as did the other two sheriff's department men, when Flo entered the room. Their mothers taught them well.

As did Flo's. "Please sit down," she said.

"Let's all have a New Year's breakfast before we worry about details." Cooper helped Harry put filled plates on the table.

"You must be cold." Harry placed two heavy mugs before them.

"Deputy Cooper, are you the senior officer?" Flo asked.

"I am."

"Jump up on the counter with me. We don't want to miss any of this." Mrs. Murphy ef-

fortlessly soared onto the counter.

"Anyone want some cookies?" asked Harry. "Every Christmas, Fair and I receive these wonderful shortbread cookies from a couple in Wyoming." She rose, opened the tin, placed rich shortbread cookies from Scotland onto a plate.

Once on the table, everyone reached for them at once, which caused laughter.

How wise Cooper was to let everyone eat, and let the warm food do its work. Her time with the churches had taught her what a hot meal can do.

"Wyoming?" Dabny bit into the glorious food. "I've always wanted to go there."

"Gorgeous. Flat-out gorgeous." Harry beamed. "We made such friends there. These are from Mimi Tate and Jim Smith. They own a ranch right up near the Montana border called Wymont. You know how you bump into people and suddenly you're friends? That kind of thing."

Cletus finished his plate. He was full and most grateful not to be talking about the huge problem by the barn door. He nudged Flo under the table.

"Deputy Cooper, I should tell you, tell everyone, why we're here," said Flo. "First, I apologize to you" — she indicated the Haristeens — "for putting Margaret Don-

335

leavey in front of your barn."

"Miss Donleavey!" Harry and Fair exclaimed.

"Yes." Flo twisted her napkin in her hands under the table. "How beautiful she was, remember? I was surprised you didn't recognize her bracelet."

"Of course." Harry's hand flew to her cheek. "But so many ladies of her generation or their mothers wore them. It didn't click."

"I nearly passed out when I saw that wonderful gold piece." Flo continued, "First. I did not kill Margaret. Esther did. Everyone was at the football game against Louisa; the crowds went wild. No one paid much attention to anything after that game. People ran everywhere, tooting horns, celebrating. Margaret was in charge of cleanup, the light stuff. Another crew would come in the next day. Al went off to celebrate with the team, the assistant coaches. Margaret and Al were a hot item. Esther knew. She watched Al like a hawk. So she lured Margaret over to her car after everyone left the lot. Said they could go to the little beer joint and celebrate with the others. Said she'd come back in the morning and help if needs be."

"Didn't Miss Donleavey know how Esther felt about Al?" Harry asked.

"I guess she did, but Margaret wasn't a person who thought badly of others, and Esther had never treated her badly. And she wanted to celebrate, too. But, you see, my sister was obsessed with Al. Esther still is to this day."

"How'd she kill Margaret?" asked Harry. She couldn't help herself.

"She drove through town, heading toward where the team was celebrating. Said she had to stop for a minute. Pretended to check a tire. Said it was flat. Margaret got out to help. That's when Esther shot her. She laid her flat in the back seat. Put a towel under her back, in case she'd bleed. She'd shot her through the heart. Picked me up, told me I had to help her. She was as cool as a cucumber. She swore Margaret did not suffer, never knew what hit her. She said it was a humane ending."

Harry asked another question, but Cooper didn't mind. "Weren't you scared?"

"You bet. I still am."

"Flo, I have to call in that we've found you or you've found us," said Cooper. "As to this entire conversation we have witnessed, good. You weren't coerced in any way." Cooper turned to her crew. "Someone write all this down. Good to have backup."

"Right," Dabny agreed as Harry rose to fetch a tablet out of the drawer along with a pen.

Noticing the button Harry had also put on the table, Flo exclaimed, "Her sweater! That was on Margaret's sweater. She had thistles on everything. Well, maybe not everything, but she was proud of her heritage."

Cooper was on the phone, reporting to HQ that Flo and Cletus were with them.

"Cletus, did you know about this?" Dabny asked.

"No. Not until Flo came to me yesterday. She was afraid of Esther."

"There are a few things I still don't understand," said Fair. He leaned forward. "Can you tell me why you brought Margaret here? And Flo, why did you or Esther remove Margaret's bones from the upturned tree?"

"Esther panicked when she heard the body was found," said Flo. "The weather worked in her favor. I let her boss me around. The first time around, I helped her because she's my sister. This time I was afraid of what she'd do to me if I didn't. We untangled poor Margaret from the tree in awful weather! We wrapped her in a plastic tarp, then wrapped another one around that. She was so light. We slid her up the hill to the old road on the spine, above here. Esther said the shed behind Random Row would be a good place for a few days to stow her until we found another hiding place. She'd thought about this. Said no one would be there. That's where we stashed her." Flo reached for another swallow of coffee. "I shouldn't have done any of this. When this first happened, I was worried that Esther would be found guilty of murder. I loved my sister. I don't now, but I did then. And over time, especially these last few months, I started to think she might kill me. If she gets a chance, I do believe she will. But who will believe me?"

Cletus vowed, "We'll find a good lawyer."

"How can I pay for it?" Flo threw up her hands.

"Don't worry about that now." Harry didn't know what to believe.

Formerly sullen, snappy, and odd, Flo was certainly in possession of herself now.

"You two stay in here," said Cooper. "We've got to go outside and finish up." She stood, as did the others.

They worked outside, taking photos, checking everything. Twenty minutes later, they all heard a big eight-cylinder motor come down the drive. A huge Suburban pulled up.

Al and Esther quickly disembarked. "Where is she?" Esther appeared very worried.

"She's fine, Mrs. Toth." Cooper smiled. "We're taking her in."

"Taking her in?"

"Yes. After all, she stole your car," Cooper cleverly replied.

"Oh, that." Esther was ready to say more when Al noticed the skeleton.

"What is that?"

Esther turned and saw Margaret's bones as well. Her face betrayed no recognition.

Cooper quietly said, "We believe it's Margaret Donleavey."

Al howled. "No. No, it can't be." He sagged against the car.

Dabny rushed toward him, held him up.

Al regained his footing, tears streaming down his face.

"How can you be sure?" asked Esther. She now looked upset but not stricken.

"Flo," came Cooper's clipped remark.

"But Flo's having mental problems. Surely she can't be counted on to tell the truth." Esther's voice oozed reason.

"I have to run her in, Mrs. Toth."

Just then, Flo, unable to stand it, ran

outside wearing one of Harry's jackets. Cletus, without any overcoat, was followed by Fair.

Esther turned to see these three. "Flo. Come on, I'll take you home."

"Mrs. Toth, I have to take her in." Cooper was firm.

"Surely not." Esther was equally firm.

"She may be a murderer or an accessory to murder." Cooper dropped one shoe but not the other.

Taking a step back now, Al appraised his wife with a new eye. He said nothing as the tears dripped off his chin.

"She drove here in your stolen car," said Cooper. "And Flo also provided us with valuable information regarding the remains." Cooper pressed ever so slightly.

Esther blanched, then color flushed back into her cheeks. "Surely, Deputy, you aren't going to listen to my mentally impaired sister and her dipsomaniac companion."

"Oh, but I am." Cooper turned to Dabny. "Better take her in now, Dab."

As Dabny gently pushed Flo into the four-wheel-drive squad SUV, Flo turned to Cletus. "Take care of Buster."

"I will," he answered. "I will. You don't worry about a thing, Sweetheart."

38

"Sunshine! I can't believe it." Harry tossed horse manure into the wheelbarrow, doors open to the barn.

"Too much white." Pewter squinted.

"Do you always have to find something to complain about?" The dog brushed past her, deliberately trying to provoke the gray cat.

Pewter reached out with her right paw to snag Tucker, who easily avoided the smack.

"Fatty, fatty," she mocked.

Pewter puffed up, danced sideways. *"You'd better be afraid. I can bloody your ears, shred your nose, and, if I feel really furious, blind you."*

"Ta, ta!" The corgi bumped her again.

Pewter, enraged, leapt toward the dog, who shot down the center aisle. Her claws clicked on the brick carefully put down in the 1840s.

Mouth open, eyes bright, Tucker charged through the aisle, ran right out into the snow, hooked a left, dropped down in the snow so only her ears showed.

"Peon!" Pewter ran after her, miscalculated the depth of the snow if she'd even considered it, and sank out of sight.

Tucker dug out, ran over to where the cat disappeared, turned around, and kicked snow all over the spitting feline. *"Weenie!"*

"What is going on?" Harry asked the tiger cat. Prudently remaining on a tack trunk, Mrs. Murphy was the epitome of good reason.

Stepping outside, Harry arrived just in time to see a gray cat with a dunce cap of snow on her head crawl out of a hole. Tucker, flat on the snow, egged her on.

The cat did look funny. Harry laughed.

"You'll pay. You'll both pay." Pewter shook her head, strode toward the barn, a study in wounded dignity.

"Tucker, don't play so rough," Harry chided.

"Every now and then, Mom, even a good dog breaks her chain." The corgi offered the old excuse.

Back in the barn, with stalls picked clean of droppings and the wheelbarrow resting to the side of the barn, Harry knew she'd need to dig out a path to the manure spreader. Each morning, Harry picked

stalls, rolled the wheelbarrow to a level spot. The earth had been dug out, secured with heavy logs. The manure spreader in good weather rested there. Harry would tip over the wheelbarrow into the manure spreader. Later, she'd hook up the tractor, pull out the spreader, and spread the manure and straw, which would be churned up, cut up, by the blades at the end of the wagon. Couldn't do that today.

Always looking for ways to be more efficient, Harry put everything to good use. Depending on the weather, she would pile the manure up, let it molder, turn it with a fork attachment on the tractor. Eventually, all this transformed into rich fertilizer, which she then shared with Miranda and Susan. She spread the rest on her pasture.

Looking up at the wall clock, she hurried out of the barn, closed those doors, dog and two cats in tow.

"I don't know where the time goes." She lifted Tucker into the old truck.

The cats hopped up, and she fired the engine. She waited just a bit, then churned out her long drive, using the ruts. Harry plucked her sunglasses from the visor.

"I need a pair of those," Pewter said.

"Fetching, I'm sure. How about cat's-eye

sunglasses with rhinestones?" Tucker suggested.

"Tucker, button your lip," Mrs. Murphy ordered. *"I'd like a peaceful ride. Besides, Pewter wouldn't look good in rhinestones."*

"You both think you're so funny." The gray cat crawled onto Harry's lap.

Lifting her elbows to make room for her, Harry started to ramble on to her animals. "I was glad to go to the barn this morning, no skeleton. Margaret Donleavey was such a good teacher. Anyone who can make Latin grammar fun has to be good. How awful to see her like that, and what a sad end to her life. I just can't believe it."

"Anyone who can make any grammar interesting has to be good," sniffed Pewter.

"What do you know about grammar?" The dog looked at her.

"I know c *comes before* d. *Cat before dog,"* the gray cat announced, oblivious to any possible errors in logic.

"So what?" Tucker really was spoiling for a fight today.

"Cats first." Pewter tipped up her chin.

The temperature at ten o'clock edged upward to thirty-eight degrees Fahrenheit. The state roads, while plowed, remained slick.

Harry pulled into the lot at St. Cyril's at

346

ten after the hour, a little late. Cooper's squad car was already there, as well as some other cars. Given what the deputy had just been through with Harry at the farm, she knew this would be a reward to the ever-curious Harry, but she also wanted Harry's take on all this later. She trusted her neighbor's insights. The two murders, along with the checks, kept bringing Cooper back to St. Cyril's, but she still couldn't figure out the connection.

Once inside the administrative building, she hurried down the hall, cats and dog after her. Harry stopped at Father O'Connor's office, quickly pulling off her coat.

Father O'Connor was seated at a small coffee table, along with Cooper and Arden.

"Sorry." Harry hung her coat on the coatrack.

She hadn't expected Arden to be there.

Father O'Connor stood. "When I called Deputy Cooper to meet with me today and she asked if you could come, I had no idea how exciting things were yesterday at your farm, Harry."

"Too exciting." Harry sat down as Father O'Connor pulled out a chair.

"You all are welcome to sit, too." He smiled at the animals.

"Thank you," they replied, but stayed on

the floor.

"Arden, it's nice to see you," Harry greeted her. "Happy New Year."

"Friday is bookkeeping day. And it's a new year. I need to keep busy." She looked at Father O'Connor and Cooper, both of whom looked back encouragingly.

"I found this." Arden pointed to an opened envelope.

Cooper picked it up, handed it to Harry. "What do you make of this?"

Harry noticed that there was no return address, just a blank envelope. She pulled it open and saw two checks inside. "Is this what I think it is?"

"It is." Father O'Connor nodded.

Harry pulled out two consecutively numbered checks that had been missing. Arden's signature was on the bottom.

"I didn't write that," Arden said, pointing to the handwriting. "I can show you."

"I can't imagine that you did sign the checks, Arden. It wouldn't make a lot of sense." Harry dropped them back in the envelope as the well-dressed woman left the room, opened a drawer in the desk next door, and returned with photocopies, which she placed on the table.

"That's my signature."

Cooper bent over, picked up a sheet filled

with images of canceled checks. "Close."

"But not close enough," Arden said defensively.

Harry took the offered sheet from Cooper, studied it, handed it to Father O'Connor, who handed it back to Arden.

"When I came in this morning, I noticed an envelope pinned to the door of the cubbyhole," she said. "I took it down, opened it, two checks. I couldn't believe it. Why would someone set me up?" Her voice quavered.

"They didn't, exactly," Harry answered.

"Why not?" Arden was indignant.

"If they'd set you up, they would have cashed them." Harry folded her hands together.

"Well, whatever you call it, I want to know who and why. Isn't there enough going on around here?"

"Yes, there is." Cooper's voice was consoling. "We should take note that your signature was not on the torn check found downstairs."

"Has anyone in the parish ever come to you and asked for funds?" Father O'Connor queried.

"No. The only requests I get for funds are from the officers of Silver Linings. The boys don't ask. We're in the black. No monies are missing. We can always use more, but the fund-raiser was very successful. The truck raffle made the difference between a good fund-raiser and a great one." Arden placed the photocopies back in a clear plastic pocket on the inside of the large business checkbook.

"Arden, does anyone have it in for you?" asked Harry. "Even if it's embarrassing, it might help to know." She had a nose for the unexplored angle.

"Not everyone likes me, but I wouldn't say they have it in for me."

"Who?" Cooper pressed.

"Dar de Jarnette once accused me of trying to seduce Max." She flipped her hair. "Absurd."

"When was this?" Cooper continued.

"Maybe six months ago. She said it as a warning. As if I would want him! I was furious. We haven't talked since, but we're polite."

"Why would she think that?" Cooper kept on.

"Oh." Arden paused. "She once said Lou was always out for a good cause or a good time and I was left alone a lot. I told her she should know."

"I see." Cooper kept a neutral expression.

"Anyone else you can think of?" Harry asked.

"Think of what?" Arden was getting testy.

"Arden, no one is accusing you of anything," said Father O'Connor. "These events are deeply disquieting. We don't mean to put you on the spot. Your answers may help all of us, including you, to discover who took those checks. Who tried to disrupt you and our trust in you at such a painful time in your life?" The priest's voice was gentle and encouraging.

Arden stood up. "I didn't mean to intrude on your meeting."

"I think this has covered whatever we might have discussed concerning the checks." Father O'Connor stood, as did Cooper and Harry, taking their cue from the priest.

"Father." Arden, suppressing emotion, stepped toward him. "Would you bless me?"

"Certainly. *In nominus* — excuse me — in the Name of the Father, Son, and Holy Ghost, may They bless you and keep you, and grant you peace."

He made the sign of the cross, the index and middle fingers of his right hand together.

"Oh, God." Harry's eyes widened.

"What?" Cooper reached over to hold

Harry's arm as her friend appeared stricken.

Without a word, Harry put her forefinger and middle finger together and made the sign of the cross.

Arden pushed Harry down and ran for the front door. She flew by Al Toth, bumping him as he manhandled Esther, dragging his wife through the building's door, which he'd forcefully kicked open.

Tucker ran after Arden, who had gotten up from her collision. Slamming the church door shut, she ran outside.

Cooper called the police dispatcher. She figured the department would have Arden cornered within twenty minutes. No point in her chasing the woman, especially since she had to now focus on Esther Toth screaming and Al bellowing.

"Father O'Connor! Father O'Connor!" Al shouted.

"Al, Al, let me go!" Esther screamed as he continued to drag her down the hallway.

Harry, Cooper, Father O'Connor, Mrs. Murphy, Pewter, and Tucker from the opposite direction converged in the hall.

Father O'Connor approached him. "Al, Al, please let her go."

Hand on holster, Cooper quietly moved behind the priest.

Harry and the animals stepped just to the side.

"Tell him," said Al. "Tell him, goddammit, or I'll break your neck." Al's anger shook the windows.

"I was wrong," said Esther.

"Tell him you killed Margaret! Confess. He's a priest, confess."

She dropped her head. "Bless me, Father, for I have sinned."

"Yes, my child." Father O'Connor hoped the words, uttered for two thousand years, would calm down Al. And perhaps Esther would say whatever she needed to say.

"I murdered Margaret Donleavey," she confessed, sobbing.

"You killed the sweetest woman that ever walked." Al gave her a shake. "Why?" His rage began to subside.

"Because I loved you," said Esther.

"Loved me. You killed the woman I loved and put me through hell."

"I made it up to you. I was a good wife."

He threw her on the wooden floor, turned, and walked out.

Shaking, Esther staggered up, sucked in a gulp of air, looked at Harry. "This is your fault."

"Get behind her," Mrs. Murphy told Tucker.

Too late. Esther lunged for Harry, grabbing her by the throat.

Harry fought, then reached into her pocket. She couldn't open the pocketknife, but the knife was heavy enough that, folded into her hand, it made her punch harder. She hit Esther with all her might as Tucker sank her teeth into Esther's calf. Cooper, who had drawn her gun, stepped into the fray as Esther released Harry.

"You are under arrest for the murder of Margaret Donleavey." Cooper quickly put Esther's right arm behind her back and apologized. "Harry, I didn't see that coming. I'm sorry."

Rubbing her throat, voice scratchy, Harry replied, "Who did?"

Father O'Connor was stunned. Collecting himself, he said to Esther, "I will pray for your soul."

Esther snarled at Harry, "If you'd kept out of it. You were even nosy back in high school. You're nosy now. Everything was fine."

"I'm hardly responsible for the wind uprooting that tree. Esther, would you have killed your sister?"

"I don't know." Esther immediately assumed a bland expression.

Cooper, quick to catch on to Harry's

design, jacked Esther's arm up enough to hurt. "Did you threaten your sister?"

"I did. She was impossible."

That was enough for Cooper. As she walked Esther to her squad car, she called Rick. By the time she'd deposited Esther at the jail, the papers were drawn up for Flo to be released. Cooper checked in with the magistrate to be sure.

After Esther spit at everyone from behind bars, Cooper hurried into Rick's office. "Did they get Arden Higham?" she asked.

"They did, right where 240 and 250 meet. She tried to ram through the roadblock. Broken collarbone but alive."

"Boss, let's get over to the hospital. Maybe she'll talk. Be a doubleheader if she did. Solve two cases in one day."

While not serious, Arden's injury did hurt. The doctors allowed the sheriff and his deputy to question her. An armed officer stood outside the room, closing the door when Rick and Cooper entered.

Cooper sat next to Arden, while Rick sat next to the deputy.

"Arden, you've carried a heavy burden. It's time to put it down," Cooper soothingly counseled.

"Is Harry all right? I didn't mean to hurt

her, but I panicked and had to get away."

"She's fine. Now tell us what's really going on. Did you kill your husband?"

"No."

"Then why did you run away from St. Cyril's?"

"Harry was getting too close when she made the sign of the cross. She was closing in on why the fingers were taken from Lou and Pete. She's clever. In time, she'd figure the check scheme — well, I had to go."

Voice also quiet, Rick asked, "Did Tyler take the checks?"

"He did."

"But he didn't steal anything. I mean, he didn't cash them, even though he forged your signature on them." Cooper pushed lightly.

She clammed right up.

Cooper leaned forward, touched Arden's hand, and took a long shot. "Did Tyler kill his father?"

"Oh, God." Arden burst into tears. Her whole body shook from sobs.

"Please, Arden, I know this is terrible, you've been through so much, but we must know. We don't want Tyler to harm anyone else or himself. He's a minor. I'm sure there will be compassion in the hearing. You need to protect him."

"That's what I tried to do. He thought taking the checks would divert people's attention. I found them in his drawer. He's suffering. You have to understand how much he's suffering. He shredded the one just to see how long it would take for someone to find it. Perverse humor, I guess. I returned the others hoping to add to the confusion. He didn't argue about the return."

"Why?" Cooper almost whispered.

"Lou and Pete bullied him for over a year. He's too scared. They were relentless. They thought they were making a man of him. Some of the other boys picked up on their disdain and they'd push Tyler around, too."

"I see." Cooper put her other hand over Arden's. "Silver Linings?"

Arden nodded. "Tyler's slight. He's almost pretty. He snapped. Do you understand? He just snapped."

"Did he tell you?" Cooper asked.

"No. I noticed sometimes he'd be bruised on his back or arms. I put it down as boy stuff, roughhousing. He tried to play football. I noticed Lou was very hard on him. After a game, Tyler was always beat up. I wanted to take him to the doctor. He had a meltdown. I didn't know what to do. Finally, he told me both Lou and Pete had been knocking him around. He begged me not to say anything, especially to his father, because he'd look weak. He didn't want anyone to know he was a victim. Other boys would call him 'faggot.' He tried to fight back. He wasn't strong enough."

"Do you think he is gay?" Cooper asked calmly.

"Truthfully, he doesn't know what he is. He's too beaten down."

"Are the other bullies adults or boys?" asked Cooper, voice steady.

"Tyler said Lou and Pete were the worst. He hated them more than any of the boys. Not that he liked them much. All my son wants to do is play games on his computer, research dragons. He doesn't want to be with people. Tyler is happier doing an equation, fooling around in the school chemistry lab, than he is with people."

Rick took over. "Arden, we want to help you and we want to help Tyler. Can you tell me how he killed Pete and then his father?"

"Tyler's a chemistry whiz. He reads everything online, he experiments. He read that potassium chloride can stop a heart. It appears natural. He made friends with the chem teacher at St. Anne's. He has use of the lab. He's so bright. I can't tell you how smart my son is, only that I don't know much of what he's talking about when he explains these lab experiments. Anyway, he made potassium chloride, filled a syringe, and waited. For weeks. When Pete Vavilov offered to take Tyler home after the big fund-raiser, Pete asked me, of course. And so did Tyler. Then Tyler asked him to pull off the road in the storm. He jabbed him with the needle in the neck before Pete fully stopped so he couldn't fight him off. Pete actually stopped the car as his heart was failing. I pulled up behind. You see, Tyler had asked me to follow them. Pete didn't know, and he couldn't have really seen me anyway. I parked behind the car, Tyler and I pushed the Explorer off the road so it looked like an accident. Then we drove off."

"I see. Was Tyler shaken?"

"No. He was euphoric, actually."

"And his father?"

"Tyler knew what I didn't. That Lou was taking Coumadin, and he kept it in the glove compartment. Tyler stole some. Then he asked Lou to pick him up at St. Anne's and drive him to the gym on campus. He gave Lou a cup of hot coffee, which he'd brought from the cafeteria, loaded with milk, sugar, and Coumadin. When he got out of the car, he told his father that Mark's mother would bring him home and thanked him for the ride. He said Lou was furious because Tyler had kept taunting him about getting old. I asked Tyler what would he have done if Lou didn't drink the coffee. He said he'd keep trying until he did."

"And was he upset?"

She fell silent, then said, "Not at first. He said he was relieved. He said if anyone ever laid a hand on him again in his life he'd take them out. Can you understand? My son has been hurt, I couldn't help him. I didn't know until the damage was done."

"Did Charlene Vavilov know anything?"

"No."

"Did her sons smack around Tyler?" Rick continued.

"No. They used to come to some Silver Linings functions, but they're both in college now." The tears started again. She caught herself. "Don't tell Charlene about Pete. What's the point?"

"Unfortunately, Arden, it will eventually come out in Tyler's hearing. He won't be tried as an adult. That should be somewhat helpful to you, but he has killed two men. Premeditated murder," Cooper informed her.

It wasn't clear if Arden had heard her. She said, "Finding out your husband is beating up your son to toughen him up is a shock that I can't begin to describe. I can't think of any woman who would knock around a daughter she considered unfeminine. Lou was obsessed that Tyler be some kind of alpha male. Tyler made his plans to end his misery."

"And the fingers?" Cooper quietly asked.

Arden grimaced for a moment, inhaled. "Hypocrisy. Tyler had a sense of symbolism. He thought they were both hypocrites, pretending to be good Catholics while being constantly on his back. At this point, my son hates the Church. He hates everybody."

"Even you?" Cooper looked into her eyes.

"Depends on the day." Arden's tears spilled down her cheeks.

39

Harry, Fair, Cooper, Mrs. Murphy, Pewter, and Tucker gathered in the kitchen at noon on Saturday. Everyone had had a good night's sleep, and Harry made lunch.

"I've spent a lot of time just lately at your kitchen table," Cooper said. "I owe you a lot of dinners."

"You don't owe me a thing."

"I am sorry I didn't see it coming with Arden. Out of the blue, she tells all. Now that I know her story, I suppose yesterday was the straw that broke the camel's back."

"Poor camel," Tucker commiserated.

"It's just a saying!" Pewter sniffed.

Cooper told them why Pete and Lou were killed. She also knew the tiny mark on the headrest of the Explorer had to have been residue of the KCl. The lab work, slow again, wasn't back on that, but she knew it. Adolescence is such a volatile time. Not that Cooper thought every pressured, angry kid is a potential murderer, but one has less mastery of one's emotions then, and killing turns a boy into the alpha dog, at least for a time.

"It's a dreadful story," said Fair. "Does Father O'Connor know?"

"Not yet. We will meet with him, Social Services, a psychologist in the area who specializes in this stuff early tomorrow. Arden will be released, but she can't say anything without jeopardizing her case because she really is an accessory to murder."

"Which brings up Flo." Harry's tone brightened.

"She's got a good lawyer. I think she'll be okay. I hope so." Cooper smiled.

"Me, too," both Harry and Fair said simultaneously, then hooked index fingers, done when two people say the same thing at the same time.

"Cletus was waiting there when she was released. I had the magistrate call him." Cooper smiled even bigger. "And he had The Terminator and Buster in his truck, as well as an old Navy duffel bag with some clothes. He took Flo home. I think he intends to stay there with her."

Harry smiled, too. "At last, some good news."

■ ■ ■ ■

That night, the animals waited for Odin. The stars were bright, the night clear and therefore cold. They'd dragged out all the remains of the lunch, as well as some dog biscuits that Tucker was willing to give up.

Odin arrived and dug in. Mrs. Murphy told him from the loft above, *"Thanks to you, Odin, two old people have made a home together, warmer than what they have apart. And two little dogs have a home, too. You've done a good deed."*

"I didn't do anything." Full, the coyote sat down.

"The bracelet that fell off the arm bone, that was what started it." Pewter then told the whole story.

"Come on down, we can celebrate." Odin grinned up at them. *"And don't worry. I won't eat you. Anyway, isn't it true that cats have nine lives?"*

"Why lose the first one to find out?" Mrs. Murphy laughed and didn't budge.

Dear Reader,

A dog. Sneaky Pie has dedicated this book to a dog. Too much catnip.

First off, the novel should be dedicated to me. I am the driving force. More to the point, I'm a cat.

And what's this about a human being beautifully trained. Is this human house-broken?

For future reference, just know all the great ideas come from me, me, me. Plus I would never dedicate anything to a dog.

Yours,

Pewter

Dear Reader,

Pewter is insufferable.

The driving force of these mysteries? Ha.

She's been sitting on her fat butt for years.

Yours in truth,

Dear Reader,

Finally a dog gets her due. Sneaky's right to dedicate this book to a dog. Where would humans be without dogs? Lost, miserable, and so lonely. For that matter, a lot of cats would be lonely, too. Many dogs are best friends to cats, not that any creature could be a best friend to the Queen of Ego, Pewter.

As to Gracie, she has a fetching wardrobe and is very stylish. Naturally, good clothes hang better on a Yorkie than a corgi but still she wears a pretty blue coat. You'd have to put a tent on Pewter. That's the real reason she's fussing.

I remain, as always, yours and the only reasonable creature in this bunch,

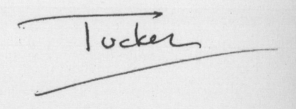

ABOUT THE AUTHORS

Rita Mae Brown has written many best-sellers and received two Emmy nominations. In addition to the Mrs. Murphy series, she has authored *A Nose for Justice* and *Murder Unleashed,* the first two mysteries in a new dog series, and the Sister Jane foxhunting series, as well as many other acclaimed books. She and Sneaky Pie live with several other rescued animals.

Sneaky Pie Brown, a tiger cat rescue, has written many mysteries. Having to share credit with the above-named human is a small irritant, but she manages it. Anything is better than typing, which is what "Big Brown" does for the series. Sneaky calls her human that name behind her back after the wonderful Thoroughbred racehorse. As her human is rather small, it brings giggles among the other animals. Sneaky's main character — Mrs. Murphy, a tiger cat — is a bit sweeter than Miss Pie, who can be caustic.